Secrets
in the
Snow

Emma Heatherington is from Donaghmore, Co Tyrone, where she lives with her partner and their five children. She has penned more than thirty short films, plays and musicals as well as seven novels, two of which were written under the pseudonym Emma Louise Jordan.

Emma's novel, *The Legacy of Lucy Harte*, was an eBook bestseller in both the UK and US.

Emma loves spending time with her partner (the talented artist and singer/songwriter Jim McKee), all things Nashville, romantic comedy movies, singalong nights with friends and family, red wine, musical theatre, new pyjamas, fresh clean bedclothes, long bubble baths and cosy nights in by the fire.

🐦 @emmalou13
📘 www.facebook.com/emmaheatheringtonwriter

Also by Emma Heatherington

The Legacy of Lucy Harte
A Part of Me and You
A Miracle on Hope Street
Rewrite the Stars

Emma Heatherington

Secrets
in the
Snow

HarperCollins*Publishers*

HarperCollins*Publishers* Ltd
1 London Bridge Street
London SE1 9GF

www.harpercollins.co.uk

First published by HarperCollins*Publishers* 2020

4

A catalogue record for this book
is available from the British Library

ISBN: 978-0-00-835566-1

This novel is entirely a work of fiction.
The names, characters and incidents portrayed in it are
the work of the author's imagination. Any resemblance to
actual persons, living or dead, events or localities is
entirely coincidental.

Typeset in Birka by Palimpsest Book Production Ltd, Falkirk, Stirlingshire

Printed and bound in Great Britain by
CPI Group (UK) Ltd, Croydon CR0 4YY

MIX
Paper from
responsible sources
FSC™ C007454

This book is produced from independently certified FSC™ paper
to ensure responsible forest management.

For more information visit: www.harpercollins.co.uk/green

In loving memory of my darling aunt Deirdre (Diddles) who left this world ten years ago. I can still hear your laugh, smell your perfume and I still smile at the wonderful memories you left us all with.

This one's for you x

My bedroom in Janet and Michael Brown's house in Dalkey back in 1996 had cosy clean bedding, a desk below a window framed with fairy lights, and a bedside locker with a lamp and an alarm clock all to myself.

Janet, my short-term foster mum, used to put Jaffa Cakes into my lunchbox on Fridays as a surprise treat because she knew they were my favourites, while her husband Michael would leave a filled hot water bottle wrapped in a pillow case by my bedroom door every night, and we'd play board games together at the kitchen table most evenings after dinner.

I remember closing my teenage eyes in that cosy bedroom on one particular evening and listening as the sea crashed in the distance and the wind battered the coastline while I was so toasty on the other side. All of this, combined with another sound coming from downstairs caught my ears and touched my soul.

It was Janet and Michael cooking together downstairs and they were laughing, really laughing, and it woke something within me. The sound made me smile from my heart, and then I realized what it was.

I felt safe in that moment. I felt safe and secure like I'd never been before and so I promised myself that I'd experience that sense of comfort and contentment at least one more time in my life—

—even if it took me for ever to find it again.

WINTER

1.

'Please talk to me, Ben. Say *something*. This silence is driving me crazy.'

I turn on the TV and flick through the channels as the fire snaps and crackles in the hearth, the only thing to break the silence of our smothering grief on this dark, cold November day.

Ben doesn't answer me. Instead he just wraps his favourite tartan blanket tighter around his ten-year-old body and continues to suck his thumb, a habit that has raised its head again just this week, after four years of going cold turkey.

'Do you want to talk about her?' I suggest, feeling my heart tug when I look at the dark rings under his eyes, his pale face, and the way he grips onto an old childhood comfort once more. 'Is that a good idea? We can talk about Mabel and some of the good times we shared?'

He rubs his eyes and snuggles deeper into the safety of his cocoon, and I frown with despair. The din from the corner where the TV flashes jolly colours and real-time images, reminding us that life, even after the death of someone you love, does go on, while for the moment it seems all in our world is frozen in time as we contemplate our next move.

I curl up on the armchair by the window and stare out to the evening's midnight-blue sky, then I pick up my phone and Google everything I can find on how to deal with bereavement through a child's eyes, an action that gives me a feeling of déjà vu, taking me back to a time before now, a time before our new life here began.

My boss and good friend, Camille, texts me just as I'm searching.

'How's the little guy?' she asks. 'And you? Keep your chin up, Ro. You're a fighter and so is Ben. You've got this.'

A familiar gnawing sensation clenches my insides, bringing back old fears, and my skin crawls with old anxieties rekindled by my child's inner pain.

I want to take it all away from him. I want him to laugh again like he used to, I want him to prank me with silly practical jokes or to make me smile when I hear him singing in the shower or in front of a mirror as he plays air guitar. I want him to irritate me with his insistence on convincing me to do something he wants and that I don't, or to make me swell with pride when his magical outlook on life wows me like only a child's can. His ongoing silence is quite literally breaking my heart, and I've no idea what to do or who to turn to.

It's been two days since Ben mumbled a reminder of how we were out of breakfast cereal, and he hasn't spoken a word since.

No demands, no requests, no tantrums and no tears. Nothing.

For a ten-year-old boy, managing to be quiet for so long when there's just the two of us in our little cottage on the outskirts of a tiny Irish village is no mean feat.

He hasn't responded to suggestions of a day trip to the new outdoor ice-skating rink in town, or shown any excitement over the winter football camp he'd spent the last few weeks looking forward to, and he never even flinched when I suggested a walk by the sea in nearby Dunfanaghy, which is always a popular pastime on the weekend here, whatever the weather.

My normally hapless, clumsy, chatty and often hilarious son has gone totally silent, but at least I can completely understand why.

The breakfast cereal reminder from Ben was on Thursday which was the same day we said our final farewell to our next-door neighbour, seventy-nine-year-old Mabel Murphy, beneath a heavy, grey winter sky in a cold Irish graveyard.

But Mabel Murphy was so much more than the little old lady who lived next door. She was our saviour and our best friend in the whole world when no one else was watching us, or noticed us, or even cared about us. She pushed her way in to fill a gap in both of our lives that we didn't even know existed when we first arrived here four years ago, numb with grief and fear and not knowing what on earth was around the corner.

'Of all the places in the world, what the hell brings a pretty girl like you here to Ballybray?' Mabel had called to me in her thick New York accent from across the garden fence when Ben and I made our way from the village bus stop to the cottages known as Teapot Row.

I looked over to see her standing in her garden with her hand on her hip. She wore pink gloves and a bright yellow rain coat, a burst of sunshine to brighten up what was a very wet, very grim winter's day. My initial reaction was to ask her to mind her own business. I'd come to Ballybray to hide for a while, to self-protect, and to plan my next move in life. I'd come to reinvent in my own time and the last thing I needed was some little old lady who dressed like she was twenty years younger poking her nose in my business.

'You do know it's a village full of old crocks just like me who are obsessed with gardening all year round, but I love it here,' she told me. 'Who knows? Maybe you will too!'

Looking back through different eyes, I can see now that Mabel was certainly breathtaking in the most unconventional way. In contrast to her yellow coat and pink gloves, she wore a deep purple headscarf that framed a face which was once that of a beauty queen, she had streaks of dark mud on her high cheekbones and a figure that defied her age.

I remember fidgeting with my scruffy duffle jacket, fixing my unruly long brown hair and scrambling in my head for an answer to her question.

I knew why I'd run away from Dublin, but I'd no idea why I chose here, and even if I had, I had no intention of explaining my reasons to a stranger.

I was thirty-six years old, newly widowed, I had very little money left after buying a house I'd not yet set foot in but had simply chosen from an online brochure, I'd a world of experience, but a head full of muddle, and I'd no doubt my boho, hippy appearance probably raised questions with a lot more people than Mabel on my grand arrival to this sleepy village. I was also very guarded and fiercely over-protective of the world I'd found myself living in, and the one I wanted to create for my son's and my future.

Ballybray, my very limited research told me, was a rural, one-street village near the north-west coast of Ireland in County Donegal, the key attributes of which were a huge lake on the south side and a wild patch of forest on the top of a steep hill known as 'Warren's Wood' on the north, even though no one seemed to know who Warren is or was. The seaside town of Dunfanaghy was just down the road, which meant we would never be far from the sea, a fact that sold it to me instantly as a far cry from the inner-city concrete jungle in which I'd spent most of my own childhood.

Between those two main landmarks, there was a small grocery shop, a bakery, an ornate little chapel, a tiny primary school, a hairdressing salon, a village hall, oh and a pub whose owners had just renovated the building next door into a vintage clothes shop with a coffee corner, which to the locals was very exciting indeed as it brought shoppers to visit from near and far.

There was no doubt about it. If I'd wanted somewhere small, quiet and easy going, I had certainly chosen the right place, which was exactly what I intended. I wanted away from the smothering smog and city life. I wanted to go somewhere where absolutely no one knew my name.

Mabel, with her splash of colour and vibrant energy, stood with her pink hand still on her hip and waited for an answer to her question.

'I – I, um, stuck a pin in the map of Ireland and this is what I got,' I told Mabel with a timid shrug. It was as much as I was giving her. 'I know virtually nothing about this place, but I've a whole lifetime to see if we like it or not. I hope we do.'

Mabel threw her head back and heartily laughed at my response, which I didn't really find to be that funny. It was the truth. It was as simple as that.

'You stuck a pin in a *map*, darling?' she howled. '*Literally?*'

'Literally,' I told her, shrugging again. 'It was a hairpin actually, but the same concept, I suppose.'

Mabel came closer to the fence between us, waved me over towards her, and when I reached her, she took my face in her gloved hands and looked deep into my soul. She smelled of outdoors, of fresh air and of new beginnings with a hint of white musk, and although I wanted to pull away, deep, deep down I also wanted so badly for someone to understand my pain without me having to spell it out.

I stiffened up at first, but despite how much I fought against it, within seconds I melted a little under her kind touch and sincere eyes.

'You and I, my dear,' Mabel said with a beaming smile, 'are going to get along just swimmingly!'

And with that gesture and her few simple words, I already felt some of my darkest worries disintegrate right then and there, even if I wasn't ready yet to let my guard down or to let her in.

I don't know if *I* found Donegal or if Donegal found me, but this move, I reckoned, was far enough to close the door on a time in my hometown of Dublin I'd rather forget about, and it was near enough to get us back there again if I took cold feet and changed my mind. I loved Dublin and always would, but life was going in the wrong direction for me there, and I had to make a choice. And that choice just happened to be Ballybray.

'My name is Mabel Murphy and I'm a blow-in too,' she told me, 'in case the American accent fell on deaf ears. I'm from New York, but I was lucky enough to marry an Irish man who brought me here about ten years ago.'

She took off her glove to shake my hand formally across the picket fence, and then she glanced around as her voice dropped to a whisper even though there was no one else within earshot except Ben to hear her, and he wasn't even listening.

'I have to warn you, though. They're probably going to fear you as much as they feared me around here,' she told me. 'They don't take to newcomers kindly, so I think we'd best stick together.'

'Really?'

'I'm kidding!' she said, her beautiful face creasing as she giggled. 'They are going to love you. It's a wonderful place to live.'

My stomach churned and the wave of anxiety that had just punched me in the gut lingered at the very idea of being resented here, even if she was joking. I didn't want anyone to fear me. I'd had enough fear in my old life.

'I'm Roisin,' I told her, trying to be mannerly despite my reluctance to become anything more than neighbour to this woman who was almost twice my age. 'Roisin O'Connor, and this is my son, Ben. We're hoping to make Ballybray our new home. A new start, whatever that means.'

I felt choked up at the very thought of it.

'Well, you are very brave, Roisin O'Connor, to make a new start, and you are both so, so welcome!' Mabel had gasped in delight, studying Ben now from head to toe, and then she smiled the most beautiful warm smile as if the very sight of him had filled her heart with joy.

I didn't feel very brave back then, but I'd go on to hold those words from Mabel so tightly for many years to come.

'I bet you're about six years old, aren't you, Ben?' guessed Mabel, which impressed my precious son greatly. He lifted his head to listen now that she'd given him her full attention, and then looked up at me with widened eyes.

'How did she *know* that?' he asked me, before turning to Mabel and smiling a toothy grin in return. 'Are you *magic*? How did you *know* I was six?'

I was totally taken aback by his reaction but I ignored it and clasped his hand tightly. Ben hadn't smiled like that in for ever. In fact, he usually cowered when adults spoke to him, especially people he didn't know.

'When you've lived for as long as I have, you get to know a lot of things. Almost *everything* in fact,' Mabel whispered with a wink and a nod, and we'd soon find out she wasn't exaggerating. 'Now, go get settled into your new home and if you don't think I'm being too pushy, I'll call in for a cuppa when you're ready. I'll keep you two right around here. You don't have to worry about a thing.'

Mabel always reminded me how she'd read me like a book the moment we met that day. She said she could see into my troubled soul, past the outgrown bangs, the heavy mascara and the wall of defence I'd built up around me and my son. She knew I was struggling. I believe that she knew me inside out from our very first conversation.

'We have a lot to do,' I told her, trying my best to be polite. 'It's nice to meet you.'

We left her to her weeding, then Ben and I lugged our

cases up the crooked pathway and turned the key in the creaky muddy green door, just the two of us, all alone in a big bad world as we took our first steps towards a new tomorrow. My hands shook as I battled with the front door key, and I bit my lip to fight back tears of absolute fear of the unknown.

'You all right, honey?' Mabel called, seeing how I was poking at the lock. 'It's been a while since that door has been opened!'

'It's OK, I got it!' I called back, my voice shaking and my insides churning as I anticipated the new beginnings that lay inside.

Leave me alone old lady, I thought, even though I hadn't the courage to say it out loud. *Just get on with your gardening and leave me and my son alone.*

The door creaked open and step one of our new life had begun.

2.

I'd known from the estate agent's brochure that No. 3 Teapot Row in the village of Ballybray was a humble little home, but I also could tell that it would be safe, far away from danger or threat of the ghost of my ex-husband ever finding us again.

The sandstone exterior with cute white wooden sash windows and wisteria had caught my eye as I flicked through properties online, and I couldn't believe my luck at the price tag. It had a small garden to the front with a little path that led to a green door – every door in the row was painted a different colour – and a back garden that had enough room for a swing and a paddling pool in summer.

We had made it this far. It was ours now, so I took a deep breath and stepped inside, trying to look at every single part of it through positive eyes.

The musty smell of the poky hallway that was just big enough for two hit me first, and I convinced myself that the tiny kitchen meant there was a lot less to clean than the house we had left behind. The living room with a circa

1970s fireplace was 'vintage,' rather than old, I decided. Yes, vintage was good. I could work with vintage.

'I love it,' I repeated to myself internally. 'I really love it.'

Truth be told, I didn't *quite* love it at first. I was absolutely petrified, but I was determined that one day I would love it with all my heart and never want to leave.

Our new home was third from the end in a row of eight semi-detached two-storey stone cottages, and I'd sealed the deal by calling up the nearest estate agent who told me my luck was in, but who also seemed baffled by my choice of destination when he heard my city accent.

I remember how I fought back tears at the enormity of it all when I walked inside and smelled the unfamiliar interior of a place I'd pledged to try to make a home for us. It was to be a brand new start, a new beginning, a place where we could be whoever we wanted to be, in a village I knew virtually nothing about and, more importantly, with people who knew nothing about me.

I would transform, I would reinvent, and most of all I would heal, because inside I was broken and Mabel knew it instantly. When the door knocked a few hours after our first meeting across the fence, Ben let Mabel in despite my efforts to ignore her, and she found me crouched in the corner of the unfamiliar living room with a face smeared in streaky tears after I'd given up unpacking clothes and given in to the terror of a future that seemed so daunting, so unfamiliar, and so utterly frightening.

'You're wading through treacle right now, girl,' she told me with deep understanding, pushing back my hair and wiping my tears. 'You're swimming against the tide, but it won't always be like this, do you hear me? You're a fighter, and you've made the right decision coming here, I can tell. Stick with it, and stick with me. You're gonna be just fine.'

She hugged me so tightly like an old friend would and she didn't let go until I felt some of my worries disintegrate in her embrace.

I gave her nothing in return at first, but she never gave up on me from that day on. She brought us hot dinners when I was having a bad day and couldn't face cooking a proper meal, she took Ben to school and sent me back to bed to rest, and she gently gave me space to do my own thing when she knew I needed it.

'Why do you care?' I asked her one day as she was fussing over a hem on Ben's school trousers. Her warmth and motherly nature were alien to me, and I just couldn't understand why she gave so much despite getting so little in return.

'Don't ever run away or be afraid of kindness, Roisin,' she told me as she repaired the hem on the little pair of grey trousers. 'You deserve love and to be loved. We all do.'

The best thing was, Mabel's words were never insincere, because Mabel Murphy reminded me every single day since then that I'd made the right decision to move to Ballybray, and that I was going in the right direction in life.

She celebrated with me when Ben got through his first

day at his new school without tears, she danced with me when I got my part-time job in the clothes shop, Truly Vintage, and she took no excuses when I mentioned how I'd always dreamed about playing the violin as a child but had never learned. Before I knew it, she'd signed me up to a weekly class at the community centre, and when I mentioned how I'd need a babysitter, she pledged that she and Ben would have a weekly movie night while I headed off with my second-hand violin case in hand, feeling full of vigour and overflowing with the magic that only playing music can bring.

Mabel steered me on the right track in every walk of life from the first day I arrived in Ballybray, and the more she told me I was winning, the more I eventually believed it.

She brought us groceries when I didn't have the energy or inclination to go food shopping, she listened to me cry when the overwhelming waves of trauma from years gone by visited me late into the night, she made me laugh until my sides ached with her witty one-liners and stories of her days in New York city as a cabaret singer. She made me believe in unconditional love when I thought my cynical old heart had been broken for ever, and most of all, she gave me a sense of family that I'd never had before. She gave me a rock to lean on, a shoulder to cry on, and friend who was always there to cheer me on.

'You're like the mother I never had,' I told her one night when she'd stood at the front row of my first concert in the community centre and clapped with a beaming smile until her hands were sore and tears dripped down her face. My *grupa ceoil* had played a classic but simple Irish tune called 'The Mountains of Pomeroy' together with tin whistles, fiddles and guitars, but to Mabel you'd have thought I'd just performed with the London Symphony Orchestra.

In return for all the love I felt from her, she told me that I made her glow inside with my warrior strength and determination to make things better. I listened to her with awe and excitement as she recounted tales of her home city of New York, of the love she shared with her late husband Peter, and by being there to share her last few years with her, she said that Ben and I showed her how to live life to the full again. We gave her a reason to get up in the morning that didn't involve her talking to herself or to the plants in her garden. She enjoyed picking Ben up from school and she looked forward to Christmas, to birthdays and to holidays like she hadn't done since Peter's passing just a year before we moved to Ballybray.

'I wish I'd come here soon enough to meet Peter,' I used to tell her often.

She would look up at his photo on the mantelpiece, which stood alongside a framed picture of Peter's very handsome nephew Aidan, who lived in America, and recall how much Peter had never feared she would be alone in Ballybray for long.

'He told me he'd send me an angel,' she used to say, clasping her frail but hard-working hands to her chest as she thought of him. 'I like to think he knew you were coming here soon after he left. He was right. It didn't take long.'

Now, four years later and only two days after her funeral when we'd said our heart-breaking goodbyes to Mabel, our cosy living room that was once always filled with her laughter, her wise words and her sometimes intense swearing when she really wanted to make a point, is drenched in the darkness of a dull Saturday afternoon in November.

Snowflakes hit the window, then melt and trickle down the pane, reflecting our mood as Ben and I sit together side by side in the quiet, contemplating what the hell we are meant to do without her. The TV is off again, the clock breaks the silence as it ticks back time on the wall, and we drift between staring into corners of the room, to looking out of the window to falling asleep for brief naps, and nibbling on snacks from the cupboard left over from her wake. We are a sight of misery and despair once more, yet I can't shake it off, and neither, it seems, can Ben.

What would Mabel say if she saw us like this, I find myself wondering? I close my eyes and hear her raspy New York accent, telling me to shake off the cobwebs of the day and go do something fun.

She was a dancing-in-puddles type of woman when it rained, a 'ditch work and let's hit the lake for a swim' sort when the sun shone, and she taught me to value every moment of time, knowing that nothing lasts for ever, so why can't I continue on with how she'd like us to be?

'How about we go outside and have a snowball fight?' I ask Ben, trying my best to sound just a little like her. I even put on an American accent for effect, but he rolls his eyes at my efforts. At least it's a reaction of some sort.

'Or we could walk down by the lake?' I suggest. 'Feed the ducks? I bet they're starving.'

He scrunches his nose and I give up with my ideas.

I feel deflated, sunk, and dead inside if truth be told. I feel like after almost winning a four-year-long game of snakes and ladders that I've landed on the penultimate square and slid right back down to number one, back in time, back to the shell of a person I was when I first arrived here.

Most of all, I feel like packing up and running away to start over again, just like I did after the last funeral I attended four years ago, when Ben was too young to care where we were going, but old enough to know not to ask too many questions.

Going to Mabel's funeral took me right back in time to when my husband had died suddenly. Only at Jude's funeral, I can't say I felt the same sorrow as I do for Mabel now. In fact, all I felt then was anger and relief.

3.

'Will I fix us some stew just like Mabel used to make?' I suggest now to Ben, hoping and pleading with him for some sort of an answer, or that he might eat something other than toast and tea or rubbish from the biscuit tins left in by well-meaning villagers for the wake. 'It won't be quite as nice as Mabel could make it of course, but I'll do my best?'

Ben shrugs his shoulders, which is good enough to make me pounce off the seat to go and attempt to make Mabel's Irish Stew, delighted with myself that I'd bought in the ingredients just in case he'd show a spark of enthusiasm for a proper meal, and happy if truth be told, to be doing something that didn't involve staring into space.

She used to bring us a small pot of stew every Saturday in winter, and Ben would lap it up in one go, sometimes asking for more before he went to bed, and if she had more she would leave it in for him rain, hail, sleet or snow. She'd a knack for making that stew, and even if it was simple and not very fancy, no one could make it taste the way she did.

I throw some cubes of steak into the pan just like she

used to and then stir them around in a dash of oil as they brown. I quickly chop an onion, adding a splash of water, then turn it down to simmer just as she'd taught me to.

'You're going to need me to write this recipe down for when I go,' she'd told me over and over again in a giddy voice. 'It's very, *very* complicated.'

I'd burst out laughing at her blatant sarcasm.

'I'll remember it, I promise.' But she'd insisted on scrawling it down on a piece of paper and sticking it to my fridge. The writing has faded since that day, but I vowed I'd never take it down as it summarized her humour so dearly. There were memories of Mabel everywhere in our home, and that's the way it would always be.

Ben turns the volume up on the TV so high it pierces my ears and I make my way to the living room to tell him off. Grief or no grief, he can't get away with drowning me out like that, but just as I'm about to say my piece, a car pulls up directly outside Mabel's house next door and my heart skips a beat.

No one ever visits Mabel's house; no one except me or Ben of course, and the kind nurses who saw her through her last months as cancer dealt its final blow.

I race to the window, trying my best not to twitch the curtains, but I feel it's in my rights to know what's going on. I still have a key to her house, just like she had for mine, but I haven't been able to step inside it since the day of her burial. I'm not sure I'll ever be able to do so again.

'Who the hell is that?' I mumble to myself, knowing that Ben isn't listening nor can he hear me over the din of the TV. The man at Mabel's house drives a fancy silver Mercedes 4x4, the type of car I'd only ever seen in a car showroom from a distance, and he steps out of his vehicle and then goes to the boot to fetch something. I try desperately to peel my eyes away in fear he might see me watching, but I can't. And then I recognize his face from the funeral, even though he never did introduce himself formally to me or my son.

He's tall, broad shouldered, with dark wavy hair. I know him. Well, I know *of* him, I should say.

It's Aidan Murphy – *the* Aidan Murphy, who Mabel loved to brag about when I'd lend her an ear to do so. Her precious nephew, her only living relative, and the one person who lit up her life even more than Ben or I ever could or would, and he is putting up a *For Sale* sign in her garden!

'Come on!' I call out over the theme tune of some American TV show Ben is now superglued to. 'You just cannot do that so soon! No way!'

I put on my boots, grab my coat on the way through the hallway, put it over my head to shelter from the snowfall outside, and march as best I can without slipping to the end of the pathway.

'Excuse me, but why are you doing this so soon?' I shout at him, recognizing a rise of panic and grief in my voice that I can't seem to control. 'Couldn't you at least have discussed it with me first? Given me some notice or warning?'

'Excuse *me?*' he replies, puzzled. He blinks back snowflakes and wipes his hair out of his eyes as he stands in the blistering cold, positioning the wooden signpost in the snow-covered muddy soil in Mabel's once impeccable front garden.

'It's the week of her funeral, for crying out loud!' I continue. 'She's barely cold in the ground, and you're advertising for a new occupant already? Didn't you mean a word you said from the pulpit at her funeral? Are you *totally* hard-hearted, Mr Murphy?'

As I rant and rave, he stares back at me in bewilderment. I want to punch him.

'Hard-hearted?' he asks, laughing as he does so.

'Yes, hard-hearted!' I reply. 'This is incredibly hard-hearted of you!'

He squints in my direction as the penny drops as to who I am.

'So, *you* must be the enigmatic Roisin O'Connor?' he says, nodding now in realization. 'I heard you were great friends with my aunt, but I'm afraid this is none of your business.'

Enigmatic? What the hell is that supposed to mean? We are face to face now with only a flurry of snow and the picket fence coming between us. Well, that and our obvious difference of opinion as to what should happen to Mabel's house this week.

'None of my business?!' I spit, knowing I'm not giving him a very enigmatic impression now, as I stand, almost frantically in tears. 'I was her best friend and she was mine!

She hadn't seen you in the flesh in at least five years, and now you rock up, play chief mourner with your glamorous wife, and two days after her funeral you stick a signpost in her garden so you can earn money from her already! How could you be so greedy? *How?*'

I've never wanted to bite my tongue so much, but I can't stop myself.

I probably know a lot more about Aidan than he realizes I do, and my impression of him isn't, let's say, very honourable, despite his tragic upbringing and rags to riches story that Mabel swooned over.

'Do you have anything else to fire at me, or are you done for now?' he asks me, checking his phone as he speaks. 'Looks like this place hasn't changed much at all – Ballybray was always suffocating with nosey neighbours everywhere. You've just reminded me why I left in the first place.'

My mouth drops open and I sigh from the tips of my toes, realizing I am very much wasting my time and that in the bigger picture it's probably not my place any more to interfere in Mabel's business. But to call me a *nosey neighbour*? Aidan is just as I'd imagined he might be. Arrogant, cold, rich, nonchalant, and far too good-looking for his own good, only unlike Mabel, I am not going to fall for his wolf in sheep's clothing appearance. If he was as wholesome as Mabel had believed him to be, he'd have waited at least until some of her more personal belongings were out of the house before he advertised for a new owner.

In my state of distress, I hear echoes of my late husband Jude's laughter ringing in my ears.

You need to learn to butt out of other people's business, Roisin! Just who do you think you are? You're always trying to save everyone else's world when the one person you really need to save is yourself!

I feel tears prick my eyes as a ball of emotion sticks in my throat. *Am* I done? I probably am, if truth be told.

I'm so tired.

Mabel's wake had been quiet but exhausting, and her funeral had wrung me out emotionally. I've had more than enough for one week, not to mention a young boy who has since declared to me that everyone he loves just 'left and died' and believes that I am probably next, before going silent on me for days.

'Oh, just do whatever you have to do, Aidan. You're right! It's absolutely none of my business,' I mumble in defeat and storm away wiping my eyes as I march through the slushy garden and back into the place I call home.

'It was nice to meet you, Roisin!' Aidan calls after me, threatening to really tip my emotions over the edge. 'Keep warm! It gives this snow storm to get worse tonight!'

I don't answer him this time, and I slam my front door behind me, the sound of it shutting giving me comfort just as it always does because I feel safe here, far away from my own past and from my own truths. I deliberately take a moment to inhale the familiarity that surrounds me, calming down in seconds. The photos of Ben on the walls at various stages of his tiny life so far and snapshots of this new chapter of my life surround me, soothing me, reminding me of how far I've come since I left the busy streets of inner Dublin.

I miss Mabel so badly already. She always had all the answers to my worries. She was a fiery New Yorker, a sharp-minded septuagenarian with an attitude to change the world, and a heart the size of the entire globe. She was Marmite, she was mysterious, and she was mine. She was the only person who believed that after all the hardship I'd been through, there was light at the end of the tunnel.

But now that light is out, I fear. The air has been sucked from within me and just like Ben, I feel like lying down in bed and shutting out the world, but I can't. I have to keep going for my son's sake, no matter how much I fear I'm crumbling inside.

I try to block out the sound of Aidan hammering in the *For Sale* sign that is still ringing in my ears, and I pledge to Mabel that I'll find a way to keep going. I have no idea how, but I go back to making her stew in search of some divine inspiration. I take off my coat and boots, go to the kitchen, where I add some stock cubes to the stewing beef, some chopped up potatoes, carrots, salt and pepper, and I allow it to simmer. As it stews, I do too at the idea of a new owner moving in next door. It just seems all too final and way too soon.

The smell of the simple ingredients warms the air and when I peep into the living room to find Ben curled up on the sofa fast asleep, I put a blanket over him, turn off the TV, turn on the soft sounds of Ella Fitzgerald, and allow myself to shed a quiet tear in Mabel's memory.

'No weeping over me, my girl!' I recall her telling me when I pushed her around the lakeside walk in her wheel-chair just a few weeks ago. 'I hope you know that I've lived a full and fruitful life, made even richer for having you and Ben beside me, so no tears please! Let there be laughter and smiles for miles and miles.'

It was easy of course to agree that there'd be smiles at the time when she was still here living and breathing, only a heartbeat away, but not so much now, when I'm empty and weak inside.

'I mean it, don't you dare fall on your knees again,' she'd said sternly. 'You're not the person I found crouching in that corner any more. You've a whole lifetime ahead of you, and you're made of tough stuff, Roisin O'Connor!'

I knew she meant business when she called me by my full name and not just Roisin. Remembering her doing so raises a smile and then my tears turn into laughter as I recall her in her glory days, out in the garden defying the elements, emphasizing that there was no such thing as bad weather, only the wrong clothes. She wouldn't have cared that the heavens opened on the day of her funeral. In fact she'd probably have enjoyed that.

'Put up an umbrella and quit moaning,' she'd have told us mourners as we shivered and complained. 'Button up your coat! It's Ireland you're living in, not the Bahamas for crying out loud.'

My reminiscing is interrupted by the faint smell of burning so I jump up quickly and add more water to the pot, stirring the stew frantically to try to save it.

Just in the nick of time, I salvage the dish and I swear I can hear Mabel tut-tutting at how easily distracted I am.

'Where is your head, lady?' she'd ask me when she'd find me daydreaming. 'There's time for dreaming and there's time for doing. Which is it for you today, Roisin?'

A knock at my front door springs me back to reality and I put the lid on the pot and turn it down to the lowest setting, then play my usual guessing game as to who it could be as I walk from the kitchen through the narrow hallway. I've always hated the door knocking, especially at night, as it opens up old anxieties and fears from my life before I found peace here in Ballybray. I open the door and almost take a step back in surprise.

It's Aidan Murphy.

A very cold, a very wet, and perhaps a little more humble-looking Aidan Murphy. What could he be looking for now?

4.

'Yes?' I say, opening the door just a little bit at first and wincing as the icy wind cuts through into my hallway.

I don't know this man and I don't need strangers calling at night, especially not him, and especially not after the way he spoke to me earlier.

'I'm so sorry to disturb you,' he tells me, peeping through the narrow slit in the doorway. 'But do you have a minute?'

I open the door a bit more to respond.

'Me? You mean you *do* want to discuss something with Mabel's nosey neighbour after all?' I say, enjoying my upper hand now. 'You're really digging a hole with your arrogance, Mr Murphy, pardon the pun.'

He at least has the grace to shudder at his earlier insult.

'OK, OK, I'm sorry for calling you a nosey neighbour,' he says, extending a cold, damp hand. Again, I open the door a little wider, I shake his hand, and a waft of very expensive aftershave mixes in the cold air. 'I'm Aidan. Aidan Murphy.'

'I know exactly who you are,' I remind him. 'I've heard a lot about you, Aidan Murphy.'

'I'm sure you have,' he sings in return. 'You probably know more about me than I know myself right now, and at that I'm not joking.'

Even though he is haughty and cold in stature, now that I see him out of the flurry of snow I can tell he is indeed a very, very handsome man and a lot older than he was in the photo that has sat on Mabel's mantelpiece for as long as I've been here. He's about at least forty years old now, I guess, noticing the fine lines around his dark eyes. He looks so much like Peter, Mabel's late husband, but from what I've seen so far he has none of his uncle's manners or charm.

'You spoke well at the service,' I say to him jutting out my chin and folding my arms, knowing I can't deny him that. 'You're a good speaker and can surely tug on emotions for someone who is so hard-hearted.'

He looks different now in his jeans and navy rain jacket, a far contrast from the slick black suit he wore for the funeral mass on Thursday. I know I should really ask him inside, but I just can't let him away with his initial approach so easily. Mabel would hate to see my stubborn streak or old anxieties creep through, especially now – especially with her precious Aidan.

'Thank you, that's – that's kind of you to say,' he says, looking through the snow at the adjacent garden of the semi-detached cottage. 'Look, if you don't mind I just need to talk to you about something and then I'll be out of your hair again for good. I'm not planning on hanging around Ballybray for any longer than I have to.'

I open the door properly and try to figure out this stranger who can barely hold eye contact with me. For someone so hugely successful in New York, he is severely lacking on people skills, but I refuse to stoop to his level, so I remember my manners.

'You're freezing.' I say, stating the obvious. 'Can I get you a cup of tea? Or some stew? You look like you're frozen through.'

It's a no, just as I'd imagined it might be, but at least I tried.

'No thanks, this won't take long,' he says, wiping his feet on the mat.

He steps into my hallway, closes the door, and I lead him past the living room where my son still sleeps off his sadness, and into the kitchen, proud of the warm, homely smell that fills the air.

My house may be small and old in comparison to whatever mansion or posh New York apartment he lives in, but I always pride myself in making a house a home with warm colours, mouth-watering smells, and a cosy atmosphere.

'It's Mabel's own recipe for Irish Stew,' I explain to him, even though he isn't remotely interested and didn't ask what's cooking. 'She insisted on writing it down for me once, even though it's the simplest thing to make in the world, but I only wish she'd passed on the secret of how hers always tasted nicer than my version ever will!'

I point towards her handwriting on the fridge and he leans closer to read it, his eyes quickly scanning across the gallery of photos that hang on to their place beside it with alphabet magnets. As he does so, I allow myself to take in his handsome physique, his hair damp from the snow, and I feel my hormones flutter at his good looks, but the feeling leaves me as quickly as it came. I am very, very much done with letting any man interfere with the life I plan on having here – just me and my son, where no one will ever hurt us or leave us again.

He stands up straight, having seen enough of my patchwork of photos from down memory lane.

'Can I take your coat?' I ask him, catching his dark eyes in direct contact properly now. 'You'll get a chill.'

He looks almost as tired as I am, dark under the eyes and his face pale and a little gaunt. Jet-lagged too, no doubt, and grieving, I suppose, in his own way.

'It's OK,' he says, still taking in his surroundings. 'I can't really stay long.'

He shuffles a bit, and I pull out a chair at the kitchen table for him to take a seat, inwardly apologizing to Mabel for our bumpy start and hoping it can only get better.

'Look, Roisin, I'm not here on a social visit,' he tells me quickly. 'So I'll cut to the chase.'

'I think I've already guessed that.'

'I've a lot of loose ends to tie up here and my plan is to do so and get back to New York as soon as I can.'

He shifts in his chair as if his skin is crawling, emphasizing that being in Ballybray is the last thing he wants right now.

He has property in Dublin, I know from Mabel's bragging, but I imagine he and his wife are staying in some plush hotel like the Westbury or the Merrion, in luxurious surroundings, a far cry from his much more modest beginnings here. His very beautiful wife, who Mabel incidentally couldn't stand, is no doubt relaxing in a spa right now while he does his mundane business here in the backwaters, and they'll have dinner by candlelight at seven and long to escape Ireland back to the glamour of their real life in New York City.

'I've just this minute discovered that Mabel has left us some sort of package to open after she died,' he says, reaching into his inside pocket. 'So I didn't want to open it without letting you know, as it's very clearly addressed to us both.'

'A package?' I ask. 'For me and you?'

My image of his glamorous wife disintegrates immediately and the mug in my hand almost slips to the floor, but I catch it just in time.

He's totally lost me on the whole 'us' revelation. I mean, I'd imagined Mabel might leave Ben and me something small in her will to remember her by, like the tea set from Amsterdam I'd always admired, or the cushion on her settee from her home in New York that Ben loved resting his head on, but what could she have left for us now at this stage?

'Yes. *Us* as in me and you, strange as it may seem,' he says, pulling out a brown padded envelope. He sets it on the table in front of him and stares at it. 'Even stranger is that I found it in the garden shed, which suggests she didn't want it to be discovered straight away, not until after the funeral anyhow.'

I lift the envelope from the table and touch her distinctive handwriting with my fingertips, feeling my heart race in my chest at the idea of what might lie inside this package delivered from beyond the grave.

Mabel was always so delicate with a pen, and every letter kicks or swirls like it is ready to dance off the page. I always felt her calligraphy reflected her vibrant past as a performer, kicking her heels up to the roar of a loving crowd in New York.

I read it aloud, with my hand on my chest, unable to contain the quiver in my voice.

'For my family – my darling Aidan and Roisin – two of my favourite people in what was such a wonderful life,' says Mabel. *'Please watch this short message together and do as I say – or else! Love, Mabel.'*

'Wow,' I mutter, in total disbelief. 'For my family? She always told me we were like her family, but . . . and she's left us a message!'

Reading her words already has me choked up and I feel my heart fill up at how she considered me family, never mind the effort she must have gone to, recording a special message just for us. I lay the envelope down carefully again on the table, stuck for words for once.

'Was she always so mysterious in her later years?' Aidan asks me in a tone that suggests he doesn't share my sentimentality. 'I mean, I knew she was capable of meddling and giving her opinion to anyone who would listen, but I never thought she'd be so meticulous in her planning for after she left this world.'

My memories of my love for Mabel change quickly to anger in her defence. Meddling? Oh, I could say so much to him right now! I could ask him why he chose to abandon and ignore her in her final years, why he didn't come to visit, knowing she was ill for months, why he had turned his back on the woman who loved him like a second mother, just the way she loved me.

'I guess when your days are numbered, all sorts of notions go through your head,' I tell him, holding the envelope once more and doing my best to remain neutral and diplomatic. 'We talked a lot about death over the past few months. She had no fear of dying even though it was staring her in the face, and I thought she'd told me all she'd wanted to, so I have absolutely no idea what this is about.'

We stare some more, and then I push the envelope across the table towards Aidan. I catch his eye, wondering how surreal this moment might be for anyone looking on right now. Here we are . . . me – a widowed, single mum with so much emotional baggage it almost makes me slouch sometimes and who'd come to this village to find solace from a life of trauma, and Aidan Murphy, a married man of great fortune and style, who'd escaped his own many years ago to make a life of huge financial success away from his own pain.

We are worlds apart in every way, from the shiny Merc that sits outside adjacent to my battered old pick-up truck, his designer clothes to my vintage second-hand dress, and his life of glamour to my humble struggles. We have simply absolutely nothing in common except the love of an old lady who for some reason wants to push us together in some sort of quest from beyond the grave.

And wedged between us is the fact that neither of us can feel any connection to each other at all.

'Open it,' says Aidan, handing me the envelope in a tone that suggests he is used to doing things his way.

I almost give in, but for some reason it doesn't feel like it's my place to do so.

'You're her *real* family,' I say, pushing it back towards him. 'Your name is first on the label.'

He runs his fingers under the neck of his shirt, bites his lips, and looks me right in the eye. He curls his lips and smiles for the first time since our hasty introduction.

'You're feisty, just like Mabel said,' he tells me, tearing open the envelope while holding my gaze.

I can't answer as I inhale deeply, waiting to see what might lie inside. I can feel her breath in the air. I can hear her voice in my ear. I can smell her perfume all around me, and most of all I can feel the intensity of Aidan Murphy's hypnotic stare.

He pulls out a silver DVD and my eyes divert towards it.

'She's left us a *video* message?' Aidan says in disbelief. 'God no. I can't watch this. It would be far too—'

'Soon,' I say, interrupting him before he says what we're both really thinking.

Sore may have been a better word in Aidan's case. It's sweet of Mabel and it's surprising, but I do agree that it's also going to take a lot of courage and strength to watch her talking directly to us when she's not with us any more, especially when one of us mightn't like what she has to say.

My own heart thumps at the thought of watching it. I'm totally lost for words and the idea of hearing her voice again, addressing me directly with whatever it was she wanted to share at this stage fills me full of wonder and disbelief at her doing this all behind my back. Mabel and I had made a pact that we'd never have any secrets. It was all or nothing between us. My mind races at the thought of what might be coming next from her.

'Yes, *soon*,' says Aidan, standing up before I can suggest we see this through right now. 'I'll leave it with you. I hope whatever she has to say brings you comfort and closure.'

My face falls into a frown.

'But you mean?' I stutter, looking up at him. 'You mean you're not going to watch it at all?'

He puts his hands in his pockets and shakes his head. He swallows so hard I see his Adam's apple move and, if I'm not mistaken, I think there might be a hint of tears in his weary eyes.

'No, I'm not going to watch it at all, Roisin. Look, I'm really sorry, but I'd better get going,' he says, shuffling as if he needs to escape from here immediately. 'My business here is just that, *business*. I don't have any inclination to allow for any emotional attachment to Mabel or to Ballybray get under my skin.'

'This is unbelievable,' I mumble. 'How could you just choose to ignore this? From your own aunt?'

I am floored by this package, but also alive with the anticipation of hearing from her again, while he, in turn, is stiff, bitter and sore.

He fidgets, pauses, and then heads for the hallway as if he can't wait to get away from here quick enough.

'It's a bit of a surprise all right, isn't it, but I'm sure it will be positive?' I call after him, realizing that if he doesn't watch what she has to say with me, Mabel's efforts aren't being received in the way she intended.

I walk after him to the door, but I don't want him to go so quickly, leaving me hanging like this. I want to talk about it, or at least to get this over and done with and hear it so we can start building our lives without her. I want to talk about Mabel with someone who knew her as well as I did, but he's leaving and can't wait to do so.

'I can't and I won't watch it, Roisin,' he tells me, meeting me at last in the eye. 'I need to get back to New York in a day or two to my . . . I'll leave it with you.'

He needs to get back to New York to his wife and his big business and polar opposite luxury lifestyle.

'Aidan!' I call as he walks down the path towards my garden gate. 'If you change your mind—'

'I won't,' he tells me without looking back, and then he disappears into the snowy, dark night, taking a tiny piece of my heart and the chance of a final connection to Mabel with him.

I clutch the envelope to my chest, wondering if I should go ahead and watch it without him, but I can't. It's not what she wanted.

'Oh Mabel,' I mutter to myself as I make my way back to the kitchen. 'Whatever are you planning now and what the hell is his problem?'

I run my fingers over her writing, bewildered at Aidan's attitude, but content in knowing she hasn't gone too far from us at all just yet.

In fact, she is very, very near.

5.

I find Ben hard at work in Mabel's back garden the next morning, rolling a snowball into a huge mound across her tiny lawn that is now unrecognizable under the thick snow. Aidan was right about the storm. It snowed all night long and there's a chill in the air that hints at more, though for now the sky is blue, and the white on the ground makes everything look bright and magical.

Ben is humming to himself, just as he always does when he is busy, and on the small stone table in Mabel's garden where we used to share breakfast, lunch and lots of conversation, I see he has laid out a scarf, a hat, a carrot and some obligatory pieces of coal for his final masterpiece.

There has always been a tangible solace in Mabel's garden and if Ben is finding comfort from being here, then that's good enough for me, so I stand in silence watching him, delighted that he's keeping busy in his grief.

'The garden is like your mind,' Mabel used to tell me when I'd find her fixing and planting at all times of the year. 'Find the time to weed your garden and you'll find the time to weed your mind. Believe me, Roisin, it works.'

A bird table that Ben once could barely reach is now almost shoulder high beside him as he stands back to admire his work so far, lost in a world of his own. Watching him play there with such ease, so at home, makes my heart pang for days gone by. This is the life he had grown so comfortable with; the peace, the love and the kindness. I pray every night that he never ever remembers the contrasting darkness of the times with his father before we came here.

This is his entire world, going from house to house, from garden to garden, and instead of the shouting and name calling from our life before, all he ever heard here was the sweet sounds of Mabel singing along to her old favourite records from her own heyday. She introduced us to the sounds of Etta James, Ella Fitzgerald, Billie Holiday and Dusty Springfield to name a few, and Ben spent so much time with her that he knows almost every word to every song.

Mabel had made a little hole in the hedge that ran between our back gardens soon after we moved in to Teapot Row. The hole had grown over the years into a 'Ben sized' opening so he could come in and out to her at his leisure, and the sight of him so hard at work now and busy in mind takes my breath away. Mabel's garden, despite the battering rain and snow of the past few days, still looks like a palette of colour from an artist's canvas, with various shades of green scattered around an immaculate little square of grass, framed with a salmon stone patio where my son used to sit and chat to her for hours on end.

'You know, we won't always be able to come in and out of Mabel's garden like this,' I try to break to him gently when he finally catches me watching him play. 'It won't happen for a very long time, I hope, but when there are new neighbours living here it won't feel like ours any more.'

He looks up at me and pauses, then goes back to his snowman.

'It's OK for today, though,' I assure him. 'You can stay here as long as you want today.'

He ignores me and continues polishing up the snowman, so I leave him to it, having made my point.

I cross back into my own patch of nature next door and I hear Mabel's words in my ear at the contrast of the two gardens – my unruly jungle versus her wondrous masterpiece.

'You'll never believe it, but lawn mowers are on offer in town right now,' she told me one day, dropping a clanger of a hint in a way only Mabel knew how to. 'Or you could always borrow mine? It's really light and easy to use. You can have it any time.'

There was no doubt about it, my back garden was sometimes an overgrown mess, but there was always something else more pressing for me to do and I just never found the time to take care of it properly. I eventually did buy a lawnmower, but its outings were few and far between.

I let out a deep sigh. Without Mabel to push *me* into things, I realize how little I'd have done around had she not always been in my ear. I was at my lowest ebb when she came into my life, and now she's gone, I worry I might be sliding down that same slippery slope already. I can feel it in the air. It's a sense of fear that is so overwhelming, like a tidal wave approaching from which I can't escape. It's hopelessness, it's loneliness, it's a huge cloud, and it's coming to get me fast.

I go inside and boil the kettle, then lean against the worktop and let the tears flow, but unlike the past few days when I've cried silently when Ben is around, this time I can't help but sob from the tips of my toes for her loss. I throw my head back and let it all out, all the frustration of what brought me here in the first place and how far I've come since then with her help. I'm so frightened again and I don't know what I'm going to do without her.

'There's a man in Mabel's house, Mum! I swear there is! He's in the kitchen! He knocked the window at me!'

I jump and wipe my tears, not knowing if I'm more in shock at Ben's revelation or the fact that he has finally uttered a few words to me at last.

'He looked cross!' he says, out of breath and full of drama. 'Maybe it's the new neighbour? Is he going to sleep in Mabel's bed? Oh Mum, I hope he isn't angry at me! I left the carrot and scarf for the snowman over there on the table!'

I dab my eyes with the back of my sleeve and feel my heart rate slow down when I realize that it's probably Aidan back again and not some intruder or some keen new occupants looking around. Or is it? Just in case, I race to the front door and look outside, ignoring how my face must look, like a swollen, puffy mess.

Aidan's car is there, just as I'd suspected, and there doesn't seem to be anyone else parked outside.

'It's fine, honey,' I tell Ben, who stands alongside me, looking outside. 'That's Aidan, Mabel's nephew. He's looking after all of Mabel's things and he doesn't realize who you are. It's OK. It's all OK. Go finish your snowman, don't worry.'

'Aidan Murphy?' says Ben, wide-eyed. 'From New York City? Can I meet him, Mum? Can I?'

'Not right now,' I say, hushing him gently. 'In fact, maybe we should just build a new snowman in our own garden, is that OK?'

He looks up at me, puzzled. It seems that even Ben couldn't escape from Mabel's tales of her wonderful nephew, but unlike how I'd chosen to imagine him with my cynical hat on, Ben had shared Mabel's view that Aidan was some sort of real life mysterious superhero.

I feel my young son's shoulders relax when I pull him in to me for a quick hug and the warmth of his touch soothes me instantly. A glimpse of sunshine peeps out from behind a fluffy white cloud above us, showing that maybe a break from the bleak weather might be just around the corner. Maybe if the weather changes for the better, our moods will too. I pray fervently for something to lift us from this sense of despair.

'I just miss her,' says Ben when we finally let go. He looks upwards, blows a kiss towards the sky and then goes upstairs to his room, and I know I probably won't see him or hear from him again until at least lunchtime, the snowman abandoned for now.

'I know you miss her, honey,' I whisper after him. 'I do too.'

She told him to do that, I remember with a smile. She told him to blow her a kiss up to the sky and that she'd catch it every time. I want to hold on to those simple connections, but since she died, so far every day is like a scene from *Groundhog Day*. Every day is a drag.

Ben will go back to school on Monday and I need to get back to work to keep food on the table, but I don't know if I can. I need Mabel. Oh God, I need Mabel.

I need to hear what she has to say. I need to hear her message.

'Ben!' I shout to my son, who probably has headphones on by now and isn't able to hear what I have to say. 'I'm just popping next door quickly. I won't be long!'

I race to the kitchen, pull open the second drawer to find the envelope that Aidan left with me yesterday, grab it and make my way next door to him. I slip and slide my way up my own pathway, race through mine and then Mabel's gate, negotiate her path, and then I knock on Mabel's yellow door with a sense of urgency as adrenaline pumps through me now at the thought of hearing her voice again.

'Roisin!' says Aidan, as if he wasn't quite expecting to see me again. 'I've told you I—'

He's wearing a white T-shirt which is splattered with paint, and is holding an old rag in his hand. I've obviously interrupted a man at work.

'You frightened my son!' I tell him, unable to let that one go before I get down to business. 'Do you always have to be so cold and arrogant? We were so close to Mabel, closer than you'll ever understand, so how dare you be so rude to him when he's struggling so badly to let her go!'

'I beg your pardon,' he says, wide-eyed and taking a step back from the doorway. 'I had no idea who the kid was. I was just letting him know I was here, that's all.'

I take a deep breath.

'Look, Aidan, I know you can't be bothered with me or anything to do with life here in Ballybray, but I can't wait any longer,' I tell him. 'I need you to watch this, like Mabel would have—'

We both talk over each other with the same breathless urgency.

'But I told you already I've no intention of—'

'We need to watch this together, Aidan, please!' I tell him, unable to listen to his excuses on why we should put it off again. 'Please. I don't want to go against her wishes by watching it without you, but I also can't just keep wondering what she has to say. I need to hear her voice, Aidan, and then we never have to see each other again. Ever!'

Aidan guards the front door of Mabel's house with his arm leaning on the doorframe and his other hand on the door itself. He looks as though he hasn't slept a wink in days.

He also looks a bit spaced out with it, but I'm on a mission and I need to pin him down to do this once and for all. After we watch Mabel's message, I don't need to see him or disturb him or interrupt his work, nor will I ever want to.

'It might help us both a little?' I continue, not budging from the subject at hand, holding up the envelope as I speak. 'Look, we can put it on and if it's all too much we can press stop. It's probably only a few minutes long. Please?'

He shakes his head.

'I'm sorry, Roisin, I can't right now,' he explains to me. 'I've a lot on at the minute and I'm not sure if I can take this all in right now. I've a lot going on in here.'

He points to his head and then to the paint on his T-shirt. My heart sinks.

'But – but it might be good for you, whatever you're going through?' I suggest. 'This message is for you as much as it is for me.'

His hand drops from the doorframe and he folds his arms.

'Roisin, I'm busy, I'm sorry!' he tells me, shouting now. 'Watch it for yourself. I'm sure if there's anything in there that's totally life changing you can shout across the fence to me before I go. Now, that's enough. Go about your own business and let me go about mine!'

I shake my head in disbelief and put the envelope under my arm. I can't believe what I'm hearing. He really doesn't want to hear from Mabel? He doesn't have time to see through her very simple wish for us to watch this together? My eyes widen. My throat goes dry and I feel tears prick my eyes.

'You . . . OK, you do your thing then, Aidan, whatever it is,' I manage to mumble in his direction. 'And then you can swan off in your fancy car back to your fancy life and sail on without giving Mabel as much as an afterthought, but for me it's not as simple as that. I *live* here and I loved her! I'm surrounded by her loss and I know yes, she was perhaps a batty, crazy old lady to some people around here, but to me she was so much more. *So* much more!'

I can't stop the tears now, and once again I realize how hideous I must sound with too much to say, not to mention how I look in my denim dungarees, my hair in a messy long ponytail, and my puffy eyes that haven't seen make-up for days.

I stomp away, deciding to do as he wishes and leave him to it, when he calls me back, his voice cracking as he does so.

'Do you even *have* a DVD player?' he shouts when I'm halfway down the path. 'I mean, who has a DVD player these days? I don't know anyone who does.'

I pause. I turn to face him again.

'I do actually,' I tell him, wiping my tears with the back of my hand. 'We're a bit behind the times here in Ballybray.'

I squint now under the sun as it breaks through a little more cloud and Aidan manages a faint smile beneath his tired eyes.

'Why am I not surprised to hear that?' he says, rolling his eyes in surrender. 'OK, OK, Roisin! I'll do it.'

'You will?'

'Yes,' he says. 'I'll get changed and will be over as soon as I can. And that's it, OK? After this we move on. We get practical. I've a lot to be getting on with and I'm sure you do too. Mabel wouldn't want either of us moping over her.'

'Yes!' I reply, almost punching the air. 'Oh, you won't regret this, Aidan, I just know it! Thank you! I'll go get it all set up! Yes!'

I slip and slide, feeling his eyes watch me for a few seconds before he closes the door, but I don't care how hideous I might look right now. I just need to hear what Mabel has to say.

Half an hour later, Aidan still hasn't arrived, and although I'm afraid he may have changed his mind, his lateness gives me time to chat to Ben about what Mabel has left behind for Aidan and me on this DVD. Despite my revelation, Ben has gone back into his reclusive state and is happy to sit it out and play on his Xbox in his bedroom rather than watch any of Mabel's message.

'Don't you at least want to come and meet Aidan like you said earlier? Maybe he'd like to meet you too?'

He ignores me, his fingers focused on the controls and his eyes fixated on the graphics on the screen in front of him. It's like someone has flicked a switch in him once more and it freaks me out as to how long this will last. I know his stand-off can't go on for ever, but I also know that I need to allow him space to get used to how life is going to be very different from now on.

'I'll just be downstairs if you need me,' I tell him, kissing his forehead before I head down to wait for Aidan.

I've pulled up my two armchairs close to the TV, I've pulled the curtains, I've lit the fire, and I have the envelope sitting, ready and waiting for Aidan's arrival. This is a massive moment for me and I've never felt butterflies like it in my entire life.

My heart jumps when I hear a knock at my front door.

'Sorry I'm late,' he says to me with no further explanation. He has changed out of his working clothes and looks casual and cool in a pale blue hoodie, jeans and trainers.

'That's OK,' I reply. 'Can I get you anything? Tea? Coffee?'

I try not to stare. After all I've heard about him from Mabel over the past few years, having him here now in the flesh is slowly sinking in that he is a real, live person and not just a figment of her imagination.

'Just water is fine.'

I show him into the living room and invite him to have

a seat while I go to the kitchen and fetch two glasses, unable to stop my hand from shaking as I fill them with water from a jug. When I come back face to face with Aidan, I see his eyes full of pain and lost in memory as he waits for what might lie ahead. He may have found the last few days just as tough as Ben and I have, even though he chooses a very different way of showing it.

'OK, let's do this,' I say, feeling the tension in the air like a thick fog, knowing he is keen to get this over and done with. He nods and bites his lip, still a tad unconvinced, and I press play, noticing how he grips the cushion beside him. I look at my own hands and realize I'm doing the same.

'Oh God, there she is,' I whisper.

And there she *is*. Mabel's oh so familiar face fills the TV screen and we both gasp at the same time. It's her. It's our Mabel, in all her glory. Our beautiful, soulful, thoughtful friend with her soft lilac silky hair, her rouged cheekbones, her cerise lipstick, and a cheeky twinkle in her turquoise eyes. I fear I might choke as a range of emotions rushes through me – sadness, happiness, relief, joy, and a heart that's smashed into pieces at her loss.

She looks as if I could reach out and touch her. She looks like her old self. She looks *alive*. Oh God. She is wearing a T-shirt that says '*I'm back, bitches*', which makes Aidan and me laugh out loud.

I shake my head. This is mad. This is so Mabel.

She clears her throat dramatically, and then she speaks, which makes us both catch our breath again.

I don't care so much for what she has to say now. I just want to hear her voice.

6.

'Hey there!' she begins, and then lets out a bold rip of laughter. 'I bet you two weren't expecting to hear from me again, were you? Oh, Aidan Murphy and Roisin O'Connor! My two favourite people who made my whole world complete!'

She blows kisses, starting off her message with a bang just as I expected, and within the first few seconds her vibrancy has me smiling through my tears.

'You know, I do feel a bit like Queen Elizabeth on Christmas Day sitting here addressing my people!' she tells us, giving us a royal wave. 'Now, I hope you two are sitting comfortably – actually, I hope you two are watching this together like I asked you to or else I might come back to haunt you!'

She can't stop laughing and I can't stop grinning, even though my nerves are in pieces.

'So, what's this all about, then . . .?' she says, asking the million dollar question we both want to know the answer to. 'Well, I wish I could say that I'm leaving you both a set of keys to my Hollywood mansion from where I made my fortune in LA, or that I'd some big trust fund set aside for Ben, or that I've a holiday home in the Bahamas for you all to share, but you know I don't. I wish I did, but I don't.'

She pauses. Her mood dips and she looks a little more serious now as she rubs her chin and thinks before she continues. I shift in my chair and glance quickly at Aidan who hasn't moved an inch, but unlike my state of awe at seeing her he instead wears a frown and is leaning forward, fidgeting as she speaks.

'I have four little messages for you, one for each season for you both in the hope that it might keep you on track on your first journey around the sun without me, and then after that I'll be out of your hair for ever.'

She laughs a little, and pauses for a moment. Then, she takes a long breath and smiles directly at the camera.

'I know each of you might feel alone in the world right now, but please remember you are my family, Aidan and Roisin,' she tells us, focusing firmly on the camera now. 'We may not be connected through blood, but we are as deep as the ocean and as close as best friends can be. We are family.'

I momentarily lose my breath at the mention of the word 'family'. I can't look at Aidan as I fear he might be struggling too. Mabel has always known I have no immediate family to turn to in my life, and I'd never even thought of it, but Aidan is the same now too. Yes, he has his wife in New

York, but Mabel was no doubt a different source of comfort to him before they lost touch in recent times.

'I also know you are both very afraid right now,' she says, hitting the nail on the head once more. 'Roisin, I know you are afraid of raising Ben on your own, but you are stronger than I could ever have given you credit for. I wanted to remind you to open your heart for God's sake and don't be so afraid to love again, my girl! You've come so far and you deserve to love everything about life, I've always told you that and it's not going to change now, so get those walls down and let someone love you for the wonderful person you are inside!'

I fetch a tissue from up my sleeve and lean my face into it, my heart bursting with gratitude at hearing her kind words again, even if she's telling me off a little. And then she focuses on her nephew again.

'And Aidan,' she tells him softly. 'Yes, you are raw and hurt, and maybe a little bit angry at what life has thrown at you, but you need to make changes and you need to take some time out right now! Aidan, it's time you put your foot on the brakes and reassess where life is taking you, because I fear it's going in the wrong direction and I believe you know that too.'

I glance across at the man beside me, constantly fearful that he mightn't want to continue with Mabel's message any more. He may be a lot more fragile than I originally thought and I can almost feel the stress that sits on his shoulders, weighing him down. He has a lot going on, he said. I really hope that Mabel's words can help him as they've always helped me.

I lick my lips slowly, rolling my fingers on my sleeves, a habit that rears its head when I'm nervous or emotional.

'I know that each of you didn't like to hear what I had to say sometimes,' she says, 'but I've always had your best interests at heart. So please take some time for yourself for once, Aidan. And be brave like I know you can be.'

Her voice shakes again and her face crumbles. She takes a deep breath.

'I know by now that I've already had my last winter in this lifetime and I'm lucky to have that knowledge,' she tells us, looking a bit stronger now. 'But some of us don't know when we are living out our last seasons, so now that I'm gone, I'd love you to do something crazy today that makes you feel alive! Do something to awaken your senses! Do something that makes you scream with the joy of life! Go on! Do it for me! Do it together and do it for fun!'

I breathe out, imagining how I'd manage to muster up the energy to do something fun and spontaneous today when the snow is thick on the ground outside and I've been feeling so low that I can barely function.

The past week has been so grim, dark and quiet without Mabel living next door, and it's pained me even to exist sometimes, but her words remind me how she always pushed me out of my comfort zone, building my confidence to help me keep going. I close my eyes knowing she is trying to do this once more.

She continues.

'I know I'll never roll a snowball again with Ben or argue with him over trivia at Christmas dinner, but he has so many more Christmas memories to make, haven't you my little monster!'

She stops, purses her lips together and closes her eyes at the mention of Ben and I wish now that I'd pushed him a little more to watch this. Maybe he will when he is ready.

'And I know that he too will be very, very brave,' she says. She pauses and manages a smile as her eyes sparkle with tears. 'Oh, how I love him so!'

She sheds a tear now and looks away as drips of emotion roll down her face, then she dabs her cheeks gently, purses her lips again, and breathes in and out slowly to regain composure.

'Oh, it's absolute balls, really, isn't it!' she says louder now, trying her best to force a smile through her tears. 'It's absolutely horrible knowing you're going to die. It's a load of . . . it's . . .'

She pauses and composes herself once again. She looks exhausted, and a whirlwind of questions are going through my head, but her next words stop me in my tracks.

'I've organized some of my better quality clothes that might suit your shop, Roisin. Maybe the two of you could go through them together when you feel the time is right?'

she says, quite matter-of-factly, as if she is racing towards the end of her message now. 'And among the clothes I've left you both a secret gift to discover together. You can chuck the rest, or recycle them or whatever, but I hope you like the little keepsake I've left for you to find.'

I gasp in wonder and anticipation at what the keepsake might be, already feeling a cloak of comfort wrap around me knowing I've something that once belonged to Mabel to look forward to.

'Yes, winter can be bleak and dark, but we can always find colour in our imagination,' she says as she finishes off for now. 'So until next season, keep safe and warm, my beautiful family. Please know you are never alone and look after each other, knowing that by doing so, I'll never be too far away, guiding you along the way, I hope, in the right direction.'

7.

Aidan and I sit in silence for what feels like ages, taking in what we can from what Mabel had to say.

'Are you OK?' I ask him, trying to break the ice between us, but he doesn't answer at first, his face changing expression rapidly as a train of thought no doubt charges through his mind.

I feel like reaching out to him with a squeeze of a hand or a tight hug just like Mabel would have done, or would have perhaps wanted me to do on her behalf, but he looks like he is in a different world and I certainly don't think he's the hugging or touching kind.

'Yes, I'm fine,' he says rubbing his forehead. 'I'm absolutely fine.'

'That's good,' I say as he stands up and stares up at the ceiling. I wait for him to ask me the same question in return but he doesn't. I do my best to digest what I can from Mabel's winter message just now. The reminder to us both to have fun and do something today to make us feel alive . . . the passing on of a keepsake with her clothing . . . telling me firmly to open up to love again, and there was a strong message for Aidan in a strict reminder to be brave, to take time out, and make changes. I know Mabel. I know she means business. She would have chosen her words deliberately and carefully with our best interests at heart.

Now, I'm wondering where we go from here.

'I'd better be off then,' says Aidan, standing up suddenly from the armchair.

'You're going already?' I ask, trying to mask how abrupt I'm finding his actions. I thought we might talk about her a little, reminisce perhaps, or at least give her message a bit of time together.

'Yes, yes, I am,' he says, looking at his watch. 'I've even more to think about now than I had before, and that's saying something. Thanks for giving me a nudge to do so.'

I pull the curtains open, wishing I'd tidied the place a bit better now that the daylight is showing up how it needs dusting after days of mourning and neglect.

'A shove, more like it?' I suggest, feeling it a more appropriate description of my earlier approach. I was hardly subtle when I begged and pleaded with him not to make me wait.

'OK, a shove then,' he says and smiles. He holds my gaze now. 'Clever old Mabel, reminding me how it feels to have no family to call your own.'

He swallows back emotion and presses his lips together, looks at the floor, then directly at me again.

'You have your wife?' I say to him, trying to remind him

that he isn't as alone as he may feel right now. 'You have a whole new world of family with her?'

'Yes,' he mumbles. 'OK, so I'd best be on my way again. Until next season, eh?'

'Sorry?'

He brushes past me and looks out through the window.

I glance after him following his eye-line. The snow is still thick on the ground, but otherwise it's quite a nice day out. It's cold, no doubt, but fresh and the type of day that would give you a rosy glow in your cheeks.

'I'll let you know when I get the next message from her. Oh, and I'll dig out those clothes she was talking about too so you can find your keepsake, whatever that might be.'

He turns to face me and looks straight at me with a force of determination, reminding me how he doesn't want to discuss this any further. Mabel has certainly hit a nerve with him, but what is it he needs to change in his life, I wonder? Why does she think he needs some time out so badly?

I feel like I've much more to discuss with him before he walks away, but I've no idea why or what it might be. He marches towards the front door and I scramble in my head to find something.

'Mabel said to have some fun,' I say to him quickly just as his hand reaches for the handle on the door. He stops. 'I think she'd like you to have fun, Aidan. She said to do something to make you feel alive today. Something spontaneous, something that reminds you you're alive.'

He looks back at me as if I've lost the plot. Maybe I have because I've no idea what I'm suggesting he does, despite Mabel's instructions.

'Fun? Here? Like do what exactly?' he asks me. 'Ballybray isn't exactly hopping with things to do, is it?'

'No, not compared to the bright lights of New York, I suppose, but . . . but what was your favourite thing to do as a child when you lived here?' I ask him, wide-eyed with hope that he might remember something. 'You must have a happy memory of the snow? Tell me what it is and we'll do it in Mabel's honour!'

Aidan stammers, scrambling I know in his mind for excuses for why he can't or why he doesn't want to.

I recognize Mabel in my own actions, words and ideas right now. She was the best person I've ever met for shaking someone out of a mindset and bringing them around in minutes.

'I – I guess I have fond memories of sledging with my dad before he died,' he says, revealing perhaps a bit more than he intended to. 'Up at – up at Warren's Wood.'

I clap my hands together like I'm some overly energetic life coach.

'Fantastic! So, Ben and I will meet you up at Warren's Wood this afternoon then,' I tell him. 'Yes, let's go sledging! All you have to bring is a towel as no doubt we'll get a soaking! We'll feel alive for Mabel, just like she asked us to.'

I take a step back. My energy is unfathomable and I know

he is trying to fight against it just like I did with Mabel so many times, but I'm not letting it go.

'Today?' he asks. 'Are you serious? Look, Roisin, I know your intentions are in the right place but sledging in the snow is the last thing on my mind right now, and I get what Mabel was saying in that she looked upon you as family, but I know absolutely nothing about you. Nothing that would make me want to stop the world today so we can go sledging.'

My cheeks burn with mortification

'Oh, OK,' I mutter, feeling a weight in my stomach. 'I – I was just trying to do what Mabel told us to. Like, there's no point in us listening to her words of wisdom if we aren't going to take heed, is there?'

Aidan scratches his head, looks at his watch, and then back at me in wonder.

'Have fun,' he says and he leaves me standing there, feeling incredibly stupid for suggesting such a thing to someone so busy. 'It's not for me, not today, sorry. Bye for now, Roisin. And thanks again.'

The door closes behind him and I feel the room spin.

I breathe out. I want to crawl into a hole and hide, or press rewind and undo my enthusiasm and suggestion to follow Mabel's instructions, but then I hear her words again, her reminder to do something today to make us feel alive.

Why should I ignore that just because Aidan doesn't want to heed her? Why should I spend another afternoon staring at the walls feeling sorry for myself like it's the end of the world?

It's not every day we have such a thick fall of snow in Ballybray, and just because Aidan Murphy doesn't want to go sledging, doesn't mean we can't. I feel a race of adrenaline pump through my veins for the second time that day, and feel some of Mabel's old verve and drive return within me.

'Ben!' I call to my son, determined to snap him out of his morbid silence, taking inspiration from Mabel as I so often did before. 'Ben, come on, get dressed. We're going sledging in Warren's Wood!'

I go into his bedroom to find him staring at me, the controls of his games console still in his hand and his mouth open.

'Sledging? For real?' he asks. 'Are you feeling OK?'

'Yes, for real, and yes I'm feeling surprisingly good!' I tell him, as I find him a T-shirt, a hoodie, and a warm jacket and throw them his way. 'We've been moping around for long enough. Let's go and live a little like Mabel would have wanted us to.'

'Cool!' says Ben, taking me equally by surprise by automatically buying into my plan. 'That's the best idea ever, Mum!'

I've never been a 'let's drop everything and do something out of the norm to raise the spirits' kind of person, but Mabel was exactly that type and I'd often wondered how she kept it going, but now I'm feeling it for real.

I know for sure that since I heard her voice again today

and saw her beautiful face so full of light and life despite the grim reality she was facing when she made her recording, my own dark days of winter are already feeling a whole lot brighter already.

Whatever Aidan Murphy decides to do from now on is, just like he said, absolutely none of my business, but Ben and I are going sledging in the snow today, we're going to have some fun, and I can't wait.

8.

'It's freezing up here, Mum!' says Ben as we trudge up the hill to Warren's Wood, wrapped up in more layers than an onion an hour later. 'I can't believe you wanted to go sledging instead of just walking around the lake like we usually do on the weekend to get some fresh air.'

My woolly hat just about keeps the wind out of my ears, but the higher we climb up the gradient of the hill, the more cutting the chill on my face feels and I'm beginning to wonder if we are a bit insane for taking up Mabel's instruction so literally on a day like today.

'It's important to change things up, and we mightn't see snow like this again for years,' I tell my son, knowing I'm trying to convince myself this is a good idea. I stop to catch my breath and turn to look down on the village below us, marvelling as I always do at the view from up here.

Ben keeps going as I take a moment to myself.

The pretty chapel steeple sits in the distance, watching over us all. I can see Ben's school, and to the far right I see Teapot Row in all its glory, then the famous Ballybray lake that rests in the background, a place that holds so many precious memories of summer walks and morning swims on my own and with Ben and Mabel of course. The sight of it all never fails to fill me up with pride and just by taking in this view I'm reminded of how wonderful my life has been since we moved here.

I see the clothes store, Truly Vintage, where I get to spend my days rummaging through high quality old dresses, suits and hats, making them look pretty again for a second chance at life. It's a place of peace and tranquillity to me, where I find my mind wandering as to who might have worn the clothes before and what their story might have been.

I love it when Camille goes off on her travels to her home city of Milan, or to places like Camden Market in London, and returns with all sorts of treasures to give a new lease of life to.

Everything looks so pretty in the snow, especially from up here, and I'm reminded how we sometimes need to step back from it all in life and look upon it from a distance to really appreciate what we have and how far we've come.

I have a job I adore, a home that is safe and warm, a healthy son who loves me, and I'm wrapped up in a community that reminds me I'm never alone. And now, although I no longer have Mabel, she has left me with a strength inside that her message has brought to the fore-front once again.

I'm doing this for her, but I'm also doing it for me and

Ben after spending days upon days housebound and feeling sorry for ourselves.

'Come on, slow coach!' says Ben in a voice I am delighted to recognize as his old self, however long it may last. Maybe he just needed some distraction and fresh air. Maybe it's my fault having him cooped up with me moping all this time. Maybe I'm overthinking again.

I try to run and catch up, which makes Ben laugh at my efforts. I was certainly never the outdoors, sporty type and any effort to be like that never fails to raise a giggle in my son, who could run rings around me. And in fact the higher we get up the steep hill towards the woods, the more terrified I am of sledging, and I realize I haven't exactly thought this through.

'You're puffed out already, Mum!' says Ben. 'I still can't believe we're doing this.'

'Neither can I,' I agree as I pull Ben's little red plastic sledge behind me. I'd bought it under Mabel's instructions when the last skiff of snow came to Ballybray, but it didn't last long enough for us to make proper use of it. Today is different though. Today our whole village is covered in a thick blanket, and from up here near the woods it looks like a magical winter wonderland.

I stop to take another look, taking out my phone to capture such a chocolate box winter scene, and it's through the screen on the phone that I see we are not alone in our idea to go sledging. Someone is coming behind us, pulling behind him a much bigger sledge with proper handles and a wooden base.

'Aidan?' I mutter in disbelief. Am I seeing things?

'I guess I'm more afraid of not heeding Mabel than I thought I was,' he says as he climbs the hill without so much as losing a breath. 'Do you mind if I join you after all?'

My stomach leaps. I certainly wasn't expecting him to change his mind.

Ben stands a few feet ahead of me as I wait for Aidan to catch up. He's beside me in no time and is certainly dressed for the occasion in a puffer coat and black woolly hat that matches his dark, thick-set eyebrows.

'The more the merrier,' I say, doing my best to keep the spirit of Mabel in the air. I'm in shock on the inside, but on the outside it's business as usual.

We clamber up the rest of the hill with just the sound of our feet crunching beneath us and the sight of our breath in front of us, neither knowing what to say nor feeling the need to make idle conversation. Mabel wanted us to have fun, yes, but Aidan so far seems as much fun as a funeral in my opinion. He has barely cracked a smile, never mind laughed at anything since we first met yesterday.

When we get as far as Ben, who is standing by the gate that leads to the mysterious wood, my son looks like he is fit to burst with excitement at our unexpected company.

'Aidan, this is my son Ben, who was afraid of freezing solid the higher we climb this hill but who now thinks this is a much better idea than I do,' I say when the three of us merge on the brow of the steep field. 'Ben, this is Aidan Murphy, Mabel's nephew who you've heard so much about. Aidan is visiting for a while from America.'

Ben extends a small red woolly gloved hand which makes me glow inside, and he politely shakes Aidan's hand.

'I think we may have got off on the wrong foot, Ben,' says Aidan. 'In fact, maybe we all did. I'm sorry if I frightened you yesterday. Pleased to meet you.'

'Pleased to meet you too, Aidan,' he says, looking up at him in awe. 'Is it true you really have your own helicopter?'

And at that my inner pride takes a swift downward dip, especially when I see the surprise on Aidan's face.

'Ben!' I say. I look back down the hilly field, which from what I can see is full of bumps and holes, and my former enthusiasm to do this is quickly waning by the second, in contrast to Ben's mounting excitement.

'This is going to be so cool!' says Ben. 'Is that the sledge that was at the back of Mabel's shed? I saw it in there. I'm sure I did.'

Aidan pats the wooden sledge and then flips it over, examining it in great detail.

'It is actually,' he says to Ben. 'It was mine when I was a kid, but I haven't been up here with it in over, I'm guessing, around twenty-five years.'

No harm to Aidan and his touching moment of nostalgia, or the fact that this was all my idea in the first place, I've now decided there's no way I'm sailing down the hill on a lump of wood or plastic that could land me God knows where.

'Who did you come up here with?' asks Ben. 'Did you have a brother? I wish I had a brother.'

I roll my eyes in apology at my son's inquisitive nature, but Aidan is all ears, and to be honest I'm shocked that he has broken his silence. Maybe coming here was a good idea for that reason only, even if I fear for my life at the prospect of flying down the hill in the snow.

'I wasn't lucky enough to have a brother or sister, but I always wanted one,' Aidan says to Ben, crouching down so he is around Ben's height. 'I'd come here with my dad and I noticed just today that he'd written our names on the back. I'd no idea he ever did that.'

He flips over the sledge again, and I see his father's name, Danny Murphy, and the date 'Winter 1990' written in black marker on the back.

'My daddy is in heaven,' says Ben. I close my eyes briefly. 'He went there when I was six but I'm ten now.'

When I open my eyes, I see that Aidan has placed his hand tenderly on Ben's shoulder.

'I'm really sorry to hear that,' he says to my son. 'But can you imagine the fun he is having up there now that Mabel is in heaven too? I bet they're having a great party and they'll be watching over us today having fun in the snow.'

I gulp and have to look away, realizing that Aidan and my son have a lot more in common than I would ever have imagined. They both suffered the loss of their dad at an incredibly young age, and witnessing this very unexpected moment between them chokes me up inside.

Ben nods and plonks down onto his sledge, ready for action, his cheeks rosy from the cold and his eyes sparkling in anticipation.

I meet Aidan's eye and blink a thank you to him for being so compassionate with my boy, trying as I do to recall the story of Aidan's own life that Mabel once told me. He suffered through his childhood without his parents, just like I fear Ben has without a father figure in his life, and for a very fleeting moment I've been given a reminder of just how much he is missing out when I see Aidan strap him onto his sledge.

'Look, I have to admit we've never done this before,' I confess, feeling once more a bit silly for suggesting we come here and then having to watch on like a clueless idiot while Aidan takes over. 'I'm not sure I'm even brave enough to sit on a sledge never mind ride on one, but I'll have fun watching.'

Aidan stands up and shakes his head.

'No, no, come on Roisin,' he says, showing a spark of enthusiasm in my company at last. 'I know every lump and bump on these fields, so you'll just have to trust me, but there's no fun in watching. Don't worry. You'll love it.'

He catches me glancing at his jacket which I'm almost sure I recognize.

'I got this in the vintage shop in the village,' Aidan says to me as he goes back to make sure Ben is well strapped in. 'One of the reasons I turned the idea of doing this down was a lack of suitable clothing, but a drive around the village solved that problem. I couldn't believe it.'

'Oh really?' I say, delighted that he has found Truly Vintage, a little huckster of a store that has fast become the pride of our village.

'Yes, so I have to take back some of my earlier comments about Ballybray,' he admits, looking up at me as he speaks. 'There's a lot more life than there was when I lived here. There's a decent coffee corner in the vintage shop too and I see the pub does a good pizza. It's all a far cry from the tumbleweed village I grew up in.'

He laughs nervously, standing up now and fixing the very smart jacket, which isn't some tattered hand-me-down, but a chic piece of clothing Camille had picked up on a recent trip to Dublin. I remember admiring it when it came in to the shop.

'That would be down to my boss, Camille,' I tell him, delighted to hear he has found my place of work. 'She sure does know her stuff. It's a fantastic place.'

'You work there?' he says, his eyes widening.

'Yes, all thanks to Mabel who, for want of a better word, "hounded" Camille, exaggerated how wonderful I was at everything from serving coffee to styling mannequins, and the rest is history. I've been there a few years now. I absolutely love it.'

When I say out loud what I do for a living, as modest as it may be, I realize how far I've come in the past few years. I really do enjoy my job and I adore spending hours dreaming of how these beautiful once-loved items of clothing took their first step to a new home. Were they outgrown? No longer suitable? Or has the former owner passed on? Moved away? I could spend my days making up imaginary stories about their provenance.

I go to tell him so as enthusiasm bubbles through me.

I am just about to go full fashionista on how Camille says I've an eye for spotting a big seller and how I've grown our social media following by almost 5,000 likes through my photography and quirky captioning, but then I hear a voice in my head telling me not to. This voice hasn't made its way there in such a long time, and it makes me stop in my tracks.

'Shut up, Roisin! No one cares about your fascination with old stuff!' I hear Jude echo in my mind. *'Just throw it out! It's rubbish. I told you, I won't live in a house with clutter. If you keep hoarding stuff, Roisin, I'm outta here for good and I mean it. You're not a second-hand teenager on the scrapheap any more. It's old and it's used. Let it go.'*

So I don't share my enthusiasm with Aidan at all.

Instead I question myself for even wanting to do so in

the first place. What would someone like Aidan Murphy care about my passion for my job in what is essentially an upper-class second-hand clothes store? My world is hardly comparable to his big city life and million-dollar lifestyle. He only bought the jacket out of convenience and because he doesn't have his own with him and he wouldn't have had time to go to the nearest designer outlet.

I feel my pulse race and my skin crawl with anxiety. This is exactly where Mabel would have told me to straighten up and be proud of what I do, but I can't, so I look for Ben. I look for a sense of familiarity.

'Are you OK there, Ben? Are you strapped in properly?'

I go to my son and fuss unnecessarily by checking the thin black belt is fixed properly. Aidan glances at me as if I think he has done something wrong. He hasn't, of course, but the imposter syndrome that has haunted me since my experience with Jude has reared its ugly head again and I need to get rid of it fast.

'Sorry, of course he's strapped in fine,' I mutter. 'Don't mind me, Aidan. Mabel always told me off for being over protective.'

Aidan looks relieved and gets back into the action.

'OK, so there's a mini slope at the far end of the hill, just over here to my left, and I think we should start off with that one as we don't want to give your mum a heart attack, Ben,' he says, totally unaware of course of the inner battle I'm fighting in my head that has nothing to do with slopes or the snow. 'Follow me, Roisin. We'll take it easy to begin with, I promise.'

I watch as Aidan pulls Ben on the sledge across the field and curse myself for my negative thinking.

'Live in the moment,' I hear Mabel tell me as she used to repeatedly. 'This is a kind, generous man who is making an effort to do something positive in the name of friend-ship so don't you dare mess it up by thinking you aren't good enough.'

I quickly push the image of Jude and the sound of his angry put-downs out of my mind and take a deep breath. It's a beautiful winter's day, I'm here with my son and a man who is the closest person I will ever know to Mabel, and we're out here to have fun in her memory, just like she asked us to.

'Go faster!' calls Ben as Aidan pulls him along on the sledge towards the spot he wants to make a start from.

'No problem, buddy!' says Aidan, pulling Ben with one hand now and smoothing back his hair with the other. 'I'd forgotten how it felt to be up here! What a magical place!'

I lift the rope from Aidan's dad's sledge and pull it along behind them, following them to the far side of the field where, just as Aidan had told us, there is a much more beginner-friendly slope that won't take the light out of my eyes.

'Come on, Mum!' calls Ben. 'Keep up!'

I put an inch to my step and try and shift my mindset.

'You have to learn to trust again, Roisin,' I hear Mabel tell me. 'There are people out there who won't hurt you like Jude did. Good people who can be your friends. Open up. Relax. Learn to open your heart again to friendship that goes beyond the little old lady next door.'

'I'm trying to, Mabel,' I whisper internally. 'I know you're right. I'm trying.'

I can feel her closer again already, guiding me on as I trundle through the snow with the sound of my son's laughter in the air. I can sense her spirit is here at the top of this snow-covered hill where we spent so many happy times together. I can feel the serenity of nature as I notice the sparkle on the snow, the chirp of birdsong and the breeze in the air. I allow it to sink in and, as I do, it fills me up inside.

I don't want to be that weak, insecure and frightened lost soul I was when Mabel found me. I want to be brave like she reminded me I could be, I want to be confident in my beauty, my intelligence, and the abilities she believed I had inside. I want to just be myself.

'Be careful!' I shout to Ben when his sledge wobbles at the top of the hill and, in true pre-teen fashion, he rolls his eyes at me in return. If ever anyone took a tally of the most common phrase I say to my ten-year-old son, it would be, 'Please be careful!'

'He's fine! Go Ben! You can do it!' calls Aidan, sounding himself now very like Mabel in his approach.

I begin to relax a little more, cursing myself that I let those old feelings of fear and apprehension return, even briefly. I hate that I was reluctant to talk more about my job in the charity shop when Aidan showed an obvious interest. I love it there. I put so much creativity and passion into dressing mannequins so they look smart and appealing to the customers, who I can now chat to freely and with confidence.

'Just be yourself,' I hear Mabel tell me from wherever she is now.

Aidan and Ben are in a world of their own and I feel like a bit of a party pooper standing on the sidelines as they get ready for their first slide of the day. Aidan looks back at me and beckons me over.

'I thought you'd be a bit more adventurous than this after your big suggestion to come up here,' he tells me, flashing a white smile. 'Come on, Roisin! Join in the fun!'

I shuffle across towards him and he takes the sledge from me into his strong arms, and then wedges it into the ground alongside Ben.

'Here, have a seat.'

'You have got to be kidding!' I tell him. My heart starts to thump at the thought. 'No way! I can just about manage ice skating on the rink in town but this . . . what if I don't stop?'

He throws his head back, puts his hands on my shoulders and guides me to sit on the sledge, then lifts my two feet into place, much to the amusement of Ben who is in absolute stitches laughing beside me.

'I think the hedge at the bottom is a good bumper,' Aidan tells me. 'Come on! This is a baby course. Just wait until we're doing the big one.'

I smell his cologne again and can't help but notice the faint dark hairs that sit below his wristwatch, his tanned complexion, and the muscular outline of the stretch pants he wears under his new second-hand coat.

He hunkers down beside me and puts his hands on my shoulders again, facing me this time.

'Trust me,' he says, when I'm all ready to go. 'If I were to put you or Ben in any danger I'm pretty sure my aunt Mabel would haunt me for ever.'

My stomach flips and at that, he goes around the back, but I freeze with fear.

'No, seriously I don't think I can do this!' I squeal, gripping the handles on the sledge. 'I'm sorry I'm just a big mouth with big ideas I can't follow through on. I need to get off.'

Again I feel his hands on my shoulders, but this time he pushes me forward and squeezes in behind me, his arms coming around by my waist where he takes my hands off the edges and takes hold of the rope. He puts his feet into two little home-made rests at the front and I try to ignore how physically close I am to him right now.

'You're not getting away with it that easily,' he tells me. I feel his breath in my ear and hear Ben's squeals of delight

Emma Heatherington

beside us. The heat of his body behind me makes me close my eyes and breathe out, as a flurry of emotions runs through me. I haven't been so close to a man in years, and I try to ignore how good it feels.

'Mum, it's a baby slope!' Ben shouts across at me, bringing me back to reality. 'I'll race you both! One, two, three, go!'

And at that, Aidan tips the sledge and we're off before I can protest any more.

'Woah!' I shout as we dip over the brow of the hill and slide down towards the hedge at what I'd feared might be lightning speed but realistically is only slightly faster than I'd ride a bike. The wind lifts the stray hairs that flow around my face beneath my woolly hat and the breeze almost takes my breath away but the rush I get, even from such a modest first attempt, is enough to get my heart racing and to my surprise, I get a real buzz as we slide down the hill next to Ben with our arms in the air.

We come to a hasty stop at the bottom when the sledges chunk into a mound of snow just before the hedge, and Ben squeals and giggles beside me, then laughs hysterically when Aidan and I manage to tip over and land on our sides, leaving me totally covered in icy whiteness. I laugh until my sides are sore.

'Are you still alive?' Aidan asks, doing his best to clamber out of our snowy mess.

'That was so amazing!' says Ben. 'I want to do it again! Get up, Mum! Again!'

Aidan helps me up, taking my hand in his and using his other hand to hoist me up gently by my elbow. His eyes dance as he steadies me, and then he helps me brush off the excess snow from the back of my jacket.

'I want to do it again!' I say to him. 'That was so good!'

'Deal!' he says, and the three of us race to the top of the hill again, the sound of our laughter the only sound that breaks the silence of the woods behind us.

It is tranquil, it's exciting, and it's as if we are lost in our own world far up high from the village and far away from the pain we've known for the past few days.

And so we slide down the hill again and again, and before we know it, the sun that has lit up our day of fun on the slopes of Ballybray goes down, and a midnight-blue sky with a bright moon takes over.

'That was the best fun ever,' Ben says on repeat as we pack up, soaked through, freezing cold, but warm inside with joy. 'Mum, I can't believe you actually went down the steepest part of the hill on your own and you didn't even tip over!'

The dark rings under Ben's eyes that I'd obsessed over for days seem to have disappeared and his once pale face is now almost a tomato shade, but the best thing is how his eyes sparkle as he speaks. I don't think I've ever seen my son light up the way he has today. His hearty laugh echoed in the stillness of the winter sky and the more he laughed, the more Aidan and I did too.

Mabel used to remark how my whole face changed when

Ben laughed, and I think that's why she made sure he always had plenty to smile about when we were in her company. It's not that she felt sorry for us in any way, though I sometimes accused her of doing so when I felt she was being too kind, but more that she loved to see other people happy. Seeing and hearing my son laughing makes me happy. I think it always will.

As we pack up before we venture on and make our way back down to the village, slightly breathless and exhausted, Aidan is smiling, Ben is smiling, and I am smiling from ear to ear. I think Mabel knew exactly what she was up to when she left us the instruction to do something that makes us feel alive. The more I got to know her throughout the years, the more I realized that nothing she ever did was accidental. Every word, every conversation, every move she made had a purpose, and that purpose was always to spread kindness and joy, or to raise a smile, usually in someone who needed it most.

She knew we would need this to get us out of the stagnant misery that had engulfed us since her passing.

It's been the most wonderful, beautiful crisp winter's day, and we are remembering her just as she would have wanted us to. I'm cold to the bone, yet I feel like so good, as if something has awakened within me and as the moon shines down on us now, I begin to thaw ever so slightly. It's hard to pinpoint this feeling I now have inside. Is it a new sense of hope, perhaps? Or could it be of a new beginning or at least a step towards a life here without her?

'I have to give it to you, that *was* fun,' Aidan says to me. He has a healthy colour in his cheeks too.

'It was amazing, thank you,' I say, and I mean it truly. 'I'm glad you changed your mind and joined us.'

'I am too,' he says.

I'm so glad that Aidan had the courage to push ahead with Mabel's wish for us to do this together, but I also can't help but wonder where his wife is while he is here, and how she might feel if she knew he was having so much fun with me and my son here today.

As Ben shivers towards me now, I remind myself that Aidan Murphy's marital status is absolutely none of my business and curse myself for my usual overthinking. I pull Ben closer to warm him up with a towel and, as I dry his hair as quickly as I can, I feel Aidan watching us.

'You know, seeing you do that just reminds me of me and my mum when I was little,' Aidan tells me, wrapping his own towel now around his strong shoulders. He dries the back of his neck and hair in horizontal strokes as he speaks. 'I remember her doing that to warm me up around this very same spot when I was about Ben's age.'

'That's nice,' I say, momentarily sensing his sadness and still scrubbing Ben's head to make sure it's as dry as I can make it. 'You must have amazing memories of your childhood here, even if Ballybray is the land where time stands still and we have DVD players and the like.'

He smirks at my nudge towards his earlier, less complimentary comments about the place he once lived.

'It's certainly a much more happening place now,' he admits. 'You really love it here, don't you?'

'It's been good for us,' I say, catching his eye again. If only he knew just how much coming here changed my life for the better.

'There's no doubt about it,' he tells me. 'I spent the happiest days of my life here too. There's no better place to raise a child than near the coast in a close-knit rural village. I have many happy memories from here, lots of which were triggered by coming up here today.'

Ben's brown eyes dart towards Aidan in a spark of admiration, and my stomach gives a leap when I see a look I recognize from many years ago. He looks at Aidan with such awe that it takes my breath away and even scares me a little inside. He looks at him as if he is the hero he's been waiting for. I need to get him home.

'OK, Ben, it's suppertime,' I say, wanting now to escape back to the safety of my life behind the green door, away from any possibility of my son becoming too close too soon to Mabel's nephew.

Call me paranoid and over protective, but I've seen that look in Ben's eyes before, and I've also seen a very different look when his father let him down. I can't risk ever seeing that again, plus Aidan Murphy owes us nothing. He could disappear in a heartbeat, and in a few days he probably will.

'But what about Aidan?' asks Ben. 'Are you going back to Mabel's house again, Aidan? We could—'

'I'm sure Aidan is very busy,' I say, avoiding Aidan's eyes this time. 'But we've all had such great fun today, haven't we? I can just feel Mabel smiling down on us already, especially at your bravery, Ben, when you tackled the biggest slope.'

Aidan pipes up, contradicting my suggestion that he may be busy.

'We could always finish off the day with some pizza? My treat?' he says, patting his tummy. 'I mean, that's if it's OK with you, Roisin?'

'Yes! Please Mum, please!' says Ben.

'Sorry,' says Aidan, when he senses my discomfort.

I breathe out and contemplate if I even have a choice right now. I'm totally outnumbered, but in the pit of my stomach, my gut instinct if you like, I am very, very afraid. I'm afraid of this feeling of euphoria, of the companionship and the laughter, of how Aidan put me at ease every time I had a moment of self-doubt up there on the hill. It awakened something inside me that has been dormant for so long, and it scares me. But then I look at Ben and—

'OK, how can I say no to a boy who is chatting and smiling again after days of silence?' I say, convincing myself I'm doing this for my son's benefit only.

But I can't get too close to this man in any way, and neither can Ben. We are all raw, we are all vulnerable, and when the dust settles on whatever business Aidan is attending to here in Ballybray, he is going to leave again. As much as Mabel has pledged us all to be family, I know my son's inner pain will want more and more of the beautiful moments we shared today.

Aidan Murphy has a life and a wife in America, I repeat to myself. He is not ours, and he never will be.

9.

'Mabel was the best at drawing cats,' announces Ben, giving his tuppence worth as he waits for his pepperoni pizza. We sit around a wooden table in Cleary's Bar and dry out by the blazing open fire in the grate beside us. 'She didn't really like them in real life, but she was so good at drawing them.'

'And elephants,' adds Aidan, much to Ben's agreement. 'She could draw an elephant like no one else could.'

I try not to laugh.

'I used to ask her to draw elephants all the time,' he says, 'and unlike cats, I think she liked them in real life too.'

I beam as Ben opens up his innocent childhood memory bank to share little snippets of his life with Aidan as if he'd known him for ever, and marvel at how Aidan chats to him at a level that makes him feel that everything he has to say is important. The scene fills my heart with joy at how relaxed and happy Ben seems in Aidan's company, but it also makes me sad, as seeing Ben light up like this is such a stark reminder of how he misses having his dad to banter with. As much as Jude did wrong by me, he and Ben shared some rare but precious moments just like this when times were good, and it pains me deeply inside that he will never have pizza and a chat with his dad ever again.

'Stop overthinking, Roisin and live in the moment!' I hear Mabel tell me, as she did on so many occasions. 'Only ever look back to see how far you've come.'

I try to relax and take the fact that we are here for what it is – we were sledging with Mabel's nephew, we were hungry, and we're finishing off in the local pub with some pizza. It's nothing more than that and nothing less.

OK, so it's not something Ben and I have done very often since we came here, but it shouldn't be something that makes me as nervous as it does, especially since Aidan has insisted it's cool and the bill is all on him. I could never afford to be so extravagant on a Sunday night with Aidan's 'order whatever you want' attitude, and while I enjoyed choosing wine without looking on the right side of the menu first for the price, a lot of this is reminding me of what we don't have in our lives. Ben doesn't have a father any more, I don't have a husband, and unlike my company this evening, I do have to watch every penny that goes out the door, leaving very little room for treats.

'Aidan Murphy, is that you!' a lively, friendly voice says, thankfully interrupting my train of thought. 'It *is* Aidan Murphy! Oh, Aidan, I'm so sorry about your aunt Mabel!

And this must be your lovely wife and family all the way from America!'

Aidan looks as startled as I am at the lady's presumption, while Ben thinks it's hilarious and laughs behind his hands.

'Thanks, Margaret!' says Aidan, standing up to shake the older lady's hand. 'It's been a while since I've been here all right, but no, these are Mabel's neighbours, Roisin and Ben from up on Teapot Row. We've been enjoying reminiscing about Mabel here as we dry off after some time in the snow.'

Margaret Madden, a larger than life outspoken lady who I recognize locally from her job on the deli counter at the Spar, claps her hands together and throws back her head in a fit of apologetic laughter.

'Sorry, of course it's only you, Roisin! You know I never even looked at your faces, I was so excited to see this young man back in town!' she says, putting her chubby hand on my shoulder. 'I'm sure you'd love to be so lucky to be married to such an eligible man, wouldn't you! Ah, you've done so well for yourself, Aidan, and your aunt Mabel was so proud. You were all she could talk about at any given opportunity.'

I swirl the glass of wine in front of me and try to disguise the twist in my stomach at Margaret's comments. She seems to think her mistake was so funny – as if someone like 'only me' would be married to someone like Aidan Murphy with all his finery. I take a sip of the wine to give my hands something to do, but it tastes sour in my mouth. I'd been enjoying it up until now, but since Margaret's outburst it now tastes just like a reminder that Aidan is from a very different world to the one we live in up on Teapot Row.

'So, how is life treating you in the good old United States?' asks Margaret, thirsty for more information and totally ignoring the fact that Ben and I are even there now. 'How is the lovely Rebecca?'

I can tell Aidan is doing his best to be polite as he fakes a smile in her direction. He hasn't mentioned his wife or family in America to me, and I fear he is being put on the spot with Margaret's questions.

'My wife, *Rachel*, is very, very well,' he says, nodding his head and giving her a wink. 'Thanks for asking. I'll pass on your good wishes when I get back home in the next day or so.'

He clears his throat and his eyes skirt around him, trying, I guess, to nip old Margaret in the bud, but she hasn't finished yet.

'Oh please do give her my regards! We've never met, but you know I saw her father Bruce interviewed on the TV when I was in New York last year! What a wealthy man! Imagine you're married to his daughter! Any little ones to carry on his great legacy?' she asks, glancing at Ben and then back at Aidan. 'I'm not sure if Mabel told me. I'm sure she would have?'

Aidan's discomfort is tangible now and it's with great relief to us all that our food arrives, thankfully giving Margaret a nudge to move on without interrogating him any further.

'No. No little ones to report, but it's been nice to see you again, Margaret,' Aidan says through gritted teeth. 'Now, Roisin and Ben – we'd better eat this up before it gets cold. Bon appétit!'

Margaret takes the hint and moves on, repeating her good wishes and almost dancing off as if she'd just met her teen idol, leaving an uncomfortable wave of silence at our table in comparison to the relaxed chat we'd been enjoying before.

'What a nosey old bat,' he says, which almost shifts the mood by making Ben laugh, and I pick up on the opportunity to get back to remembering Mabel, just as we were earlier, but despite my efforts of telling stories of the time we went ice skating, to our days picnicking by the lake, Aidan has closed up again and I can feel his urgency to get away from here as fast as possible.

The evening passes with stilted efforts to converse, and at almost seven thirty I realize I still have to iron Ben's school uniform, make sure he has all his books ready after his brief absence from school for the funeral, and make up his lunch for the next morning, so I'm glad, as is Aidan, when it's time to get the bill and make our way back home to my own little haven on Teapot Row.

'It was very kind of you to treat us this evening,' I say to him for the third time when we reach our garden gate. 'Ben had a ball and so did I. Please don't let people like Margaret Madden get to you, Aidan. Some people really *are* just nosey neighbours around here, and your private business in America is just that. Private. But try not to let it upset you.'

He kicks the snow under his feet as Ben makes his way up the path to open our front door, his fingers 'almost frozen to death' on the short walk home from the pub.

'The little guy is exhausted,' says Aidan as he watches him turn the key in the door ahead. 'He misses his dad a lot, I'm sure, as do you too, of course.'

'Ben really does miss his dad sometimes,' I say, feeling a familiar twinge of emotion grip my insides as I struggle to hide how it's not the same for me. 'It's so hard on him, but he's done so well since we moved here. A fresh start and a step back from everything is sometimes the only medicine. Helps us see the wood from the trees. I know it worked for me more than I could ever have imagined.'

Aidan pushes his lips together and nods his head in agreement.

'Did Mabel advise you to do that?' he asks, with just a hint of sarcasm in his voice.

'No, actually, she didn't,' I reply, looking him straight in the eye. 'I made the decision to come here all by myself and was lucky to have landed Mabel as my next-door neighbour, but I do believe that was her advice to *you* in her message earlier today – that you might need some time out?'

'Touché!' he says, staring across at the house he grew up in. 'On that note, I think I've hung around here for long enough so I'd better get packing. Goodnight, Roisin. It's been a nice day, all in all. Thank you.'

10.

'You're in a good mood!'

Until Camille points it out to me, I have absolutely no idea that I'm singing along with the radio at the top of my voice to Fleetwood Mac's 'Everywhere' as I prepare a coffee for our local postman Mickey.

As well as sorting and displaying the most magnificent previously loved clothing in Truly Vintage, I also get to choose my own retro playlists, and prepare coffee and treats in a little corner by the window we call The Nook, which is only ten square feet in space, but is a little slice of heaven. The Nook hosts a coffee machine, a compact wooden trolley with all the trimmings, and just two square old school desks with dinky painted wooden chairs for those who want to shop but also stop and watch the world go by.

It has proven a popular spot for a morning visit from some of the locals who aren't shopping but who just fancy a window seat and some company, and Mickey the postman is one of our very welcome regulars.

'Did I see young Aidan Murphy knocking around the village?' he asks me as I make up an Americano for him. 'I thought he'd be long gone back to his millionaire lifestyle across the sea by now.'

It makes me smile at how the older generation still refer to Aidan as 'young' even though he's definitely kicking the ass of forty, but it's sweet at the same time.

'I think he's going back in the next day or so,' I tell Mickey, fetching his favourite Danish pastry. 'I don't think Ballybray is big enough for someone like him, is it?'

Mickey rolls his eyes.

'It was good enough for him for long enough,' says Mickey, flicking open the newspaper in front of him. 'Mind you, I don't envy him being married into that family. I heard it's not all as rosy out there as it might seem on the surface!'

Now it's my turn to roll my eyes, and I go back to my singing which doesn't seem to faze Mickey, but Camille knows I'm in higher spirits than I really should be this morning, considering all the trauma of the week before.

'It sounds like someone had a good weekend,' she says in her magnificent Italian accent that I'd often like to bottle up and keep. 'It's so good to see you smiling again, Ro. You've had a rough few weeks.'

I wipe my hands on my apron and carefully bring Mickey his Americano which he takes with two sugars and a Danish pastry every Monday at the same time. The smell of freshly brewed coffee always fills my senses and I have to say I enjoy this part of the job almost as much as I love to sort through the trinkets and items of clothing that arrive almost on a daily basis.

'We had a surprisingly fun day yesterday,' I tell her, unable to hide my beaming smile. 'We had a—'

'Sorry, *cara*, just a second.'

Camille doesn't get the chance to hear about my weekend or how unexpectedly pleasant it turned out to be as she's distracted by an inquisitive customer who wants to try on a gold fringed flapper-style dress from the window display.

'It's a real beauty,' says Camille, in full sales pitch mode now as she talks with her hands to emphasize her point. With her bubbly, enthusiastic approach and around the clock European charm, I often believe she could sell snow to Eskimos. 'I picked it up at a market near the Louvre in Paris just last season. It's what I call a "head turner" or what the French call *un tourneur de tête*.'

My heart sinks as I watch the lady take the dress to the changing room, taking my dream with her. I've had my eye on that dress since it came in last week, and I curse myself for putting it in the window, or for not buying it before now. The only thing that stopped me of course is that the social scene in Ballybray wouldn't really lend itself to such attire, but I couldn't help but dream about wearing it one day and I even sneakily tried it on when I'd the place to myself just before Mabel died. It fitted like a glove. As Mabel would have said, I looked 'like the best version of myself' in it, but it just wasn't meant to be.

'There's nothing like a woman in the right dress,' she used to say to me when she told me of how she almost made Peter Murphy's head spin when she turned up unexpectedly one night in New York wearing the most amazing red dress. He proposed to her on the spot and they never looked back. It was the most romantic story I've ever heard, and I had her recount it over and over again, as I knew she needed to tell it as much as I loved to hear it.

Thinking of Mabel and her whole journey through life from New York to Ballybray, and now watching how life in our little village trundles on in its usual Monday morning rhythm with ladies shopping and regulars calling for coffee makes me feel guilty for a moment for being in such chirpy form without her.

Shouldn't the whole world stop in her honour? Don't they know that nothing around here is ever going to be the same again?

But everything, to an extent, is very much the same.

Postman Mickey tells me, just as he always does, about his busy morning and about his nemesis Dipper Donnelly, the dog in the posh house by the lake who growls at him so much that his glasses fell off with fear again this morning, and of how he danced around the garden to avoid the attack. It's the same story as last Monday, and will be the same next week too.

There's a comfort in familiarity and routine, in the repetitive patterns of village life. And once again I'm reminded of how I found my tribe here, and of how far I've come.

Ben went to school without a whimper this morning, which was the opposite of what I'd expected to happen. He was itching to tell his friends about the sledging fun he'd had at Warren's Wood and how Aidan bought him a whole twelve-inch pizza all for himself, and a strawberry milkshake in Cleary's Bar afterwards. He was also eager to tell his teacher of how his new friend Aidan had a real helicopter in New York City and that he promised Ben he would take him for a spin in it if we ever get to go there.

I'd tried to quash this promise to save his ultimate disappointment knowing I couldn't afford a night away locally never mind a trip to New York, but Ben was having none of it and was already picturing himself skipping up 42nd Street and climbing the Statue of Liberty.

'So . . . who is he?' asks Camille as I stare into space moments later, leaning on the worktop at the coffee corner. Mickey still sits by the window procrastinating as usual, and the lady who tried on the gold dress leaves with her new purchase wrapped in one of our stylish deep purple paper Truly Vintage bags.

'I've no idea who or what you're talking about,' I say to Camille, standing up straight now and fixing my green jersey maxi dress.

'Come on, Roisin!' she sings. 'You know how much I live

in hope that someday you'll tell me of a dashing hero who has come to Ballybray to sweep you off your feet! Just make it up! Tell me something to knock my socks off!'

I raise an eyebrow. Camille knows that the last thing on my mind these days is ever to do with a man of any sort. She raises an eyebrow back in my direction.

'Ben and I had a very unexpectedly pleasant weekend after a horrendous week, and I'm just so glad to feel a bit stronger and more positive,' I explain. 'Mabel left me a lovely video message by surprise and it changed my mood completely. It was so nice and comforting to hear her voice again; sad in a way of course, but also quite lovely.'

Camille leans on the counter, thirsty for more.

'Ah, that's so sweet of her!' she says, twisting her dark brown curls in her fingers as she speaks. 'I would say I'm surprised, but I'm not. So what did she say? What sort of mischief is that rascal up to now?'

I don't get the chance to answer her as I jump up a little too quickly from my wooden seat in the little coffee corner as the bell sounds and Aidan Murphy unexpectedly walks in through the door.

'Aidan?' I say, unable to hide the surprise in my voice at his unannounced visit, but the two oversized bags he is carrying explains why he is here.

The bags contain the clothes Mabel was referring to in her message, of course – the clothes she wanted to pass on to the shop and the promise of a keepsake for both of us, as she said, lies within them.

My tender heart leaps at the thought of going through her most personal belongings, and I'm not sure if I'm prepared to deal with this so soon, and by the look on Aidan's tired face in front of me, I'm not sure if he is either.

11.

'Good morning Roisin,' says Aidan, and I catch Camille swoon a little at the sight of him. 'I was just passing, so I thought I'd drop these in. You don't have to go through them now of course, but I found them in Mabel's wardrobe and I'm thinking it's another job done before I leave for New York.'

I swallow hard and stare at the bags in Aidan's hands with mixed emotions.

As nervous as I am about seeing her belongings, I know Mabel will be smiling down on me right now, knowing that behind all the sentimentality involved today, there's nothing more I love than a new delivery to the shop. She used to compare me to a magpie, as I am always thinking of how everything can be reused instead of just sent to the scrapheap. She'd encourage me and admire my taste for being able to spot the eternal beauty in a special dress, a hat, or a pair of shoes that could be brought back to life.

Jude, on the other hand, hated me wearing anything second-hand. He turned his nose up at the thought of wearing the same outfit twice, never mind rummaging for a gem in a vintage shop, and he'd have freaked out if he'd ever known how I used to spend hours in my favourite little streets in Dublin, piecing outfits together from next to nothing, and saving a fortune into the bargain. It was my secret hobby. It was a true passion. It was the real me that I was never allowed to show.

'Thanks, Aidan,' I say to him, trying to remain business-like and not let my emotions show. 'This is Camille by the way. She's the owner and brains behind Truly Vintage. Camille, this is Aidan Murphy, Mabel's nephew. He's – he's been sorting out Mabel's things.'

'Nice to meet you properly, Aidan,' says Camille, shaking his hand, all bangles and rattling jewellery as she does so. 'I hope the jacket did the trick yesterday?'

'It did, yes, thanks. I was lucky you open a while on Sundays,' he says, changing the subject immediately by indicating the two huge bags in each of his hands. 'So, these bags were carefully labelled by the lady herself to come here if you don't mind? Just let me know where to put them and I'll leave you both to get on with your day.'

'No, no!' says Camille, taking a last sip of her coffee and clearing away her coffee cup. 'You don't have to race away. I know this is hugely emotional for you, so please don't feel you have to rush off.'

'It's fine,' we both say in unison.

'Honestly, it really is fine,' adds Aidan, for good measure.

'But it's such a personal thing to do,' insists Camille, looking from me to Aidan and back to me again. 'Believe me, I cried my heart out when I finally cleared out my parents' home after my dear papa died. It can feel like the end of the world, so Roisin, why don't you take Aidan upstairs and go through what you think we can make use of, and I'll man the fort down here? Take your time. Take all the time in the world, and I promise not to disturb you till you're done, unless you need coffee.'

I shoot her a look to say I appreciate the gesture, but I don't want to force Aidan down a path he is uncomfortable with.

'I suppose it shouldn't take very long, should it?' he asks me, taking me very much by surprise. 'She did say there's a keepsake somewhere in here for both of us, so I guess I should probably find that before I go.'

'OK then, let's get it over with,' I say to him, delighted that he's finally taking Mabel's instructions seriously.

We go through the poster-clad door that stands behind the main shop counter and climb the narrow wooden stairs, heaving the bags as we go up to the room where all the excitement in my humble job happens. I normally get such a rush when a new batch of stock arrives, but this is different of course. These are bags full of memories from someone who I loved deeply, and it's going to be a killer to live and breathe her belongings once more.

Mabel loved clothes.

She had some pretty wacky items, some very random purchases that she bought for shock value as a 'woman of a certain age', like slogan T-shirts and bright colours that were normally reserved for the young. But she also had a very fine collection of coats, scarves, shoes, boots and dresses that defied time, mostly purchased during her time in New York or when she and Peter would go back there to visit friends.

I lead Aidan into the room upstairs and await his reaction with a smile.

It's a huge attic space, with wooden beams running along above our heads, white walls that display framed art deco posters collected from Camille's travels, huge vintage leather trunks that hold costume jewellery from all around the world, hat stands that display colourful pieces in an array of different materials, and rails of clothing, all separated and filed by size, era, colour, style, you name it.

Camille and I spent months developing our systems, which means that every item of clothing lucky enough to wait for a place on the Truly Vintage shop floor is easily found, recorded, and ready for action.

'Nice room,' says Aidan, standing right in the line of a stream of sunshine that beams through the small circular window as he takes it all in. 'You know, I used to walk past this building on my way to school every day when I lived here, and I never once stopped to admire its architecture.'

I can't help but glow from the inside at the look on his face.

'I love it up here,' I tell him, watching his jaw drop in wonder at the treasure trove of colour, clothing, and reams of stories in front of him.

He runs his hand across the rails, taking it all in, then lifts out a brown suede jacket, holds it under his chin and looks into the free-standing gold-framed mirror that stands under the window. He puts it carefully back, reaches for a hat from a stand and positions it on his head, adjusting it in the mirror as he speaks.

'Homburg, 1940s?'

I take a step back.

'Spot on,' I tell him in bewilderment.

'My father had one almost like this,' he says to me, putting the hat back in its place with all the tenderness and respect it deserves. 'My parents had a cabaret act back in the day, and they wore all sorts of clothes from every generation. I'd almost forgotten about the clothes they used to wear, but seeing some of this stuff up here is taking me back in time.'

For a man who could, it seems, buy anything in the world he wanted with a price tag that would make your eyes water, his genuine interest in what we do here with second-hand goods makes his interest all the more impressive.

'There's quite a view too,' he says, going to the circular window and looking outside. 'Look, you can still see the tracks from our sledging yesterday up on the hill by the woods.'

I join him, having to stand very close to see out through the small window, stretching up on my tiptoes to see properly.

He points up to the hill where the snow still sits just as it did yesterday. I feel his hand rest on my shoulder and he pulls me in for a closer look.

'Yes, I see it now,' I tell him.

It's like every moment he spends here in Ballybray brings him back to his glory days where carefree times were spent with his parents and grandparents before he lost them all.

'I probably take that view for granted,' I confess, marvelling once more at the beauty of the village I now call home. 'But seeing those tracks now just reminds me of all the joy that can be made in such a simple place. There we were yesterday, leaving our secret memories in the snow, and soon they'll melt away, never to be seen again.'

We stand there for a moment in the stream of sunshine which sparkles with dust, shoulder to shoulder, both lost in grief, both blinking back the sadness in our eyes, and I recognize the deep pain that runs in the same direction through our veins.

'I'm so glad you convinced me to go sledging yesterday,' says Aidan. 'It's nice now to look back at how we did that in her memory.'

I glance across at the bags of Mabel's clothes, knowing it's now or never.

'So, shall we do this then?' he asks me, taking a deep breath.

I can only nod at first as the thought of it once more overwhelms me.

'Stepping stones, I suppose,' I reply, unable to hide how I'm just a little bit breathless right now. 'Every little thing we do these days is another step forward to life without her, and another thing that she wanted us to do.'

'That's it,' he says, and so we make our way to the centre of the room where we sit on the floor and make a start.

I pull the first bag of clothing towards me, my stomach in a tangle of nervous jitters at the thought of what lies inside.

I close my eyes.

'Oh, I can actually smell her perfume,' I say, feeling my eyes well up a little already. 'I hope she knew how comforting that smell was to me on days when I really needed her.'

I look up at Aidan apologetically. We haven't even started yet, and I fear I'm going to be an emotional wreck.

'You really loved her, didn't you?' he whispers, his own eyes etched with pain and regret. 'You know, I did too, and being here is reminding me of how happy I was in those days. Maybe it's why I can't wait to get away again. Everything I loved here is gone.'

I pause with my hands resting on the top of one of the bags of clothes, holding on to this moment where Aidan has finally opened up to me on what being in Ballybray really feels like for him. It isn't as suffocating or small perhaps as he pretends it to be, and maybe, just maybe, being here is much better for him than he realizes.

I want to remind him of Mabel's words to him, of how

concerned she felt about him, and how she told him to take stock of his life by taking some time out.

'You know something, Aidan?' I say to him. 'Mabel may have seemed meddling sometimes, and I know life in a small village can be suffocating to someone who is used to the anonymity of city life, but what I know about her is that she was rarely wrong in her advice.'

For once, he is all ears.

'That's why I wanted to do exactly what she said in her message yesterday, even though getting up and out of the house was the last thing on my mind,' I continue. 'It helped me so much, it helped Ben, and I think it helped you too.'

'It did I suppose, yes,' Aidan says as he opens the other bag of clothes in front of him with great trepidation. 'It reminded me of some happy times that perhaps needed to be reawakened.'

'I'm glad it did,' I tell him, lifting out the first item. 'Now, let's see what she has in store for us this time.'

12.

'Well, if this scarf could only talk!' I swoon half an hour later when we are still having so much fun rummaging through Mabel's bag of memories. 'Oh, the stories it would tell!'

I swirl Mabel's turquoise, brown and white silk London headscarf around my neck and pout like a movie star, reminding me of the eternal influence of Bridget Bardot in Mabel's wardrobe.

'She always had that little touch of sophistication that money can't buy,' says Aidan.

Both of us have been completely overwhelmed, but are now enjoying immensely how we can relive so much about Mabel by sorting out her clothes. We have separated everything so far into two piles – one that will stay here at Truly Vintage, and another that we'll recycle at the nearby clothes bank in town.

'You've a real eye for this stuff, haven't you?' says Aidan, looking on as I handle each item, giving them the care and attention they deserve.

I fold the silky headscarf carefully, knowing it will be snapped up by some eagle-eyed shopper in a heartbeat.

'I have to admit, a lot of clothes aren't made like they used to be,' I say to him, 'but the way we dispose of everything without a second thought frightens me sometimes. My late husband Jude was a prime example. A lot of our disagreements came from a vast difference in opinion on what I wore and how I looked.'

I close my eyes tightly in instant regret. I didn't want this to be a time when Jude would creep into our conversation, and I'm sure that Aidan doesn't need or want to hear my tales of woe about the man I married and couldn't wait to escape from. It's the first time I've mentioned him in Aidan's company, and my face flushes with remorse.

'I'm – I'm sorry to hear you lost your husband so young,' says Aidan, just a little bit awkwardly. 'I didn't want to mention it until you did, but it must have been tough on you. And Ben, of course.'

'It can be tough, yes,' I mutter, fiddling now with the silk scarf. 'I'm dealing with it as best I can on so many levels, but Jude and I had a very complex, complicated history that went on for a lot longer than it should have before he died.'

We sit in brief silence.

'And Mabel's death must be bringing a lot back?' whispers Aidan. 'I'm sorry. It's tough.'

He tilts his head, acknowledging how I've opened up ever so slightly for the first time about my turbulent past.

'It has, yes,' I tell him, wanting to close the conversation as quickly as I unintentionally started it. 'But it's not straightforward. This is a very different type of grief with Mabel. It's not at all the same thing.'

We don't speak again for a few seconds, both tangled up in thoughts of how painful the subject of loss can be.

'You know, when I look at your son I see a lot of my younger self staring back at me,' Aidan says with gentle trepidation. 'Losing a parent so young definitely shapes you for life. I know it did for me, anyhow, and I'm sure losing your life partner is just as difficult. I know you are going to miss having Mabel's support to lean on.'

I busy myself by taking out a wonderfully soft cashmere camel coat with an over-the-top fur collar that brings me back to when Mabel first marched me down to meet Camille to ask for a job here.

'She was a very determined woman,' I say with a smile. 'I'm so sorry, Aidan, but can we talk about Mabel instead of my ex? Grieving for Mabel is a very different process than what I feel for my husband's passing, and I would much rather remember her with the love she deserves. I doubt she'd want my late husband stealing her thunder.'

My forehead is creased into a frown that Mabel used to call 'the look of doom', and I consciously change my expression.

'Of course,' says Aidan, changing tack immediately. 'OK, let's stay focused on the job at hand here and the legendary

Mabel Murphy. So tell me about this coat. I don't think I remember it?'

I breathe out a very obvious sigh of relief, and then we both erupt into a fit of nervous laughter.

And so I launch into the story of how Mabel was fed up looking at my long, pale face one day, and equally was fed up with me talking about the dire state of daytime TV in Ireland and my tendency to lie on the sofa, day in, day out while Ben was at school.

'Did you move here to get a life together or to simply exist?' she'd asked me crossly one afternoon in March. 'You're better than this, Roisin O'Connor! You've a whole life ahead of you that I only wish I had! Get up and get out! I'm taking you to Camille once and for all!'

Aidan is all ears, and is especially impressed at my facial expressions, my New York accent, and how I can mimic Mabel right down to the way she used her hands to illustrate her point.

'She had threatened me with Camille ever since I let it slip that I used to sneak in here and drool at the rails of clothing in Truly Vintage, wishing I'd someday have the courage to follow my own passion and dreams for upcycled fashion, arts and crafts,' I tell him. 'Before I knew it, I was being led by the hand like a school girl right to the door. She was wearing this coat that day. I'll never forget it.'

The meeting with Camille, who was about to go on holiday at the time, was as it turned out perfect timing as she was desperately seeking someone she could trust to run the shop while she took time out, and the rest was history. Mabel always had that sixth sense to know when two people would work well together, and she was bang on the money with Camille and me.

I hadn't looked back since.

Aidan pulls out a very cool pair of green velvet flared corduroys next, and it's his turn now to share a memory of Mabel in her finest hour.

'My uncle Peter was so madly in love with her,' Aidan tells me, his face full of awe and admiration. 'It was sickening to the outside world because let's face it, a love like that comes only once or comes never at all for most of us mere mortals, but they had a deep, deep chemistry that could be felt in the air. They clicked, you know. They just clicked. It was pretty magical to be around.'

I imagine a younger Mabel in the corduroy flares, her bouncy blonde curls like she had in her photo albums, and Peter's handsome stature watching her as if she were the only woman in the world. She *was* the only woman in the world for him.

'Ironically, Peter used to warn me off marriage every time I spoke to him on the phone,' Aidan says, his turn now to fall into a frown. 'When I told him I was getting married to Rachel, he asked me so many questions, telling me of the pressures nowadays on young people and how we plunge into things without thinking. I thought it was because he didn't believe in marriage, but it was in fact the opposite. He believed in it so much that he didn't want me doing it for the wrong reasons. Disposable vows, he called it. Divorce on tap. He warned me not to get married if I was going to throw it down the drain a few years later. Anyway. That was Peter!'

And then he stops. And he looks away.

I can tell by Aidan's tone of voice and how he stopped that he has already said more than he intended to. I want to prod a bit, to ask him more, but he looks like a rabbit caught in the headlights.

'If only we all had even a little bit of magic in marriage like Peter and Mabel had,' I say, trying to lighten the mood now by holding up a quite hideous luminous floral jumper that was definitely for a separate pile of clothing we'd decided would go elsewhere.

'I do believe in that magic,' says Aidan, a faraway glaze in his eyes now. Then he looks right at me. 'I believe what he said now more than ever. I think we can all have what Peter and Mabel had, if we're lucky enough to find or marry the right person.'

'And have you found the right person?' I ask him, wondering about his relationship with Rachel, his wife of I'm guessing, about six or seven years now. He stops and thinks and then shrugs it off.

'I don't think I have,' he says sadly now. 'But like you, I'd rather just talk about Mabel.'

13.

I try not to let my jaw drop at Aidan's honesty about his marriage and we go on to share so many stories as we sift through Mabel's collection of pussy-bow blouses, pleated skirts, and chunky knitted cardigans, with Aidan telling me of how he was so mesmerized by Mabel's accent when he was a young child, and of his uncle Peter's stories of New York that gave him a longing to try out a life in America.

He tells me how Peter and Mabel were treated like movie stars when they'd come to visit his grandparents in the little house on Teapot Row, and how the excitement that led up to their homecoming was second to none.

'My grandfather would start rearranging furniture and polishing every surface so that the smell of the house was like something from an ad for Mr Sheen,' he says with a spark of nostalgia, 'and as for my gran, she put all her energy into fixing up the spare room, making it cosy and shopping for a list of food and drink only found in Ireland in the hope that it would make Peter want to bring his new

American wife home for good sooner rather than later. Everyone was in awe of Mabel, but my grandmother just wanted her son to come home.'

I listen to him open up so much about his childhood as we sit there, cross-legged on the floor, our minds drifting from the past to the present in a comfortable flow. His parents, Jean and Danny, were always on the road for work, travelling the length and breadth of Ireland with their two-man show, which meant that Aidan spent more time than others may have with his grandparents. He chokes back tears as he skims past the hole his parents' deaths left in his life, and I don't dare pry any further, then he laughs out loud as he remembers a family wedding where someone turned up in the same outfit as Mabel, and how his grand-mother said it would take her down a peg or two.

'I realized when I was very young that the mythical Irish mother who thinks no one is good enough for their son just might be true,' he says, as I put Mabel's clothes on hangers and file them into our railing system.

'Guilty!' I say, holding my hands up for effect. 'Having a son is like having your heart slowly broken, one day at a time.'

Aidan laughs at my analogy.

'I'm not sure my grandmother ever thought Mabel would fit in here in Ireland,' he says, 'but she proved them all wrong, didn't she? It's not everyone who prefers life here to the buzz of New York City.'

'Like you?' I ask, unable to skip past this one.

He thinks for a moment.

'I love both places,' he says, 'but this will always be the place I'll call home, even if I am hard on Ballybray sometimes. It has a much gentler pace, and that reflects in its people.'

'Even nosey neighbours like myself and old Margaret Madden?'

He tells me fondly about how he used to run home from school when he was Ben's age, grab a football and go straight back outside for a kick with his friends, and of the time his uncle Peter bought him his first pint in Cleary's and how he got drunk on gin there and hasn't touched it since.

And all the time as I fold and listen, one minute my guts will burn with envy at how idyllic his memories of growing up here are in comparison to the topsy-turvy childhood I'd had, and the next my heart is broken and sore for the sudden loss of his parents in a tragedy that Mabel told me should have been prevented.

Aidan stops, as if he's come to the end of his memories that both move him and pain him in equal measure.

'Are you sure you really want to cut the cord with Ballybray by selling the house?' I ask him, hoping I'm not overstepping the mark. 'It all sounds very final to someone who loved it here so much. Like, wouldn't you prefer to still have a base here in your home village in case, like Peter and Mabel, you might like to return here one day?'

He shakes his head, brushing fine dust from the floor

off his jeans. His black shirt is covered in white marks from the chalky floor, and I have to fight my instinct to help him wipe it down.

'It's not quite as simple as that, Roisin,' he whispers, scrunching up his nose as he speaks. 'I wish it was, but it isn't, because my life is very different now to what it was like when I lived here . . . things have changed immeasurably.'

I lick my lips and brace myself, feeling my words tripping on my tongue, but I need to know.

'Has Rachel, *ahem*, I mean, has your wife ever stayed here?' I ask, unable to help the stutters and stammers that come out. 'She might like it? It's so lovely here in summer, as you know of course, and—'

He laughs and totally interrupts my big speech.

'Yes, and the lake is a treat on a summer's day and the woods light up on top of the hill when the sun shines through the trees and you'll never find a welcome as warm as the one down in Cleary's where the sounds of the fiddle and the whistle fills your senses. And sure Dunfanaghy with its golden sands is just around the corner.'

'Are you taking the piss?'

'I'm sorry, but I just couldn't resist,' he says in apology. 'You sound just like my grandmother used to when she was trying to convince Peter to stay at home for good. Gosh, my gran could have got a job in the tourist board for how she used to sell Ballybray before he'd board a plane back to the States!'

119

'Oh . . .' I say, admitting defeat. 'I'll take your word for it and say no more about it then.'

He changes the subject back to the clothing and I remember his honesty from before about his marriage. I wonder why Rachel couldn't have stayed with him after the funeral to help him through these final moments in Ballybray. Maybe she had work commitments, or family stuff to get back for, or maybe she just didn't like it here in Ireland. It is a direct contrast to what she was used to, but wouldn't she enjoy a change of pace, like most people do from time to time?

Somewhere in my heart of hearts I've a feeling that no matter how much Aidan protests and denies that there is any other way around selling a house that's been in his family for generations, there's a lot more to his decision than he is letting on. And that something just might be to do with his marriage in America.

14.

The keepsake for each of us has still to come our way, and in true Mabel fashion she leaves it to the last, right at the bottom of the bag she had so elegantly packed with every single item folded and presented with the care they deserved.

'Do you think this is it?' Aidan asks me, watching as I lift the very last item from Mabel's bag of clothing. I can feel my heart rate rise as I peek inside and I look back at him in bewilderment.

'Oh my . . .' I mumble, totally overwhelmed. 'Oh, Mabel! This is just—'

I take out a heavy, red beaded dress, with fine shoulder straps and a deep V-neckline, which wouldn't look out of place in any high-end boutique even nowadays. I nod slowly and my heart gives a leap as I recognize it from a story she once told me with tears in her eyes and a smile on her face. It was one of my favourite stories of hers, one I asked her to tell me many times over.

It's the dress she wore that made Peter's eyes almost pop

out of his head. It was the dress she wore when he spontaneously proposed to her in New York City.

'Oh, Mabel!' I say, lifting the dress out with tender loving care, fingering the fine silk base and the tiny beads that decorate the bodice so tastefully. I stand up from the floor and hold it under my chin, my mouth open with glee at how I'm actually holding a piece of history in my hands. The skirt drops and falls into place, and swirls as I sway, hugging it now close to me. I can barely speak. I'm right back in time.

I close my eyes and I picture the scene. I feel her anticipation, her excitement, and the romance of it all.

'Wow, that's a pretty amazing dress,' says Aidan, looking up at me from his position on the floor. 'That's a piece of history, right there.'

I can hardly speak and I want to dance around the place with the man of my dreams in this dress one day. I want to feel the love that she felt, and I want to know that there's magic and companionship out there for all of us, if we find the right person.

'There's something pinned to the back of it. Is it a note?' Aidan tells me. 'I think she's left this dress for you.'

My eyes widen and I try not to let my hopes build up. Could this be the keepsake I've been waiting for? Could she really have wanted to pass this on to me?

I find a small envelope pinned to the side of the dress, then sit back down on the floor as Aidan and I exchange glances of anticipation, both eager to see what is coming next.

I put my hand to my chest.

'I'm nervous,' I say, unable to get a grip on my emotions. 'I know how much this dress meant to her, but I'd no idea she still had it.'

From the envelope, I slide out a photo, which has a note paper-clipped to the back. I look at the photo first and Aidan shuffles over beside me, sitting so close that our arms touch.

Slowly, I open my eyes and look down at the photo in my hands to see Mabel, wearing this very special red dress looking back at me. Her hair is a pale blonde, styled in soft messy waves, long parted bangs, and a small bouffant. Her eyeliner is winged and feline, while her lips are pouting and full. She was an absolute beauty, but it's not Mabel who steals the show in this photograph. It's the man beside her, and it's the way he looks at her with a mixture of admiration, awe, and lust. It's like nothing I've ever seen before in my whole life.

I flip over the photo and I read aloud a note written in Mabel's neat hand.

Aidan, this photo is for you, my darling boy. I know how much family means to you, so this is my favourite photo of your Uncle Peter, taken on the night he proposed to me in New York. We called this photo 'the look of love'

– I don't think I need to explain why! But I want you to have it for reasons that only you can interpret. I hope it gives you direction and guidance for the rest of your life.

We love you, Aidan. We always will.

'Wow,' I whisper. 'Gosh, they really were like something from a movie, weren't they?'

'That's pretty awesome,' says Aidan as he takes the photo from me and we both stare at it a little longer.

I catch my breath and he reads aloud to me now.

Roisin, this dress is now yours, my little rose. I know you will wear it well, but please do so only when you find a man who looks at you the way my Peter looks at me in this photograph. I know he's out there somewhere for you. Promise me you'll never give up on finding him, and when you do, that you'll never let him go.

Mabel x

I bite my lip as tears prick my eyes, and I look up at Aidan. Our eyes lock, and for a fleeting moment I can hear my heart beat in my chest and my hands shake as I take the photo back, still looking at Aidan, who is looking at me.

'Anyone for coffee?'

Camille's voice echoes up the narrow stairwell and I hear her footsteps on the wooden stairs in what is perfect timing.

I have no idea what just happened, but what I do know is that Aidan has made his way to the window again and is staring outside. Something is bothering him deeply – something that perhaps has nothing to do with Mabel or Ballybray. I can tell by how one moment he is laughing and joking then the next he just switches off, that he has remembered something in real life that is anchoring him down.

Or maybe it's just grief, and I'm putting two and two together and coming up with five.

'Yes please, that would be amazing, thanks Camille,' I manage to respond.

I try to distract my mind from Aidan's pain by picturing Mabel, in her beauty and prime, linking Peter's arm as they walked down 42nd Street, looking very much the pretty woman with her gorgeous man beaming with pride beside her. Jazz music spills out of open doors, trying to lure them into basement bars, but they're too caught up in each other to notice. I can hear Mabel's thin stiletto heels *click-clicking* on the sidewalk, her infectious bursts of laughter as she throws her head back so seductively, the way she looks up at Peter beneath her luscious lashes, stroking the warmth of his woollen suit on his arm as he blows cigarette smoke into rings into the night sky.

And then I look down at the photo, and the red dress that lies draped over my lap in real life, here in Peter's home town of Ballybray all these years later, and I'm in absolute awe.

I don't think I'll ever find a man to look at me the way Peter Murphy does Mabel in that photo. I don't think I'll ever find a man who could make me feel the way Peter made Mabel feel.

Promise me you'll never give up on finding him, and when you do, that you'll never let him go. 'I won't,' I whisper to Mabel and I hold the dress up to my cheek, drifting back in time to her heyday when she found the love of her life in New York, all the way from Ballybray here in Ireland.

Like Aidan said, this dress holds a little piece of history and it's a part of Mabel's life that I'll treasure for ever.

'I can't tell you the relief I feel now that that's done,' says Aidan, as we pack a few loose items back into the brown canvas bags he had brought them in some moments later. His hair is dishevelled, as though he's just up out of bed, and I feel as if I've just run up the steep hill at Warren's Wood without stopping. I can feel a faint river of sweat trickle down my cleavage, and Aidan's brow is dotted with tiny little glass beads. I'd forgotten how warm it can get in the attic storeroom, especially with the heat blasting at this time of year.

Camille's interruption with her offer of coffee was perfect timing and it burst the hazy bubble and pulled us out of the fog of memories we had become so lost in.

'It's another little step in the right direction,' I say, agreeing with Aidan wholeheartedly, now that my nerves have settled and a shot of caffeine has taken the edge off the intensity of our reminiscences. 'It was a lot less painful than I thought it might be. In fact, dare I say it, I quite enjoyed it, despite my fears.'

'Same,' says Aidan, as he helps me to gather up our empty cups and picks up his jacket. 'It was nice to hear your stories about Mabel. I enjoyed your company, Roisin, once again. Thank you.'

I swallow hard and lead the way down the narrow wooden staircase, gripping the hand rail for fear that I might fall as my legs wobble after sitting for so long.

I feel a pang of guilt when I think of his wife so far away, unaware of the intense moments we just shared locked away for over an hour together, bonding over memories and stories, but then I remind myself that there's nothing wrong with enjoying someone's company.

Aidan enjoyed my company today, just like Camille does when we work together, or like Mabel did when we'd talk and talk for hours on end. There's absolutely nothing wrong with that and I don't need to look into it any further.

And I'd enjoyed his company too. A lot. Yes, I had and I'm not afraid to think it. I do my best to control my roller-coaster emotions of guilt and fear that I've done something wrong as I take the last few steps and breathe to overcome my overactive mind.

'I hope I didn't bend your ear too much on my trip down

memory lane,' he says to me as we approach the door of Truly Vintage on his way out. His next mission is to take the rest of Mabel's clothes, stuff that didn't make it into the shop's collection, to a recycling centre or a charity store who may have use for it. 'I've a habit of talking way, way too much when I get started.'

'It's an Irish thing,' I jest, shrugging my shoulders. 'I bet you're a lot quieter back in New York, but when you come here you let loose and let all that Irish charm run free.'

Back in New York with your wife, I almost add, but I don't, and then to my surprise Aidan fills in that gap for me. He scratches his head.

'Rachel would disagree wholeheartedly that I'm quiet in New York if you told her that. She has reminded me on numerous occasions when I should be keeping quiet instead of rabbiting on. That's her expression, not mine.'

'Really?'

'Yes, really. Let's just say that my wife never did quite grasp the ins and outs of the Irish culture and her experience of how we like to talk and talk and talk is a bit mind-blowing for her,' he tells me.

Do I detect a hint of bitterness or resentment in his voice? Or is it rather the whole classic 'she just doesn't get me' excuse that so many are known to make when a relationship takes a dip?

'She would have given my grandmother a heart attack with her absolute refusal to live anywhere other than New

York,' he continues. 'And to think my grandmother thought Mabel was a threat all those years ago.'

Ouch. There are so many things running through my head right now, and I don't even recognize my own voice when it comes out. It sounds like a pathetic squeak and is at least three octaves higher than usual.

'Well, Mabel surprised you all, so maybe Rachel will too?'

He stares at me now, and I catch my breath.

'She won't. Believe me, she won't.'

There's so much more I'd love to ask him, but I don't seem to have control over what is going to come out of my mouth next.

'I have to say I was a bit surprised she didn't hang around after the funeral to help you organize all Mabel's stuff,' I say, knowing I'm totally going into the none-of-your-business zone, but Aidan just looks baffled in return.

'Rachel wasn't at the funeral, Roisin,' he says, dropping his voice down to a whisper and shrugging his shoulders as if it was no big deal, but I can feel the hurt that radiates from him.

'Oh?'

'She's in New York, working,' he tells me. 'My wife has never been to Ireland, never mind Ballybray, and she probably never will.'

His forehead creases as he opens the shop door, letting a wintry breeze cut through us both, and I get the impression he wants to leave quickly before I interrogate him any more. So, who on earth was the glamorous blonde lady that stood next to him in the church pew? I could have sworn it was Rachel.

He closes the door again and I wait for further explanation, but I won't be getting any more information today, it seems.

'Look, on a totally different level and staying with life here and now in Ballybray,' he says, quite unfazed by my questioning, all things considered, 'it's Thanksgiving tomorrow and I thought before I sell up the house and move on, it might be nice for us to have one last dinner in Mabel's kitchen knowing how much she loved Thanksgiving? I'll cook.'

'Oh.' His invitation takes me by genuine surprise.

'You don't have to if it doesn't suit,' he says quickly, almost as if he's changed his mind already.

'Sorry – yes, I'd – of course. I'd really love that and I think Ben would love it too,' I tell him quickly. 'We'll look forward to that. I'll – I'll bring dessert. Thank you.'

'Tomorrow at five thirty, is that OK?'

He is back to being monotone and focused, while my head is still on all things Rachel.

'Perfect,' I tell him, doing my best to stay present, but I can feel a headache coming on after the intensity of today. 'That's very kind of you. I'll see you then.'

I watch him walk away from my workplace, his handsome figure with his dark head bowed down against the flurries of snow, and then I go back to work to try and shake off my headache. I start off by placing Mabel's silk neck scarf carefully on a mannequin in the window and snap it for our social media, knowing it will sell almost immediately, if not locally, to one of our growing online followers.

But all the time I'm doing so, I can't stop wondering about Rachel, and how much I loved going through Mabel's clothes with her husband, and the time we just spent together. It's odd that she's so far away, not knowing what's going on in his world at such a vulnerable time.

'Can I visit Aidan this evening? Please, Mum?' Ben asks me when he bounds into the shop after school. 'I want to find out more about New York City! My teacher was there and she says it's so cool and we should definitely go there!'

I hold the bag with Mabel's precious red dress in my right hand and I can't wait to get it home and put it away safely.

'Let's get you home and see what homework needs to be done,' I tell my son, trying to divert him from something he has probably been dying to do all day. 'You'll see Aidan tomorrow at a special Thanksgiving dinner in Mabel's memory. He's invited us over, so you'll have to wait until then.'

Ben punches the air in delight, then his face falls as he realizes he has to wait twenty-four hours for that, but I hurry him on as we say our goodbyes to Camille then leave the shop to walk the half mile home to Teapot Row.

The sun begins to bow its head over Warren's Wood in the distance as we walk under the deep November sky.

'And Brandon says his mum has been to New York three hundred times, but I don't believe him,' Ben tells me as we walk hand in hand quickly against the nip in the air. 'Brandon tells lies all the time and I'm so sick of it. He always has to beat my stories, every single time.'

I wonder how long Ben's obsession with New York and Aidan Murphy will go on for, and that old familiar grip of fear clasps within me, letting me know how important it is to protect Ben from any further feelings of abandonment when Aidan disappears from his life very shortly. Maybe I shouldn't have agreed to the dinner. Maybe we're spending too much time together already. Maybe I shouldn't be sledging and dining out and dining in with another woman's husband, no matter how fragmented their marriage may seem from afar.

'And when I asked Miss Tennyson if one person could really go to New York three hundred times, she laughed and—'

'Hang on, honey, just a second,' I say to Ben, quite literally stopping us both in our tracks as I look ahead.

Daylight has really dropped down fast as we approach Teapot Row. I see Aidan's silver car parked in its now usual place under the yellow glow of the street lamp, but when I get closer I notice something is different, something is missing which makes me stop right there to take it all in.

It's the *For Sale* sign outside Mabel's house.

The *For Sale* sign is gone. Aidan, it seems, has changed his mind.

15.

I don't set eyes on Aidan Murphy until it's time to go next door as promised at five thirty the following day, which gives me the space I desperately needed to gather myself and build up some emotional strength from deep inside after sorting out Mabel's belongings.

But even though I haven't seen him, I did hear some rather heavy chat coming from next door when I was tidying at the back of my house, meaning he was either on a very intense and heated phone call, or he was letting off some steam to himself. I don't know him well enough to decide which of the two it may have been, but he did sound very frustrated.

Ben and I, on the other hand, spent a very relaxing afternoon baking an apple pie, which was the only thing that prevented him from bounding next door ahead of our invited time. As we walk the short distance now to Mabel's house, the heat of the pie in my hands and the warm, sweet smell of apples mixes with the crisp evening air and calms me right down, helping me regain some composure for the evening ahead.

'Knock, knock!' I shout, just like I always used to, hoping the moment I do it that Aidan doesn't mind us letting ourselves in. I'd suggested we knock properly and wait, but Ben was already ahead of me and Aidan shouted a hello from the kitchen where he is still cooking up a storm.

The first thing I notice when Ben and I step across the threshold of Mabel's cottage isn't the smell of food or the sound of Aidan's voice, but the black suitcase in the hallway all packed up and ready to go. I stop. I do a double-take and almost drop the masterpiece of dessert I'd spent so long making.

'Is Aidan going home already?' Ben asks me, but I can barely bring myself to answer. It's for the best all round, I tell myself. It's definitely for the best.

The next thing that hits me is the delicious smell of roast turkey and ham, and as it's our first time inside this door since Mabel left us, I also can't help but sense that already the whole house feels different even though it's only just over a week since she was last here.

Photos that once lined the narrow little hallway, mostly of Mabel in her cabaret days and of her wedding day to Peter, have been removed, leaving a faint line of dust where they used to sit on the wall. The paint, a shade of green she used to describe in a posh voice as 'pistachio' was darker beneath where the framed photos once took pride of place, and the coat stand that stood in the corner is now empty and lonely without her vast collection of colourful coats to keep it company.

'Come on in and have a seat. I'm almost ready to serve up,' says Aidan, looking very much at ease considering he is cooking in someone else's kitchen. He has a tea towel over his shoulder and wears a fitted navy T-shirt, blue denim jeans, and white tennis shoes. I try not to stare at his muscular back as he leads us inside.

'I'll just leave this here, but mind, the dish is still hot,' I say, leaving the apple pie on the worktop. I have butterflies, but I'm glad at the same time that Aidan's stay is coming to an end because the longer he stays, the more Ben seems to enjoy having him around, and that frightens the life out of me.

The smooth sounds of Ella Fitzgerald that used to grace Mabel's kitchen have been replaced by Aidan's rather elegant classical music choice, which we follow as he leads us into the poky kitchen at the back of the cottage. To my relief, nothing much else has changed in here just yet, apart from a few cardboard boxes that are stacked in the corner, still to be filled in the big clear-out. It's still a little bit cluttered, with Mabel's green and white checked oven glove over the oven door and a selection of spices to the left, the tree of mugs to the right, and the bread bin that never had bread inside but always had a loaf or two sitting on top instead. The little ornaments that lined the windowsill are still there in their random display, with everything from porcelain ladybirds, a robin, a frog and even a little pig dressed up as a chef. Seeing these makes me smile.

'The first thing I wanted to do when I moved in here was declutter this kitchen,' she told me once when I questioned where on earth such a fine collection of ornaments came from. 'But then I remembered how every little trinket in here has its own story to tell, and Peter loved living amongst his own home comforts. Young Aidan will always enjoy them too.'

Judging by the cardboard box that says 'ornaments' I'm not so sure Aidan shares Mabel's sentimental ways, and I feel a touch of sadness that these little porcelain animals and ceramic insects have seen their final days.

Mabel's table centrepiece of a large, silver candelabra stands proudly as it always has and I hope that Aidan, even if he is about to clear the place out for whatever is going to happen next here, is able to find some comfort with these remnants from his childhood surrounding him. So much of Mabel's interior design was kept 'as was' in honour of Aidan's grandparents, who lived here before she and Peter did, and although I know she didn't always see eye to eye with her mother-in-law, she respected her memory enough to leave some of her trinkets still in their original place all these years after she'd left this world.

'You look as if we should be eating in a fancy restaurant and not in Teapot Row,' Aidan tells me as he pulls out a chair for me to sit down. My eyes automatically divert to my dress, which, apart from my attire at work earlier that day, is certainly a huge step up from the fleecy pyjamas or the denim dungarees he had previously seen me in.

Ben takes the seat opposite me, a place he always sits when at Mabel's table, and without thinking he plays with the wicker table mat, rolling it up and making it into a telescope, just like he has done now for years when he comes here.

I tut and roll my eyes, giving the effect of '*oh this old thing*' in response to Aidan's subtle compliment towards my efforts, but I have to admit, I did choose my outfit carefully this evening as I wanted to feel and look good for the first time in a long while.

I didn't dress to impress Aidan. I dressed to impress myself, of course, knowing that I have been dowdy and miserable for weeks now, and that it was time I started making an effort again, just as Mabel would have wanted me to. I'd made an effort for work again this morning, and I made an effort for tonight's dinner, and it has absolutely nothing to do with Aidan. If I look good, I feel good. It's as simple as that.

But am I being truthful by thinking this way or am I becoming the woman that every other woman hates? Am I turning into the type of woman who flirts around another woman's man; the one who preys and waits on an opportunity to make him look at her just like the way Aidan Murphy is looking at me now? Please God, I hope not.

'I have a thing for floral tea dresses,' is the only neutral, middle of the road response I can come up with to acknowledge his roundabout compliment. 'I find them very comfortable and snug.'

Aidan pours me a glass of cold Sauvignon Blanc and he

barely gets the chance to finish filling the glass when I take a long chug. I haven't drunk white wine in ages, and I just know it will go straight to my head, but I need something to settle my runaway train of thought.

'Are you going back to New York tonight, Aidan?' asks Ben, very comfortable in his surroundings now he is right back in his happy place. Aidan serves dinner on Ben's favourite plate, a hexagon shape made of white bone china. Ben believed it to be from the country China and of course Mabel spun him a yarn about how it had some sort of magical powers that made those who dined from it go on to do marvellous, magnificent things.

'I'd – well, I'd planned to leave tomorrow afternoon,' explains Aidan as he serves up my food and lastly his own. He glances at me, as if to gauge my response, but I don't give anything away. I can play the perfect poker face when I need to. God knows I've had to do it so often in life. 'I'd hoped to stay a little bit longer, but something has come up in work that I'd best be there for.'

'Aw! Does that mean we're getting new neighbours already?' asks Ben, already tucking in to his succulent turkey, with gravy dripping off his chin. I pass him a napkin to wipe it since he has already tucked his own into his jumper, which I know he believes makes him look posh.

'Well, I'm not very sure of that yet,' says Aidan, shifting in his seat a little. 'I was all set to sell the house as quickly as possible, but . . . well—'

I feel it's time to take the reins and rescue him from any awkward explanations as to why he has taken down the *For Sale* sign outside, reminding myself that it's not really our business.

'Let's talk about all that later, is that OK, Ben?' I suggest, sensing Aidan's immediate relief. 'Now, eat up before your delicious food gets cold.'

The chat over dinner has a distinctive air of a long goodbye, with the only saving grace being the exceptional food and Ben's constant chatter about facts of New York that he has been obsessing over since he first met Aidan.

'There are twice as many people living in New York City than there are in the whole of Ireland,' Ben tells us, talking with his mouth full on more than one occasion despite my reminders not to. 'Isn't that crazy? I can't wait to go there. I just know it's going to be so cool when we visit. Can someone really go there three hundred times though? I do think Brandon is lying.'

I roll my eyes in mock apology.

There's no doubt about it, my boy is becoming smitten with New York and with Aidan Murphy and I'm terrified at the crash of reality that's about to come our way when he is gone. I've never been to New York City and I very much doubt I'd be able to afford to go there anytime soon, but for now I'm just glad that Ben has something to get excited about even if it's just a pipe dream.

'I really hope you can come and visit me some day, for sure,' says Aidan, shooting me a wink. 'And I'll try and dig out that helicopter Mabel told you about, Ben.'

We finish our evening in front of a roaring fire in Mabel's sitting room, with Ben lounging around like he owns the place, which for long enough, he was very much made to believe he did. Aidan doesn't seem to mind at all that he helps himself to a train from a wicker basket of toys that sits in the corner of the room, beside a fringed standard lamp that I realize would look so good in Truly Vintage if the time ever comes for it to find a new home.

I want to know why Aidan isn't selling the house after all, but I don't dare ask. The wine from dinner has relaxed me no end, and I'm enjoying the buzz it gives me, taking away the urge to analyse or make any interpretation of Aidan's every word, his every move or his every glance in my direction.

'Those toys are as old as I am,' says Aidan, watching Ben.

At ten years old, Ben had long outgrown playing around a floor with a train set, but I always said that no matter what age he was, he always turned into a little boy again when he visited Mabel's house, and no one minded. Here, no one ever judged his preferences and he didn't have to pretend to like Minecraft or whatever the latest video game was. It was back to basics at Mabel's, and he loved it.

'Wait a minute. Are these your toys, Aidan?' I ask. 'I never even thought to ask Mabel where they came from, but I guess that makes sense.'

Aidan nods, still staring at Ben, who is in a world of his own.

'I was ten when I moved in here for good,' he says, lost in thought. 'And no matter what toys I had outgrown by then, that little green train set was timeless to me. Man, life just flies by, doesn't it?'

I can feel an internal glow as the glass of wine I'm cradling takes its sweet effect and I sit back on the sofa across from Aidan, watching him watch Ben as if he is watching his younger self.

'Losing your parents at that age is unbearably sad,' I whisper, then realize that Ben is of course within earshot and that at his age, listening to adult conversation is one of his favourite pastimes, especially when he gets to stay up a little later on a school night. The last thing I want to do now is talk about death in front of him when we're all having such a relaxed evening.

'It was,' agrees Aidan, shrugging it off and snapping out of his flashback as quickly as he zoned into it. 'So, what are your plans for Christmas then? I know it's going to be different this year for all of us, but you'll do something nice, won't you?'

The thought of Christmas without Mabel makes my stomach churn, but Ben lights up.

'I'm getting a robot and a Nintendo and I'm not sure

what else yet, but I'm going to write my list soon, aren't I Mum?' he says, kneeling up on the floor with eyes wide as the moon.

'And that answers my question,' says Aidan. 'I always thought that Christmas was only Christmas when there's a kid in the house.'

'It's going to be different for all of us, that's a given,' I say, trying to keep things light. 'As I'm sure this all is for you too.'

I'm already dreading waking up in the morning with that old familiar sensation of loss that will hit me all over again; the hollow feeling that sits deep inside which comes with such a devastating change. I dread looking out of the window and seeing the empty space where Aidan's hired car has been, right in the place where Mabel's funny little green VW Beetle used to sit before she sold it earlier on in her illness. Most of all I dread knowing that this house next door to me will be still and silent again, and that the path of grief and sadness will be walked on without anything to prop us up, for at least the foreseeable future.

16.

I check the time. It's almost nine and as it's a school night, I realize we'd really better get going.

Normally at this time, Ben would be tucked up in bed dreaming, and I'd be on the sofa in front of the TV, flicking through channels robotically, checking social media repeatedly, and wondering was it too early to go to bed. Jude and I used to watch TV together at night, but it normally ended in a row over something I'd said or done that day that had upset him, so the peace of switching off the telly, turning out the lights, locking the doors, and going to bed without an argument mid-week had become quite pleasant.

But being with Aidan is different. He can strike up a conversation about anything, from music of the nineties, to Italian cuisine, to the best video games on the market these days that Ben would enjoy. An evening in his company, even if it has broken our normally regimental bedtime routine, has been a much more positive and all-round wholesome experience than I could ever have expected.

'I think it's time for bed, buddy,' I say to Ben, who dramatically lies on the sofa in protest.

'But!'

'No buts,' I tell him in my best mummy voice. 'Aidan has a long journey ahead of him tomorrow and we've had a great time, but you're normally fast asleep by now. Aidan, I can't believe you wouldn't let me do the washing up. I wish you'd let me help before we go?'

Aidan shakes his head.

'No way, and anyhow I need to keep my mind busy, believe me,' he says emphatically. He yawns and I echo him, which makes us both smile.

'You're tired,' I say, stating the obvious. 'Dinner was delicious. Thanks again.'

'I'm a little bit tired, yes,' he admits. 'But I've also a lot on my mind, so washing up a few plates and saucepans will help distract me from wandering around this house and feeling sorry for myself.'

I put on my coat as Ben pretends he isn't going home and hugs his favourite cushion on Mabel's settee, just the way he used to do when we'd have dinner here in days gone by. It's a simple, round, pale-grey velvet cushion she bought in a high street store, but Ben always got great comfort from resting his head on it while he and Mabel would watch a movie or sort out the world's problems with their many deep and meaningful conversations.

'I know, how about you take that cushion home with

you tonight?' Aidan asks Ben, and I swear I don't think I've ever seen my son look so overwhelmed at a gesture before. 'You can keep it. I think Mabel would like that.'

Ben opens his mouth to respond, but the words don't come out and I recognize the way his lip quivers, just like any mother's instinct would recognize, that he is going to cry.

'That's very kind of you, Aidan,' I say, trying to give Ben some space to compose himself, but he's way beyond that already.

His chin wobbles, his mouth twitches, and then he pulls the cushion up to his face, burying himself in it to disguise his feelings, which makes my heart break for him. I feel a wave of panic, just like I did when he was little and he fell, or when I had to tell him Mabel was leaving us, or when he told me he was once being picked on at school in days gone by. It's an instinct mixed with fear and protection, but whereas I stand there frozen in those few seconds of real-ization, then rush to his side, Aidan is already there. He puts his hand on Ben's back and comforts him instantly, just like he did with me a few nights before.

'It's OK to cry, little guy,' he tells Ben to the back of his silky brown head. 'You don't ever have to hide it when you feel sad or a little bit overwhelmed. It's better to let it all out. That's it. Have a good old cry.'

I crouch down in front of Ben and put my hand on his little hand as it grasps the cushion.

'I just want her to come home,' sniffles Ben. 'I just want Mabel to come home.'

His little voice pleads with us and I feel so helpless watching on. All I can do is be there for him through this, I know that, but a tinge of anger bubbles inside me at how there is absolutely nothing I can do to take his pain away.

Soon, I'm crying softly too. I glance up at Aidan, who reaches his other hand across to me and squeezes it tightly. I know Ben's reaction is all very normal and natural, but I still can't help the anxiety that eats at me inside. There's nothing, simply nothing as frightening as seeing your child in pain and knowing there is nothing in the world you can do to take it away. All you can do is be there for them, listen to their fears, and allow them to express any emotion they feel necessary.

Despite knowing all this, when I look at my broken child, so affected by the weight of grief twice now at such a young age, it chills me to my very core and I want to scream out at how unfair it all is.

'You were Mabel's very, very, special friend,' Aidan says, finding the words I can't seem to. He softly rubs the back of Ben's little yellow hoodie as he speaks in such warm, reassuring tones. 'There's nothing like a good cry. You'll feel better after, I know I always do.'

I wipe my eyes, feeling useless as I cry almost as much as Ben does, but I know my anguish is coming from the past as well as what is happening now. An unwelcome flashback to my time with Jude floods my mind. He couldn't cope when Ben showed emotion through tears or tantrums, and he'd end up having his own tantrum in turn, shouting sometimes over our child's tears. He'd tell me afterwards that it was my fault. I was raising a 'sissy', and he'd tell Ben that 'big boys don't cry', then we'd argue over which of us was right and which of us was wrong and Jude would insist it was my fault because all I ever did was cry and cry.

'No wonder your mother abandoned you,' he said to me once as I cried into my pillow one night after a particularly tough evening of name calling and abuse, all because he'd had a bad day at work and needed a punchbag to make him feel better. His words cut me right to the bone and I vowed it was the final straw, but the next morning there was an apology, a cooked breakfast in bed, and a trip to the swimming pool planned for our very excited son. And so I stayed. And so it continued . . .

I feel a lump wedge in my throat now, a huge boulder of anxiety at the memory of how his words used to hurt me so deeply. He'd tangle me up in an argument I could never win, and if someone had asked me about it afterwards, I'd never be able to convey how he played me like a fiddle, making me dizzy with my own words and tangled up in his.

And now, here I am watching on as this gentle stranger who only came into our lives a few days ago, has already taught my son the complete opposite. Ben leans into Aidan and does what he was so frightened to do for so long now.

He cries for Mabel and in turn I cry for him, and soon Aidan is filling up too. He grips my hand a little tighter and I close my eyes, wishing I could lean on him for just a bit longer.

Here we are, just the three of us, Mabel's family as she called us, crying floods of tears in her little sitting room, each of us so distraught at her loss but each of us also knowing that she has brought us all together with a bond that is so strong, no one will ever be able to break it. Not even a mysterious wife in America who never had the joy of knowing Aidan's wonderful aunt or his family home the way I did. She will never know the fun and laughter that knowing Mabel was, or the way she could light up a room without saying a word, or how she could sort out a problem just by standing beside you. This is a part of Aidan's life that only Ben and I will ever understand here in Ballybray, and knowing that makes it just a little bit easier to let Aidan go back to his other life where he belongs.

He will never be *ours*, but this moment will always be ours together and for that I'm very, very thankful.

'Roisin,' he calls, just as Ben and I have said our goodbyes and wished him well for his return to the States a little while later.

'Yes?' I say, turning towards where he stands in Mabel's doorway, rubbing his forehead with one hand as if he is squeezing back a mound of tension.

'Look . . . this might sound a bit crazy and maybe it is.

Maybe I'm not thinking straight at all, but my head is a bit mangled and I suppose it's a mix of emotions and—'

'What is it, Aidan?' I ask him, worried now. I totally understand what he's saying, but not sure what he wants from me.

'I've been thinking about Mabel's messages to us and – well, everything so far has made me feel better, so I've decided . . . I've decided to stay here for a while and try to get my head around some of the bigger things going on in my life,' he tells me, and I can almost see the tension on his face fade away as his words spill out.

'OK,' I nod, a bit shocked at this last-minute U-turn.

'So, I'm not going to sell the house so hastily,' he continues, 'and I'm not going back to America tomorrow. I'm going to stay in Ballybray, away from all the madness over there, and try to figure things out from here.'

'Oh,' is about all I can find to say at first, and I'm unable to disguise my surprise at his decision. I can't deny it, I do like the idea of him being here rather than Mabel's house lying empty, plus we've had some nice times together so far, but I'm also, for the first time, quickly trying to digest just how bad things have been in America for him. 'Well . . . well, you take your time and do what's best for yourself, Aidan, and you know Ben and I are right next door if you need us.'

His face breaks into a wide smile of relief, I assume at getting some sort of reassurance that he's doing the right thing.

'Thank you, Roisin, that means a lot,' he says, his frown disintegrating and his voice a lot softer than the gruff arrogance I was first met with only days ago.

I walk away, trying to answer Ben's flurry of questions at Aidan's announcement as we slip and slide in the snow back home.

'Is Aidan our new neighbour? That's so cool! Does he love it here like we do? I wonder could we go sledging again. What do you think, Mum?'

I have so many thoughts running through my head, mostly of how Mabel has guided us all lately, and so I secretly acknowledge thanks on what has been a surprisingly pleasant Thanksgiving Day to her for watching out for the three of us in more ways than she will ever know.

'Just for a little while,' I tell my son who is wide-eyed and eager at the thought. 'He will have to go back to America one day, but not just quite yet.'

SPRING

17.

'Would Aidan like to come to the beach with us, Mum?' Ben asks me on a bright, sunny Sunday in March.

With the weather picking up, Ben and I make an effort every Sunday morning to continue a tradition we had with Mabel where we walk on the beach in Dunfanaghy at the beautiful Killahoey Strand after breakfast, putting the world to rights, or at least our own little world to rights, as much as we can.

Aidan has been settling in well next door, keeping to himself when he wants to sometimes for days at a time, but popping by for the odd coffee or a chat over the fence.

'I suppose it might be nice to ask him,' I reply, touched at Ben's kindness. I'm not sure how Aidan spends his Sundays, but I do know that it can be a very long and lonely day for many, so I take the bull by the horns and go across to Mabel's house to ask him.

He opens the door, a bit more taken aback than I expected, and I get the impression I've landed at exactly the wrong time as he has his phone in his hand and looks as if he was in the midst of quite a heated discussion.

'Thanks all the same,' he says in response to my invitation, with just enough edge to make my face flush. 'I'm in the middle of something really important, Roisin, so not today, sorry.'

I leave, feeling rejected and a bit embarrassed, and vow I'll never ask him again, telling myself that Aidan Murphy's purpose for being here is not to fill the gap that Mabel has left behind in our lives and never will be.

Some days I find myself wondering what on earth he gets up to next door, but then I remember how small the world is now, especially in his line of business where everything can be coordinated and managed online or by telephone. Some days I forget he is even there at all, but as the new season settles in, so does Aidan, and eventually he does take up the offer for a Sunday walk on the beach when Ben puts him on the spot as I am fetching my coat.

'You really should come with us. It's really good to blow the cobwebs off the week before and get ready for the week ahead,' I hear him say over the fence to Aidan, who has just come back from his morning run. 'That's what my mum says anyhow. I have a Frisbee. It's brand new, but Mum isn't really good at catching it. She tries her best, but I just end up giving up and kicking my ball instead.'

The lonely only-child's remark is enough to at least guilt Aidan into joining us this time.

'OK, I'll meet you down there,' he says to Ben, catching

me listening in from my position at the front door. 'My grandparents weren't very good at Frisbee either when I was your age, so I'll see you there and we'll show your mum how it's done.'

As well as Sundays by the sea, I begin the new season with a bang by making a decision that this will be the one where I finally put my energy into doing something I feel passionate about, and so far it's keeping me up late at night, but it's making me very excited indeed.

I've thought of names for my future brand of home-made candles and I stay awake at night, dreaming of one day stocking some of my supplies in local shops including Truly Vintage of course, in addition to some of the unique little gift shops in nearby Dunfanaghy.

'There's something about this smell that reminds me of Mabel,' Aidan tells me one Sunday morning as we walk the Strand with Ben. I'd brought a candle in my handbag to see if I could pluck his business mind to help me come up with a brand name. 'It's so simple, yet so her.'

'That's it!' I say, stopping in the sand as the answer came to me. 'It's simply Mabel. I've got it! *Simply Mabel*! Thanks Aidan.'

'Nice to see I'm useful for something,' he says, looking very gloomy in comparison to my upbeat enthusiasm at my big revelation. He closes up and walks over to a sand dune before I can dare to ask what might be on his mind.

Our push and pull mode of communication continues

like this every Sunday, but I'm quite happy with the distance we've created even though we live so closely. He's a married man, obviously in some sort of despair with whatever he has on his mind; it's not my place to intervene, nor is it my intention to. I've Ben to focus on and my own mental health, and I'm quite happy to keep a comfortable space.

I start the new season by writing daily affirmations in the spare room, which I made a 'room of one's own' in true Virginia Woolf style, to become my new workshop. I also practise my violin in there until my fingers bleed, I write poetry to express the anger of my past and the hope for my future. I meditate and I swim. I walk and I cook. I even garden, and it's when I'm trying to figure out the best way to attack a patch of weeds by the fence that I overhear Aidan, who is pacing the garden on the other side.

'I don't know how much longer, Bruce,' I hear him plead. 'Yes, I know the time difference is shit but I'm doing my best. Jesus, give me a break! I've just lost the last family member I have and I'm sorry if it's affecting the business, but I'm barely sleeping to try and keep up. I just need some space. I need this space and so does Rachel. You know it.'

I crouch down, unable to erase what I've just heard and praying that he doesn't notice me so close by.

'Fuck!' I hear him as he hangs up on the call and then the back door slams as he goes back inside. It's later that afternoon when he lands at my door, trembling and exhausted.

'What's wrong?' I ask him. It's a gorgeous spring day, the

clocks have just gone forward to give us an extra hour of daylight, and yet Aidan stands in front of me looking like it's the end of the world.

'I was wondering if you'd time for a chat?' he asks and I step aside to let him in, then lead him out to the back garden where I've taken great pride in trying to mirror Mabel's masterpiece next door now that we don't have it at our disposal to dine outside.

I put the kettle on and bring him out some tea and home-made scones, another of Mabel's recipes baked by Ben, all the while wondering what has made him take this change of pace of communication.

'Sorry, I hope I'm not interrupting your day,' he tells me, squinting in the sunshine when I join him. 'I know I don't like being landed on sometimes, so don't be afraid to say if you've to go somewhere or if you're busy.'

I think back to the conversation I overhead earlier from the garden.

'It's Saturday, it's my day off, and I like to do as little as possible around Ben's sporting timetable,' I explain to him as I pour us some tea. 'He's horse riding at the moment with his best friend, Gino, after spending the morning playing soccer. He's a better social life than I do, no joke.'

Aidan's face has softened now, relieved perhaps that I can take the time to lend him an ear.

'I've been under a lot of pressure since I got here, so first of all I want to apologize if I've made you feel like I was pushing any of your kindness away,' he says, 'but I'm really not used to it at all. My life in New York is the polar opposite of any sense of neighbourly community or having someone who cares. I honestly don't even know my neighbours' names over there.'

I can barely relate. When I think of how close Mabel and I were, I can't even imagine a life where you were totally anonymous, with no one to call upon.

'It's not the same in New York at all, at least not in my circle,' he continues. 'My wife's family are money orientated and the more I distance myself physically from their demands, the more I see just how cold I've become after being immersed in that world for so long. I wasn't brought up like that. Our home here in Ballybray was full of warmth and love and I've closed the door on that over the years. I'm trying to open it again.'

I have no idea where he is going with this.

'Aidan, I'm not expecting anything from you at all,' I say to him. 'We spend time together on Sunday mornings at the beach, which Ben absolutely adores, but don't ever feel pressurized to do any more.'

'But Mabel wanted us to have some sort of family connection, and I think I should make more of an effort. Can I treat you and Ben to something? Is there anything you need?'

I'm absolutely baffled now.

'Anything I *need*? Like what?'

'Well, I don't know,' he says, looking around him for some

inspiration. 'Like, is there anything you need for your home or your new studio? Anything I can—'

'Aidan, I don't want you to *buy* us anything,' I say to him with a nip in my voice I don't even try to disguise. 'I don't ever want or need you to *buy* my friendship, and I'd very much doubt that's what Mabel meant when she said she'd like us to get to know each other!'

My blood boils at the very idea.

'Sorry, I'm not very good at this,' he says, knowing he has hit a nerve. 'I guess I'm used to a life where buying gifts is a way of showing gratitude.'

'Well, that doesn't work with me,' I let him know. 'In fact, I'm exactly the opposite. The last thing I desire is for you or anyone to try to buy your way around me!'

He shifts in his seat, searching for the right thing to say.

'OK, so that's no excuse, but I ran away from my life here looking for something I never did find in New York,' he says, his voice breaking now. 'I ran away trying to fill a void I could never fill over there, no matter how much money I earned or how much my father-in-law Bruce has told me I'm his right-hand man, because I know deep down he doesn't care about me, Roisin! He only cares about how much money I can make his company, and so does his daughter!'

Ouch.

'I don't want to be like him,' he says, a little softer now. 'He's not my true family and now I've absolutely no true family left, Roisin. Mabel is gone, and she's asked me to get to know you and Ben, and I've no idea where to start. I'm sorry.'

I take a deep breath. So does Aidan.

We sit opposite each other with only the birdsong in the garden to break the blanket of silence that surrounds us as I think of what to say next.

'Maybe you should stop trying to be something or someone you're not comfortable with,' I suggest to him, pouring more tea just for the sake of doing something with my hands. 'Maybe just take this time to get to know the real you a bit better? You can't buy friendship and you can't buy family, Aidan, but you know that now. Just be yourself, and don't try so hard to impress the wrong people.'

I see how his shoulders relax now he's got this out in the open and, as the afternoon passes, we open up more and find we've a lot more in common than we thought we ever could have.

He tells me more about his job and how demanding it is sometimes, how he has lately really felt like packing it all in and downscaling when the pressure became too tough.

'It's like living in someone else's cocoon, with high expectations you never seem to reach and even when you do, they only raise the bar until you're so dizzy and don't ever think you'll find your way back to earth again.'

He opens up about the social life in New York and how he sometimes finds it too busy and fast, and how he likes to disappear when he can to a tiny Irish pub he'd found just to get a sense of comfort he often craved in such a huge, anonymous city.

'You've no idea how much I appreciate the humour from home or even the familiarity of our own accent,' he says with a smile. 'Of course I can't even admit to Rachel that's where I've been. That would be the ultimate sign of weakness to her.'

'Why?' I ask him. 'Wouldn't she like to get to know more about where you come from, even if it's only over a drink in a pub that makes you feel welcome?'

He laughs off the suggestion.

'Control,' he admits to me, and I raise an eyebrow at his admission, his story all too familiar. 'It's all about control at the end of the day in her world, and I'm so glad to be out of it, if only for a while.'

We talk until it's time for me to pick up Ben from his horse riding lesson in Dunfanaghy, and Aidan agrees to come with me for the ride, a gesture I find much more endearing than any offer of money or material goods.

'See, it's as simple as this,' I say to him as I drive my rusty pick-up truck towards the seaside equestrian centre. 'Ben is going to be over the moon to see you, so be prepared for some mighty fine showing off on his part.'

I catch Aidan smiling out of the window as we drive along the coast and something touches my heart at the sight of it. It's as if he is very slowly, day by day, minute by minute, going back in time to a much slower pace of life in his mind and, from what he's told me, it's exactly what he needs.

And so as the days of spring pass by, instead of pining every time I miss Mabel or when I feel like I'm drowning without her or if I too need an ear just to have a mild rant about something, I go into her kitchen and have a cup of tea with Aidan, dwelling in the place of her warmth, love and generosity. We sit together, we put on the awkward heating system or light the fire, and I do my best to wean myself off her love and guidance, little by little, feeling her breath on my back as I grow stronger and stronger without her.

We talk about music, we talk about movies, and Ben loves to tell Aidan all his really important news such as who in his class has a secret girlfriend, and his excitement for his eleventh birthday in August where he is torn between having a boys' only soccer-themed party in the community hall or a bouncy castle in the back garden, which may or may not be cool enough for his friends.

More recently our chats have turned to the mysterious location of Mabel's next message and the excitement and wonder of what it might say.

'Have you checked the drawers in her bedroom, or you know the place she kept all her correspondence?' I ask Aidan, when spring is most definitely well under way. 'Or looked in the cupboard above the fridge? It has to be around the house somewhere.'

'I've looked everywhere,' he tells me, and I know it's true. 'Absolutely everywhere.'

Between us, we haven't left a stone unturned as we search Mabel's home for clues as to where the next message might lie, and I even take the opportunity to while away some time looking through some of Mabel's photos. When I come across one of Aidan and his wife Rachel, I realize the mysterious lady who stood next to him at the funeral looked nothing like Rachel at all. They were both blonde, yes, but Rachel's features are much sharper and she is a lot taller than the woman I'd mistaken her for.

My stomach flips a bit when I see that Rachel is a beauty queen, that's for sure, in her full-length navy ballgown, and Aidan looks so dapper in his tux by her side. I analyse every inch of the photos, hoping I'll spot something that will give me some sort of deeper insight into their relationship. Aidan hasn't kept it a secret that their marriage is in trouble, but it's the one area I tiptoe around still, knowing it's as painful for him to talk about as my past with Jude is to me.

'Maybe it's not a video message this time?' he suggests on our most recent search of Mabel's home. 'Maybe it's something totally different and we're looking for the wrong thing, but whatever it is, I'm sure it will turn up soon. Good old Mabel, keeping us on our toes. She doesn't half like to keep us waiting, that's for sure.'

We give up and open a bottle of wine in the garden where

we while away an evening, telling stories and wondering what Mabel's next message might reveal.

'I've always thought there was something she wasn't telling me,' he says, allowing his imagination to drift off in a direction I'd never even have thought of. 'As I grew older, there was always something on the tip of her tongue, or lingering in the air when I'd spend time with my uncle Peter. Maybe I'm clutching at straws when I say that, but it may have something to do with the row my dad and Peter had on the night of the accident my parents had. Now that Mabel is gone, I'll never know, will I?'

I look at the pain on Aidan's face and want to reach out and touch him, just to let him know that I'm right beside him for whatever will come next, but I refrain, not wanting to push him any further. He has opened up so much to me over the past few weeks, and I already feel us growing closer, just as Mabel wanted us to so badly.

'Let's just wait and see, eh?' I suggest to him. 'I'm sure Mabel's next message isn't too far away.'

18.

Mabel's message for springtime comes on a bright morning in early April, just as Ben and I are leaving for the school run.

We are running late as my normal morning routine of making sure he has everything he needs for the day ahead – PE gear, an empty cereal box and an egg carton to make something for the craft table, dinner money for the week ahead, and a signed form for a forthcoming school trip to the zoo – takes longer than usual, due to an extra late night I'd spent researching online for branding ideas for the new business venture I'm working on for the near future.

I have the message here at last, courtesy of the postal service this morning. It's a huge mystery as to who may have posted it.

The daffodils Mabel planted in her garden next door bob their yellow heads to bid us good morning as we leave the house for school and work. The sky is a magnificent shade of azure, and there's a fresh, clean nip in the air and definitely an overall lift in our mood, but it's the padded envelope in my handbag that came through the post that excites me most about the day ahead.

And now, as I drop Ben off at the school gates, try and fail to kiss him goodbye as he tells me off for embarrassing him in front of his schoolmates, I race back through the village to work, where I'm delighted to find the shop quiet with only the hum of the radio in the background and the sound of Camille's footsteps upstairs.

'Is that you, Roisin?' she calls – our normal morning routine when I get here just after nine.

'Yes, carry on what you're doing,' I tell her. 'I'll take over down here.'

But Camille comes down the stairs straight away and stops in her tracks when she sees the beaming smile on my face.

'Have you won the lotto, or am I missing something else equally wonderful?' she asks me as I make my way to the coffee dock for a caffeine fix. 'You look like you've had a great start to your day.'

'Something wonderful *has* happened to me this morning!' I say, taking the envelope from my handbag and waving it in the air. '*Ta daaa*! It's Mabel's springtime message! She arranged somehow for it to be posted – after all our frantic searching. Oh Camille, I'm so excited to see what she has to say next!'

Camille takes the cup from my hand and playfully steers me towards the front door of the shop, grabbing my coat and keys on the way past and stuffing them into my hands.

'So, what are you doing here then? Go home right now and watch it!' she says, without taking no for an answer when I try to reply. 'I know you're not going to be much use around here until you do, so just go, and get Aidan, and watch it before you spontaneously combust!'

I squeeze Camille into a bear hug and race out of the door, barely catching my breath until I get home to Teapot Row to tell Aidan the good news.

'It's here!' I tell him when he opens the door in his dressing gown. 'You'll never believe it, but it came through the post today, which is so intriguing and amazing! Let me know when you're ready and we'll open it together.'

I squeeze the padded envelope just a little, like a child trying to guess what's inside a birthday present. I can feel the circular outline of a DVD again and I'm careful not to push too hard, as my veins rush with excitement at what Mabel will have to say to us this time. So it is another video message. I feel my skin tingle in anticipation of what she might have in store for us. We have both been waiting for this for so long.

'So, how have you been?' Aidan asks me when he calls in to watch Mabel's message about twenty minutes later. He never fails to ask me that very simple but very meaningful question, no matter how tired or stressed or busy he is in his daily existence next door. 'I thought this next message was never going to come. It's nice to see you.'

'I've been really good since I last saw you, what was it, about two days ago?' I laugh, trying to think if I've any news since. 'We've been so busy in work so the time has gone by a lot quicker than I'd expected.'

'Let me guess,' he says, scratching the side of his nose before going full drama mode. 'After a top sales record in Truly Vintage, a lot of running around after Ben, some mighty fine home cooked cuisine in the kitchen, and a bit of creative genius in your new workshop upstairs, you are bursting with new energy and a mission to keep everyone smiling? Am I right or am I just jealous of your ability to for ever be wonder woman?'

Aidan's humour and mock awe at how much I seem to pack into my day is often the way we kick-start our conversations, while I in turn will take the opportunity to tease him about how he doesn't seem to do anything except work on his laptop, eat takeaway, and sleep a lot.

'It's called parenting and it's never-ending,' I tell him, marvelling at how he is of course spot on. It's only when I hear it all back that I realize my life is a lot busier than I give myself credit for. 'Being a mum is a full-time job in itself.'

He listens as I recall Ben's latest obsession with all things equestrian and remarks that I look tired, which I take completely the wrong way of course, despite knowing it's true, then backtracks by trying to compliment the yellow dress I am now modelling, all set for our big reveal from Mabel.

'You've changed the living room around a bit,' he says, observant as always and never missing a trick. 'Wasn't the sofa better where it was?'

I fleetingly feel as though we are just like an old married couple, the way we talk about everything so casually and smoothly these days. We bicker too, especially over very broad subjects like commercialism or waste, which I feel so passionately about, and which he is learning to be more mindful of as he learns to live a little bit more humbly here in Ballybray, far from the millionaire lifestyle he'd become accustomed to in the States.

He takes a seat on the sofa, which I've temporarily moved under the window, but to be honest I'm not so keen on it there myself and agree now with him totally. It was better where it was.

'You must have gone on some sort of mad spring cleaning session, did you?' he teases as I bend down to put the DVD into the player below the TV. 'It smells good in here too. Very fresh and definitely not as musty as it can get next door sometimes. I tend to forget how old these cottages are and how little it takes to—'

'Can you please be quiet for one second?' I joke, eager to get on with the job at hand, and I take a seat beside him just in time for us to be greeted once more by the wondrous voice and delightful face of our beautiful Mabel. 'I'm so freakin' excited to see her again. Who could have posted this? I've so many questions!'

I curl my feet up beneath me, Aidan glances at me with trepidation, and I press play on the remote control, all ready to hear what Mabel has to say to us next.

Despite having had all morning to prepare for this, and having months of knowing it was coming our way, I can't help but feel so deeply sad when I see Mabel before us again. I lift her soft grey velvet cushion from where Ben had left it on the sofa just beside me, and I clasp it to my chest, closing my eyes for just one second to squeeze away the pain.

Apart from the hideous but quite hilarious colourful Easter bonnet she wears on her head, which I recognize as one of Ben's masterpieces from school, Mabel seems to have recorded this new message around the same time as the first one, which means that she still looks quite healthy and well in comparison to how she had become before she died in November past from the cancer that gripped her so quickly and cruelly.

I'm so glad she recorded it at the start of her illness. No matter how wondrous her messages are and will always be to have and treasure, to see her deteriorating season by season in front of me all over again would have been too much to handle. I'm glad she had the foresight to do what she wanted to do so that we can still remember her in her prime.

'So, how are you both doing, my little daffodils?' she asks, in her oh so familiar, warm and soothing tones with just a hint of laughter. 'I hope you've been looking after each other just like I asked you to.'

I nod, I smile and I shake my head at how she has no idea how much magic she has created from beyond the grave. She has absolutely no clue how much her wisdom and foresight has made living without her just a little bit easier, and how her message and guidance has helped me through each day as I've remembered how positive and encouraging she always was. I shudder to think of how I'd have coped over the past few months without Aidan next door to call upon and to lean on, to express my fears to and to know that I'm not alone in missing her, and I only wish she could hear my response to her question to how we have been.

I want to tell her about Ben's new horse riding hobby, of how he has his eye on a new surfboard after trying it out with his friend Gino and his dad on the beach, and of how he still blows a kiss to the sky to her every night before he sleeps, and how he cradles this cushion when he needs a 'Mabel hug'.

I really do hope she is watching us, watching her, and I know she'd be so happy that Aidan has taken the time out to stay in Ballybray and look after himself here for the foreseeable future, however long that may be.

'So,' she says, clearing her throat before taking a sip of water. 'My first message was, I guess, a sort of introduction of sorts between you two. I know you're probably wondering how I have it all so impeccably planned, but what I want to say is that there's no point searching the house for the rest of the messages, guys.'

She lets out a raucous laugh and pats her delicate leg as she does so.

'You *were* doing that, weren't you, Roisin?' she says, shaking her head. 'I just knew if I left them lying around you'd be tempted to take an early peek at each one and that wouldn't work at all!'

My eyes widen at her intuition and I giggle at the thought of me searching every nook and cranny of her house in vain.

'They aren't in the house, honey, but don't worry, I know exactly what I'm doing,' she continues. 'You will get them. You'll get them all in good time.'

Her eyes light up with excitement and I feel so much better to know how we both have played a part in making her passing from this world a bit more controlled and slightly more bearable in her eyes. I can only imagine the fun she had putting these videos together, and also the pain she was in as she did so, knowing she would be speaking to us in a one-way conversation that she would never get to know the results of.

'Look, I don't claim to know it all about life,' she continues. 'In fact, I don't think anyone ever does know it all, and I'm not setting out to lecture either of you on how to live your own lives, but what I do know is that the whole damn thing goes in a blink and I'm so thankful I've had a bit of warning that my time is almost up.'

She clicks her fingers to emphasize her point and I breathe in. The whole concept of the fragility of life is exactly what has been occupying my mind recently. I'm beginning to wonder if she anticipated how her death would raise these questions in those she left behind?

She removes the silly Easter bonnet, which makes me take her a lot more seriously, but her hair is sticking up a little at the front and I want to fix it for her. She was always so particular about her hair.

She shifts a bit now in her seat, then leans slightly forward and clasps her hands together, just like she always did when she had something really important to say to me. She stares at us too for effect. It works, as I'm all ears.

'I've a simple message for you as the joy of spring fills the air,' she says. 'To yourself you should always be true.'

I can see Aidan shuffle at the edge of my vision.

'If you hide your true self, it will follow you, it will haunt you, it will whisper in your ear in the morning, it will roar at you in the middle of the night,' she tells us. 'It will trip you up all through your day and throughout your whole life, because the truth will always get you in the end. No matter how fast you run away from it, the truth will always win, and your true self will always be revealed.'

Mabel talks slowly, emphasizing her words with her pale wrinkled hands and with her sparkling turquoise eyes and, as always, I'm totally engaged with everything she is saying as I quickly reflect on my own path in life over the past almost forty years.

I have tried to cover up the truth many times, but it always did get me in the end.

When I was just eight years old, my grandmother begged me to come and live with her, and I said no. I didn't tell her the truth about my mother's drinking. I lied to her about what I'd had for dinner. I lied about the bruise on my arm that I said had happened when I'd bumped into someone in the playground at school.

I lied when I was a teenager to my teacher who asked if I had enough dinner money to see me through the week, and I lied to her again when she asked if I was hungry.

I lied to myself when I left university early, thinking that all I needed in life was already all in my head.

I lied to my friends when they asked me if everything was OK with Jude, and when I seemed so agitated and irritable at times. I lied about feeling unwell when he wouldn't let me see them any more.

If I'd told the truth to my grandmother back then, she'd have saved me from a childhood of pain. If I'd told the truth to my teacher, I wouldn't have had to go so hungry I'd sometimes be sick. If I'd told the truth to my friends about Jude, I wouldn't have been broken into a million pieces of glass and then been blamed for making him bleed.

Mabel's voice lilts into a merry tone of reflection.

'You know, my husband Peter once took me to visit the most delightful little village across on the east coast of Ireland called Breena where he and his only brother Danny worked for a hot summer on a farm when they were young men in their twenties,' she explains, recalling Peter with such joy as always. 'We had the most wonderful time there. We walked the pier, we sipped a beer and we dined on the finest foods overlooking the ocean. Peter said it was the happiest times he and his darling only brother spent together and he cried to me that day over a fear he had of a truth never told, but one he never could tell even to me, not even on his dying day.'

She stops again. She pushes a strand of hair out of her eyes, closes them and then continues her story with her hands clasped to her chest as if in prayer.

All I can hear is the ticking of the clock in my living room and eventually the intake of breath as Mabel lifts her fine, porcelain hand and wipes a tear from her eye. She was seventy-nine years old when she died, but to me she was eternally youthful, wise and beautiful. And she always knew the right things to say.

'Aidan, I'd love you to go there and follow your father's footsteps he took when he was such a young and carefree man,' she says, her eyes brightening at the very idea. 'Go with him, Roisin. It's a gorgeous place, and when you're there, have a pint in Sullivan's Bar and reflect on his short and beautiful life. Connect with him there if you can.'

I grip the cushion and bury my chin into it, as so many thoughts run through my head as to what Mabel might be up to this time. It's a much more cryptic message than before, and I have no idea why she might want us to take such an adventure together.

'Enjoy a day away this spring and I'll see you again in summer, OK?' she says with a little wave, and then she blows us a kiss with a smile. 'In the meantime, please look after each other, now and for always, and remember always, always be true.'

19.

The TV screen goes blank and I wait for Aidan to react before I say a word, but he doesn't speak at all. He just sits there contemplating, rubbing his chin in deep thought.

There's a lot to take in this time in a very different way than there was from Mabel's winter message. I know how much she always emphasized to me about being true to myself down the years, but I think for Aidan this was a much more deliberate personal message which has many layers of meaning for him.

His shaky marriage in America, his job over there, and all the pressures it entails from what I've gathered through snippets and hints along the way, and now a hint to his past that there may be a truth untold with his father and his uncle Peter . . . And why the expedition to this place called Breena? What is she hoping we'll find out there?

'I've no idea what you must be feeling right now,' I say, struggling to find the right words to make him feel better or want to talk, 'but I do know that what Mabel just said has got me thinking of all the times I could have made my life better by telling the truth. I think that was what she wanted to say most of all. She really wants us both to be true.'

He rubs his lightly stubbly face with his hands now, then sits forward again and pushes his dark hair back off his face, holding it there until when he lets go. It doesn't flop into place like it normally does, but instead falls down slowly like dominoes until he pushes it away again, lost in thought.

He breathes out. And then he speaks at last.

'The secret . . . I knew it. I remember a lot of whispering and hushing when my parents were killed,' Aidan tells me, leaning his head now in one of his hands. 'I was so young, only ten years old, so I'd no idea what was going on, but in the years that followed, I'd heard about Peter and my dad working on a farm together from my grandmother. I guess she was trying to reinforce to me just how close they once were and that's how she wanted to remember them, as brothers in arms rather than the rivals they become in later years.'

Rivals? Surely not. I had no idea, but I nod, totally understanding how a mother would want to think exactly that way when she'd lost one of her precious sons so tragically.

'What I did question on any given opportunity as I grew older,' Aidan confides in me, 'is why I wasn't in my parents' car on that night of the accident.'

'Oh, Aidan.'

I've never heard about any of this – not from Mabel and definitely not from Aidan.

'You see, I should have been in the car that night too, Roisin,' he tells me, his face etched with despair as he sits staring into the empty fire grate in front of him. 'I did eventually get an answer to that question when Mabel told me the truth when I first went to New York and she felt I was strong enough and old enough to hear about it.'

'I'm so glad she told you,' I say, gently encouraging him to trust me with this most painful memory that is already bringing tears to his eyes. He loosens his shirt collar and takes a deep breath.

'My folks had returned to Ballybray to pick me up from my grandparents after a weekend on the road, as was often the case,' he remembers with a slight tremble in his voice, 'but when they arrived, a row instantly broke out between my dad and Peter, who was over to visit. They hadn't got on well for a long time, and this was a normal occurrence when their paths would cross.'

He rubs his face again and takes his time, not knowing how much it's breaking my heart to see him recount such painful times from his childhood, as if it was yesterday.

'I was . . . I was taken out for ice cream the moment tensions were raised,' he explains, 'but my parents stormed off, saying they'd only be back later when Peter was gone. They never . . . they never did made it back for me, ever again of course.'

Oh no. I close my eyes, trying to absorb the trauma that must have unfolded around a very young Aidan that night as the worst thing possible came to his family's door when he was just a little boy.

'Roisin, I know that if Mabel hadn't taken me away that evening to protect me from their argument,' he says, swallowing his emotion, 'if she hadn't used her instinct to get me offside, I'd have been in that car and I'd have been killed too.'

I hold my breath.

'Mabel, in her wisdom to take me for something as simple as an ice cream, saved my life,' he whispers, his voice cracking. 'My dear aunt Mabel saved my life.'

He swallows. He looks away, and then he lets out a long, deep breath of relief to have shared his story.

'Wow,' I whisper. 'I had absolutely no idea. She never, ever said.'

I realize now how much of this all makes sense. No wonder Mabel was so protective and close to Aidan through his younger years. No wonder she was so proud of him as she watched him develop from the terrified youngster he was that night to the determined young adult and then the successful man he went on to become. No wonder she loved talking about his success like it was the be all and end all to everything, because to her, he was so special.

And no wonder her loss is taking its toll on him as much as it is on me.

We sit in silence for a few seconds, saying nothing, but at the same time, saying it all as we digest Mabel's words and her mission for us this springtime. I want to reach out and touch him, to tell him I'm glad that he wasn't in the car on the night his parents were so tragically killed, and I'm so grateful for Mabel's intuition that night, and honoured that he felt he could share his story with me.

And so for the first time since I met Aidan, I do just that. I reach across and I touch his hand to show him that I do care about all he has been through and all he is going through now as he tries to figure his life out, both his past here in Ballybray and his future in America, whatever that may hold.

'Thanks, Roisin,' he whispers to me as we sit here hand in hand with Mabel's words still echoing in our ears. 'You've been good for me lately.'

'And you've been good for me too, Aidan,' I tell him, feeling a tiny bit awkward now, and so I let go and fix my hair, then stand up wondering what I can do to shift the energy around us. 'Look, I'm sure Camille will understand if I take a bit of time out this morning. Do you fancy a walk on the beach to clear our heads and try to make sense of this all?'

He looks up at me and smiles with so much gratitude in his eyes it touches me in a way I wish it wouldn't. The more I get to know him, the more attached I feel we are becoming, and in my heart I know that is very wrong and will only end in tears. I keep telling myself that one of these days I'll create some distance between us to save all the pain that is inevitably coming my way when he decides to pack up and leave and go back to make amends with Rachel.

'I'd love to walk on the beach,' he says, standing up tall beside me, so closely I imagine I can hear his heart beat. 'I'll just get my coat.'

I walk barefoot along the sand, carrying my shoes. The spectacular Killahoey Strand is one of the area's majestic Blue Flag beaches and, when I look ahead at the glorious backdrop of Muckish Mountain as it meets the sea, it doesn't take a psychologist to know why being here always fills me with good feelings.

Aidan strolls along a few feet away from me in a routine we normally save for a Sunday morning when Ben usually leads the way and dictates the pace, yelling at us to keep up as the wind blows in his face and the sea air gives him a healthy glow, but today it's just the two of us and it feels very different.

'I can't stop thinking of how close my dad and Peter once were when they were young and carefree in that little town on the far side of the country,' he says to me when our footprints meet along the water's edge in a natural rhythm. 'And I can really see now why Mabel and my own grandmother preferred to remember them both from those times, rather than the bickering mess they became in their later lives. Imagine only having one sibling and to lose them after a stupid row. It just doesn't bear thinking about.'

We walk along the golden sand on auto pilot to a sand dune where we have sat so many times in recent months, watching the waves lap along the coastline.

'I think you only feel the loneliness of being an only child when your parents are both gone and you realize you need someone to lean on or turn to in their place,' he tells me, pulling some grass from the sand as he speaks. 'Not that I even remember what it feels like to have a parent to lean on. Both my mum and dad are just blurry faces in my memory now or smiling distant strangers in a photograph. It pains me to admit that, but it's true.'

He lifts a stick from beside him and makes shapes in the sand as the waves crash in the near distance, a sound that I will never tire of.

'Me too,' I tell him, knowing that although our stories are so very different, they both make us feel the exact same way. 'I always wanted a big sister or brother to replace the parents I never had in real life. Someone to guide me along the way, or to tell me off, or someone to call when I'm in need or just to vent to when I'm feeling sad or angry. Mabel filled so many gaps for me in the short time I knew her. I trusted her. I could tell her anything and she, in turn, could tell me the truth right back.'

The truth – I remember again her emphasis in her message on how important it is for us always to be true, and it almost makes my head spin at how often I've refused to be true, particularly in all the time I pretended to be happy when I was really stuck and trapped in a soulless and destructive marriage.

'You know, I once overheard a conversation my grand-parents had when I was a young teenager, one that I wasn't supposed to hear,' Aidan tells me as he looks out onto the dark blue water in the distance. 'They were whispering one night in the kitchen, which was always a cue for my young ears to tune in, but they were saying how they believed my mum and dad loved each other so much that sometimes I got in the way, so it was maybe a good thing they never had any more children to fight for their attention.'

My mouth drops open and I look his way, but he just keeps staring ahead as the pain of this memory replays in his mind like a broken record.

'Ah, Aidan, I'd doubt if that was true,' I try to reassure him, touching his arm briefly to show some support. 'Your grandparents were probably trying to deal with their own grief and were thinking out loud for the sake of it. Grief can make us act in many strange ways and say many strange things, believe me.'

He turns his head around to face me at last – his strong, handsome face that has become so familiar to me by now. I know every crease when he smiles, I know the way his eyes light up when he is winding me up, I know how his voice cracks when he wants to scream but chooses to grit his teeth instead, and I know how his brow furrows when he needs space or some time alone. And most of all I know when he laughs during our lengthy conversations on random topics that often lead to arguments or disagreements that he's someone I could never fall out with, no matter how hard things got.

'Do you really think so?' he asks me, and I realize that whatever I tell him now is enough to change a mindset that has lived within him for ever.

'I know so,' I say, nodding with no doubt in my mind. 'Your parents sound like wonderful people and it would take two wonderful people to make someone like you, Aidan Murphy.'

He throws the stick away and our eyes both follow it as it lodges into the sand below.

'Ah, you've a way with words, Roisin O'Connor, and you always know when to say the right things,' he says, unable to mask his smile now at my attempt at a compliment. 'But you've been a good friend to me lately, despite our rocky start, and I'll never forget it.'

I smile too now in return, and we sit here on the sand dune, shoulder to shoulder, feeling a little bit lighter in our hearts and minds.

We *are* good friends now, and I don't think we've acknowledged that officially until this moment, but we are really growing very close, and the more time we spend together, the more evident it's becoming, and the more evident it's becoming, the guiltier I feel inside at how his wife is so oblivious to the connection and bond we share here in Ireland.

'So, will you come with me to Breena and see what sort of journey Mabel wants to send us on this time?'

'Of course I will,' I tell him, as if it was ever going to be a question. 'I'll come with you, and I'm sure Ben will love to as well. We'll make a day of it and go there in Mabel's memory.'

20.

'Are you sure you don't mind?' I ask Camille on Saturday morning when I drop Ben off with her at the shop. 'I'd really love him to come with us but he's determined to ditch me for a better offer with Gino.'

It's only gone 10 a.m. but Ben has already locked heads with Camille's son Gino and they're swapping football cards in a state of excitement, their bags packed alongside them as they await her husband Paddy's arrival to take them on a very last-minute camping trip and horse riding expedition in County Sligo. Well, it's last-minute for Ben, but not so for Gino who has been looking forward to this for ages.

Camille reaches out and fixes the button on my dress. I've chosen a royal blue maxi dress, my favourite gold wedges, and I too have a bag packed for my day away to Breena with Aidan.

'If you ask me that again I'm going to be very cross with you, lady,' warns Camille. 'Look at those two. Do you think Ben is going to cause me any extra trouble? They're like two peas in a pod and I think Paddy might be even more excited to have another member of the team. Plus, the weather is perfect for camping today! How are you feeling?'

'Really good, thanks. Today is all about Aidan so I'm just going with the flow and I'll be happy to keep him company,' I tell my boss, who over the years has become a very close confidante and a real tower of strength to me. 'I just want to do as Mabel tells us and see where it leads to.'

I say my goodbyes to Ben, warning him to remember his manners and most importantly to have fun and stay safe, then with a final hug for Camille, I leave Truly Vintage and set off home where Aidan is ready and waiting for our day away.

I don't know if I'm more nervous or excited, but when I see Aidan pack up the car in the distance, my jitters calm down and I want to get on the road as soon as possible.

Now, as Aidan holds the car door open for me and I climb inside its cool, cream leather interior, I remind myself that I'm simply going on a day trip to a place that means a lot to a very dear friend, even if it's in a way he hasn't discovered yet. He sits in the driver's seat beside me, starts up the engine and I put my head back on the head rest and look over at him.

'You OK?' he asks me, patting my hand gently.

Everything in Aidan's world always begins with asking me if I'm OK, and I'm slowly getting used to it.

'I'm really good,' I tell him. 'I'm beginning to relax at last. I'm looking forward to today.'

'So am I,' he replies. 'It will be nice to have a change of scenery. As much as I've enjoyed my downtime and walking on the beach, some nice food and a stroll around a different place sounds nice.'

We cruise along the road out of Ballybray, heading east and hugging or at least skimming the northern Irish coast-line on any given opportunity, and the route, which will take just over two and a half hours in total, will take us through many picturesque towns and villages that I've never heard of.

Aidan's music playlist is made up of a variety of artists, from classics by Prince and Fleetwood Mac to some 'Irish Trad' to set the mood of our road trip, and some rock legends like AC/DC to keep us on our toes. It's a spectacular spring day outside and we pass lush green fields with sheep and lambs, towns bustling with shoppers, along country roads and dual carriageways on our journey to visit the place where his father and uncle spent their young years together in happiness.

Driving along like this on a sunny day brings me back to childhood trips to the beach with my own grandparents when I was very, very young and I'm shocked as the memory comes flooding back to me. I taste cold, juicy strawberries and cream, I feel the light breeze on my face and the sun on my skin and I hear my grandfather's country music on the radio as I sat in the back seat, my bare legs swinging along in time to the beat.

I'm brought back to happy memories I'd long buried, and having them come to life like this sparks a sense of contentment that has for too long been masked by all the pain of my past. Being with Aidan has had this effect on me, I realize. It's like years of darkness that have taken over my mind have been pierced with little speckles of lighter moments that are now being brought back to life.

'So what are you expecting from this trip?' I ask him, checking my lipstick in the mirror on the sunshade of his car as we cruise along. 'Is there anything you specifically hope to gain, or are you just letting Mabel guide the way like I am?'

He changes gear as he comes to a junction and I can't help but notice his arms as he does so, a sight which makes me lose my breath a little.

I've become so used to being so close to him in many ways, but sitting here up high in his Mercedes 4x4 feels a bit more intimate than usual.

'I dunno, I guess I'm excited about seeing the place my dad and uncle spent their summers in before I came along,' Aidan tells me, reminding me of the roots of our trip. 'My uncle Peter was a role model to me ever since I lost my parents and even though I know he and my dad didn't see eye to eye in their last while as brothers, I always knew that if I followed Peter's advice, I'd never go wrong. He was a good guy, and Mabel was a fine lady, so I'm easy and open to whatever today brings.'

'Great,' I tell him, not expecting him to divulge any further, but as the spring sunshine beams through the windscreen, Aidan hasn't finished answering my question just yet.

'He made me promise when I told him I was marrying Rachel that I wouldn't make a mess of it, and that I'd treat her well,' he tells me, as he remembers a conversation from days gone by. 'But I know now that he just wanted me to realize that as far as he believed, marriage was for life and as the vows say, till death do us part. He didn't want me to make a mistake and marry the wrong person. He told me he wanted me to love my wife the way he loved Mabel, and I have to be honest, I lied to him. I said that I did, but I knew that wasn't true.'

I almost choke on my reply. He mentions Rachel so rarely, that every time he does bring up her name my heart stops.

'Aidan, you don't have to compare your love for your wife with someone else's relationship,' I say, trying to ease the pain of his admission, 'and at the same time, you certainly don't have to stay with someone for the rest of your life if you really feel you've made a mistake.'

I'm taken aback at how he has divulged this to me, but now that he's started he doesn't seem to want to stop.

He pulls in to a lay-by where a family is having a picnic in the morning sunshine, puts down his window and leans back in his seat, thankful, it seems, to take a quick break from driving.

I feel sticky and sweaty beside him, so I put my window down too and push my sunglasses up onto my head.

'That's all I ever really wanted most in life, just right there,' he says, nodding his head towards the mum, dad and two little daughters who are battling against a light breeze to keep their food from blowing away. 'I yearned for what I never had – a family of my own. Don't get me wrong, I also want the high-flying successful job I've worked my ass off to find, but I always thought I'd have a family unit to go along with it. I suppose you could say I wanted it all, but then, what's the point in aiming for anything in life if you don't aim high?'

I take a deep breath. There's so much of what he is saying that resonates with me. All my life I felt like I was looking in through a window where everything was so much better on the other side. People with nice steady lifestyles, mothers and fathers who loved each other as well as loving their children, no worries about where you were going to live next or what might be coming to trip you up. It was all I ever wanted too, but instead I was dragged up by a mother who battled addiction, forced to grow up before my time, and pushed from pillar to post in foster families who I'd cling on to in desperation for the unconditional love that I so badly needed.

'I'm so sorry it didn't work out that way for you, Aidan,' I tell him, and I really mean it. 'But why didn't you just come clean and own up about how bad things are across the water instead of trying to pretend? Mabel would have understood. Mabel would have backed you through anything, Aidan, and you know that. You didn't have to go through it all alone.'

He shrugs, knowing what I say is true.

'She would have, I guess,' he agrees, 'but she and Peter had built me up so high, they'd made me believe I was the golden child they never had, and when I thought of how Mabel spoke to me and about me with such pride to everyone and anyone who would listen, I just kept putting it off until it became a lie that I was OK to live with from afar. And when she got sick, I couldn't land it all on her in case the worry made her worse, then I realized I'd probably never see her again. I told her a lie that things were so good and, just like my dad, she died not knowing the truth. She died not knowing I loved her.'

I go to speak, but he isn't finished yet. I twiddle my hair. I look across at the happy family to see the mother attempting to salvage a sandwich that has fallen on the ground, then giving up and throwing it in the bin, her face puce with temper.

It makes us both laugh even though we really shouldn't.

'I knew Mabel built me up to be some hotshot property developer with a beauty queen wife who was just about to announce any day the pitter patter of tiny feet and the next generation of the marvellous Murphy boys,' he says.

'She sure did,' I tell him with a playful smile. 'But Mabel

knew you loved her, Aidan. She never once spoke ill of you, no matter what was going on between the two of you. She knew you loved her and she really did love you. She wouldn't have left us both these wonderful messages if she didn't.'

We stare across at the picnickers again.

'So much for happy families,' he laughs. 'Someone's in trouble.'

The stressed-out mum is now packing up with a vengeance, one of the little girls is crying, and the dad is opening the boot, ready to make their big escape.

'I don't think anyone has it worked out perfectly,' I suggest to him. 'Not even those who appear to have it all. We're all just finding our way, really, aren't we? We're all just doing our best.'

I feel his eyes on me and I can see his chest move up and down as he breathes. Our eyes lock and he smiles and for a second I think he is going to reach out and touch me. I can almost feel his touch and his energy that radiates between us and lingers in the air.

I feel palpitations and my breath shortens as claustrophobia and panic engulf me. I can't take this any further. He's a married man who is taking a break to sort out his life. He's raw, he's vulnerable and so am I despite my outer bravado. My hands shake and a fine blanket of perspiration washes over me.

'Yes, we're all just trying to find our way,' I agree, trying to brush off any further analysis of what has really been happening between us lately. 'We are close, just as Mabel would have wanted us to be.'

He looks out of the windscreen as the happy family drive off.

'Yes, I suppose that's it,' he tells me, trying to reassure us both that the underlying tension between us isn't as scary as it seems, but the truth is so much more than that. There is an undeniable pull between us and it's ramping up by the minute and by the hour of every day we spend together. I can't set myself up for this fall and I don't want to see Aidan hurt either, plus I'd be going against every moral I've ever held if I gave in to falling for another woman's husband.

'Would you mind if I jumped out just to stretch my legs?' I ask him, totally breaking the mood just as I intend to. 'I think I could be doing with a bit of fresh air.'

'Sure thing,' he says, a little relieved, I think. 'In fact, I might just need the same.'

I climb out of the car, glad to feel a breeze on my face and my lungs fill up again, which instantly calms me down, but what Aidan has to say next is set to make my pulse race again as he closes the car door behind him.

'My marriage is over, Roisin,' he tells me from where he stands just a few feet away. 'I can say it out loud at last that it's over and it has been from the moment I decided to stay here. I feel free from the clutches of the Bowen family at last. Well, almost. I'll need to go back there and make it all final, but I've a plan in place and it feels good.'

I feel a trickle of sweat form on my brow and my heart palpitates as I watch him smile at his new pledge of freedom. He snatches a glance my way and I try not to reciprocate as a wave of trepidation ripples through me. Knowing he was married, even if his marriage was in trouble, was like a safety barrier between us. But now?

Well, this changes everything, and it scares me so.

21.

By the time we get closer to the village of Breena, a harbour town located not far from the famous Glens of Antrim overlooking the Irish Sea, we've well recovered from Aidan's revelation, not to mention our moment of discomfort beforehand, and we've covered a lot more about our past lives, loves, and fears.

It's funny how riding in a car with someone on any sort of a lengthy journey can spark off the deepest of conversations. The hum of the road, the faint company of the music, and the carefree ways of being out of your own environment can often lead to some pretty interesting chat. I've always found it happens with Ben too. There's nothing like a road trip to loosen the conversation cogs and get two people really talking and, although I'm nervous, I find myself talking about how I wished I'd had the courage to leave my marriage to the one person who almost ruined me – Jude.

'I was too afraid, so I really admire your decision,' I say to Aidan, now that he has opened up about his own marital situation. 'I just couldn't bring myself to take that step even though I was screaming inside to escape.'

'That's exactly how I've been feeling, Roisin,' he says, with such animation. 'I was putting on a front – an act, and I couldn't keep it going any longer.'

It's as though we've both released a valve of admission and relief where we can't say enough about how good it feels to be free.

'I lived in such denial, walking on eggshells around someone who I can see now was controlling my every move,' I confess to Aidan. 'He was like a ticking time bomb, always ready to explode, and it took me a long time to recover from the emotional damage he caused me. Mabel played a big part in helping me move on from it all. I'll never forget her for that.'

Telling Aidan about my marriage is like ripping open a book from the past, tearing through well-fingered pages, wearing them out all over again and reading aloud a story that is normally so painful to tell, but with him lending me his ear it seems so much easier.

'My husband, Jude, told me he was my saviour after my very turbulent childhood where I longed for my mother to stay sober enough to love me,' I tell him, trying to ignore the lump that has formed in my throat as my past threatens to choke me again. 'She did her best, that's what I've been told to tell myself. She could only ever do her best.'

Aidan listens without judgement and only ever asks

questions when he thinks they're the type I'm comfortable with giving an answer to. He knows when to prod, when I want to open up more, and he knows when to pull back and let me leave out parts of my life with no big analysis or explanation.

'Roisin, I'd never have guessed that about you at all,' he says, his strong arms steering us along the road to Breena. 'You always appear to have it all so together. Tell me your secret.'

He laughs a little, knowing of course there is no secret.

'Sometimes when I look back I've no idea how I stayed sane never mind together,' I joke in return. 'I talked it out a lot with social workers through my teens and took any support they could offer as I ducked and dived through the system, but talk about jumping from one disaster to another. I believed every word my husband told me, and I suffered for it deeply once I found a way out of the fog. I'll never make that mistake again.'

I close my eyes to fight back tears, then try and distract myself by looking in my handbag for some gum. I offer some to Aidan and he accepts, catching my eye for just a second before he has to watch the road again, but in that moment I know he sees me now in a very different light.

'You're pretty amazing, really,' he says, and I gulp back tears as a tsunami of the past threatens to suffocate me once more. 'You've been to hell and back emotionally, yet you still find strength and have faith in seeing the good in others.

You're a good person, Roisin. I see more and more of why Mabel thought so much of you every time I spend time with you.'

I can only nod and pretend I'm staring out of the window to disguise the tears that fall down my face.

'Thanks, Aidan,' I manage to whisper. 'That's really nice to hear.'

'Do you ever see your mum now?' Aidan asks me tenderly now as we sip coffee overlooking Breena harbour, both of us so glad to have reached our destination and to be able to see what made his dad and uncle fall in love with the place so much all those years ago. 'Do you keep in touch with her still?'

I take a moment with my reply and look out at the Irish Sea, which is tranquil and peaceful today, much calmer than the rugged, wild waves of the Atlantic I've grown used to in County Donegal.

'She's living her own life in Dublin in a way that only she can understand,' I say, stirring my coffee and trying my best to remain dignified. 'I've tried, Aidan. I've tried until my heart bled sore, but there are only so many times one person can let you down before you have to walk away for your own sanity. It's for the best and I honestly believe that. I've made peace with her now in my own way and I need to protect myself and Ben from any further hurt. Her rejection was like a knife in my heart every single time she turned her back on me, and I'll always have the scars to prove it.'

He looks at me so helplessly and I try to shrug it off. Talking about my mother will never be easy, but for some reason I seem to be able to empty out my feelings with Aidan, and he is the same with me.

He tells me more about his relationship with Rachel and the way their marriage has fallen apart after only three years.

'There are times when I've felt like such a failure by hiding away here since Mabel died,' he says, when we're on the subject. 'I really, *really* wanted my marriage to work, but it takes two, you know, and like Mabel said, there's only so long you can run without having to meet the truth face on.'

'Tell me about it,' I say, fidgeting with the buttons on my dress. 'I know exactly what you mean.'

'I've told them all in New York how I've been feeling,' he explains. 'I've told Rachel and her dad that I simply need this break away from them all to sort my head out and to find the strength to see this through. And I've told them that there's only so long I can live under their . . . I've told them there's only so long I can be under someone else's control to live my life in a way that's so uncomfortable and wrong. I was suffocating, Roisin, and so was Rachel, but being here has helped me breathe again, just like I hoped it would.'

My eyes widen as I dig a little deeper in my mind as to

what he might be hinting at when he speaks about control and feeling suffocated under a regime instilled by others. It sends shivers down my spine as I connect with exactly what he means and I feel a wave of protection for him burn inside me, as if I want to confront whoever it is that's making him feel so vulnerable and used.

'Did you – did you feel trapped in your marriage?' I ask him gently. 'Have you been staying with Rachel against your own will?'

My stomach twists at the familiarity of it all and my eyes sting as old painful memories churn inside me, curdling like sour milk so I almost gag. It reminds me of how I used to assure myself that Jude's actions towards me were only because he cared, and at least he didn't push me around. Then, when he did push me, at least he didn't hit me. Then when he did hit me, at least he didn't leave a mark. And so the cycle went on and on.

'That's one way of putting it,' he says, laughing with a hint of disbelief. 'I was most definitely staying against my own will. But anyhow, I plan to go back to New York by summer and sort out my affairs, both privately and professionally, before I start all over again, God knows where. I can't emphasize how being away from it all has really given me the space I needed to see everything so much more clearly. It's made it hit home just how much I've been living a lie.'

He exhales long and slowly, as if he is releasing so much tension through his confession. Of course I'd already guessed that his marriage to Rachel was struggling, as he's spent so long here in Ballybray avoiding the very subject at almost all costs, but to hear of his reasons has stunned me a little.

'Good for you to recognize that and do what's right for you,' I tell him, knowing exactly what he's been through in his own heart and mind. A seagull lands at my feet and waddles along picking up invisible scraps from the ground before flying away to pastures new. 'And how does Rachel feel about it all? Does she know why you're doing this?'

I can only imagine how frightened, yet heartbroken at the same time, Aidan must feel having told her.

He laughs nervously.

'For me, it's like a tonne of bricks has been lifted off my shoulders after carrying around the weight for far too long,' he says, clasping his hands together and stretching out in front of him to release some of his pent-up tension. 'And I know she is glad it's over too, as the whole set-up was becoming toxic for us both. I should have moved away about twelve months ago to give us both some space, but I was too tied up in work and too tangled up in my own head to think straight.'

'I understand.'

'Mabel's death gave me a reason to come home, and as much as I thought I'd want to race right back there after the funeral, within a few days it was the opposite,' he admits. 'Coming here made me wake up to the fact that Rachel and

I were never in love like a couple should be. It's helped me make the changes I should have made a long time ago.'

We both take a moment to reflect on our own pasts, each on the same wavelength at how devastating a marriage break-up can be on so many levels, and I contemplate and recall just how difficult making that move – whatever the reasons – can be.

My interpretation of what was for the best in my marriage was really what was for the worst, and acknowledging as much is a bitter pill to swallow. I should have left Jude long before he died, but I didn't. It pains me so much to admit that.

'And what do you think a couple who are really in love should be like?' I ask him, my mind still a little bit stuck in the past. 'Is there a magic recipe, because if there is I'd love to know it?'

I laugh as I say this, knowing that no one really has the answer, except perhaps their own version of what true love is.

'Ah, that's the million-dollar question, Roisin,' Aidan replies, laughing a little now too.

'It really is, isn't it?'

We both hold each other's gaze, breathing in synchronized harmony as a veil of tension hangs in the air between us.

'The other person should be someone who grounds you,' he says eventually, his eyes hypnotizing me now like never before, as if he's cleared a fog between us and is ready to show his true colours at last. 'He or she should be someone who soothes you, someone who you want to run to for comfort and who you can comfort in return, and they should be someone who you think about first thing in the morning and last thing at night in the best way. Someone you want to share your best and worst moments with.'

He stops.

'I'm afraid that's the best I can do in my attempt at a million-dollar answer,' he whispers, and I feel like the world has stopped spinning around us.

His arm brushes against mine and the touch of his skin sends a tingle right through me that I try to ignore.

Someone like you, I almost hear him say, and a wave of panic washes over me once more.

'That was . . . that was a pretty good effort,' I say, my voice croaking as the familiarity of all he just said sinks in to my mind.

I can't deny how comforted I've felt by Aidan's presence today. Being in his company alone like this has soothed me. He has made me feel at ease, and I feel we're growing closer every time we talk to each other with honesty and trust, almost as if we're exposed now to the truth.

'I think it's time we started exploring this beautiful place, like we were instructed to,' I suggest to him. 'Or else we'll have the wrath of Mabel to deal with, from wherever she is right now. What do you think?'

I stand up quickly to try to shake off the intensity between us and the acceptance that some sort of attraction or at least a connection is bubbling just beneath the surface of denial, threatening to burst through.

'Yes,' he says, taking a deep breath and looking to the heavens with his beautiful eyes. 'That's probably a good idea. Let's see what sort of magic Breena has to offer once and for all.'

We stroll casually along Breena's little pier, imagining we are following in the Murphy brothers' footsteps where colourful pleasure boats and fishing boats bob along under the afternoon sunshine. It really is like a living history, with every inch of the place we explore, and I feel like I'm in a different world from the one we are used to in Ballybray.

This was where Peter Murphy hung out before he even met Mabel. This was where Danny, Aidan's dad, spent his summers long, long before he met Aidan's mother. It's like stepping back in time, to an era that is long before our own and it's special on so many levels, but most of all to Aidan, who has lightened up so much now that we've shared our deepest secrets of our past and present.

And I feel lighter too.

Maybe it's the company I'm in, maybe it's because we've normally Ben to distract us or entertain us in equal measure when we spend time together, but today it's just the two of us to focus on all the things we've wanted to say for so long. I feel so liberated and free to just be Roisin and not a mother or a widow or an ex foster kid or a victim. I am 'me' and with Aidan I feel I still have something to give, be it a shoulder or companionship or friendship, sharing this gorgeous new place where his father once spent such happy times.

A tourist information board tells us that the settlement in the local area of Breena is believed to go back as far as 6000 BC, which explains the almost medieval feel to the town, a treasure trove which is quite hidden, nestled under the green cushioned hills of Glencoy, one of the nine Glens of Antrim.

We drink more coffee as we casually stroll around, we people-watch as much as we can, and we hoke through a thrift shop where I try on a pair of denim flared jeans that I can't resist buying, while Aidan finds a scarf almost identical to one his uncle Peter used to wear, which makes me howl with laughter when he tries it on.

'You look like Popeye the sailor man!' I tell him, and he agrees, and buys it anyway 'for the craic'.

We relax, we chat more and, as we look around us, we try to imagine what those two young men from Ballybray might have got up to here in Breena in their spare time all those years ago.

'Do you feel closer to your dad having come here?' I ask Aidan after a glorious afternoon of doing very little, simply walking around and taking in the scenery, shops and stunning location. 'I can feel a presence of some sort even though

I never knew them, but some people would call me batty for saying such things.'

We sit down on a little bench along the sea front to eat an ice cream, the light breeze in our hair and a rosy glow on our faces.

'I believe in that wholeheartedly,' he tells me as we sit contentedly side by side, watching as gulls feast on scraps and gather in clusters around our feet again. 'I think it was important for me to do this, just to acknowledge within myself that my dad and Peter are both reunited somewhere now, and have hopefully finally put their past behind them.'

'That's nice.'

'I can just imagine them sauntering around here, laughing and joking and probably checking out the local girls of course,' he says. 'They were so close, my grandmother said. Isn't it funny how two people who really love each other can still cause each other such unnecessary pain?'

I pause.

'I don't think love should cause us pain,' I whisper. 'I think love should be the very opposite, don't you?'

I think of my mother when I say that. I think of how much I also tried and failed to convince Jude that I was worth his love, more than his temper and fist. I'd given up on ever knowing anything else until I found the maternal love I had from Mabel. Being with Aidan is easy and so effortless lately, like I've found a kindred spirit who accepts me just as I am with no games, no fuss, and no fear whatsoever. He has been such a comfort to me, and I know I've been the same to him too, even if we never admit it.

'I can see the hurt in your eyes every day, Roisin,' he tells me as we watch a little red boat called *Bold Venture* set sail. 'But I also see an inner strength that completely blows me away.'

'Really?'

'God, yes,' he says. 'I really mean that. To have come through all you have and to still look at the world in such a positive light is something rare. It's something that impresses me every single moment we spend together.'

I focus on the ice cream in my hand, doing my best to accept his compliments right now. We sit so closely that anyone passing by would think we are a romantic couple, and the more the day goes on, I confess to having imagined a few times that we are.

'Ah, I'm just the same as everyone else, really,' I say, as usual trying to play down any compliment that comes my way. 'I'm just playing the cards I was dealt with and I try and make the best of it. None of us knows what's around the corner, which is probably a good thing.'

I look at him shyly, feeling the warmth of his arm by my side, at ease with his presence. I've had it rough in life, yes, but so has Aidan. We are two wounded soldiers, wading in waters so troubled for all our lives that it's become all we are used to, each of us searching for a love we've not yet found.

I wanted my mother's love so badly, but she wasn't able

to give it as she battled with her demonic addiction. I wanted the passion and love of my husband that he promised in the beginning, but he drip-fed me poison and scarred me for life with his bullying and abuse.

The only love I've ever fully trusted is Mabel's as she had no ulterior motive and I could be myself without apology or any expectation in return. And of course I feel loved by Ben and I love him unconditionally in the fierce, maternal way that means I'd quite literally die for him.

Love is a cluster of many things, but being here with Aidan today is frightening me into thinking that after spending so much time with him over the past few months, I may be growing close to him. And for that very reason, I need to be extra careful. There's no way I'm going to set myself up for a mighty fall, by letting my guard down to a man again, especially not a married man. No way.

'So, do you think we've achieved whatever Mabel intended by asking us to come here?' Aidan asks me just as I think we've seen all there is to see in Breena. 'She did mention we visit a bar called Sullivan's, so we should probably do that before we call it a day.'

I don't want to say it to Aidan, but I've a feeling that Mabel's mission for us here today isn't quite fulfilled yet. I know it has certainly brought us closer together and has been fun and carefree, plus it's been a lovely way to remember his dad and uncle, but could there be something more?

'She did, that's right,' I recall, wondering if we'd passed it at all as we explored the town's cobbled streets. 'OK, let's finish off the day by going there just like Mabel said to. I'm kind of hoping they serve food too. Are you hungry?'

'You have the most amazing way of reading my mind, Roisin O'Connor,' he says, flashing me one of his heart-stopping smiles. 'I'm starving. Let's go there and see.'

We walk along side by side on the final chapter of our journey with a spring in our step. I sense for a moment that Aidan is going to take my hand, but he doesn't.

I don't think either of us really want this day to end just yet.

22.

I'd imagined Sullivan's Bar to be a typical cosy Irish pub, but instead we are met with a rather chic, family-run establishment decorated in cool, modern grey tones, dark wooden tables, and a tempting chalkboard gin menu.

'Welcome to Sullivan's. A table for two?' asks a young lady who greets us the moment we step inside. The smell of fresh fish and chips makes my mouth water and loud Celtic music fills the air. The venue certainly takes us both by surprise and was definitely not what I expected.

'Yes, please,' Aidan replies, as we follow the waitress past bustling tables packed with young couples and families, all immersed in noisy conversation.

She shows us through to a separate, much quieter area where the ambience is more relaxed and spacious and I can see the relief on Aidan's face already.

'We're so busy all day,' the young lady tells us, 'so I'm afraid this is all the space we've got here in the bar. Is this OK for you?'

We both nod emphatically, delighted to be seated in the more traditional end of the establishment, which is more along the lines of what I expected. Cosy snugs instead of high tables, and music that feels much more like an underscore than a soundtrack.

She hands us two giant menus and I realize I'm a lot hungrier than I thought I was.

'Ah look, Ben's favourite is on the menu,' says Aidan, pointing out a basket of scampi to me. 'He could live on that every day, he told me.'

My heart warms at how well Aidan knows my son by now. They've had many adventures together over the past few months, mainly beach related where they'd head off and kick a ball on the sand, or talk tactics from Aidan's Gaelic football days when he was just a boy living here.

'It's going to break his heart when you leave in the summer,' I say to Aidan, but I instantly regret it when I see how his face falls.

'Let's not talk about that right now,' he replies. 'I don't want to even think about it. So what do you fancy to eat? I'm starving!'

I can feel Aidan's eyes follow mine from across the table as I scan down a delicious selection of home-cooked dishes, squinting my eyes as I try to find something that suits my inner conditioned budget.

'Let me treat you,' he says and when I look up at him, he's all smiles. 'You've no idea how much it means to me that you've come here with me today, Roisin. So, what do you fancy? Steak? I remember you saying it was your favourite.'

I have another look and my taste buds tingle at the very idea of my favourite dish, one I don't get the opportunity to sample very often as I've always sacrificed my own choices to make sure Ben gets the best I can afford.

'Sounds amazing,' I tell him, and before I know it, we're tucking into the most magnificent feast, washed down with a delicious glass of Merlot, and I don't think I've ever felt so content with anyone in my whole life before.

'Don't beat yourself up for feeling some relief and happiness when it comes,' I remember Mabel pleading with me before she died. *'You've been beaten up enough in life, Roisin. You can be happy now. Let him go. Let all the hurt of the past go and enjoy the good times ahead.'*

Being with Aidan has made me realize just how much meeting a kindred soul can make all the difference in good times and bad times. He is the opposite of anything I've ever known, and I can feel my heart squeeze in pain every time I think of him leaving. The way he looks at me so tenderly, the way we make each other laugh, and the sense of safety I get when he's around is undeniable, but I know I'm potentially walking into uncharted territory.

'That looks good,' he says to me, nodding at my plate. 'I can see why my dad and Peter liked coming here, though I'd say it was a different vibe back then. I can only imagine the shenanigans they got up to around here in their early twenties! Can you picture it?'

I take a moment to remember Aidan's father and Mabel's husband Peter to whom our little expedition today has been dedicated, and I thank them for bringing us to such a magical little place where we've bonded in a way I'd never have imagined possible.

'To Danny and Peter and all their shenanigans when young, free and single,' I say, raising my glass of wine, and Aidan clinks me back with his pint of Guinness. 'And to Mabel Murphy who always has the best ideas, even when she's not with us any more.'

'To all the Murphys of Ballybray!' says Aidan joyfully, 'and to Roisin and Ben O'Connor too!'

We lift our glasses to have a drink, and as we do I can't help but notice how a lady behind the bar stops and stares our way as she overhears us. She's a bit older than we are, mid-fifties, I'd guess, and she looks over a pair of stylish winged spectacles in our direction.

I'm sitting directly in her eye-line and as she goes about her business for the next half hour or so, wiping down her counter and polishing glasses behind the bar, I can't ignore the look of disbelief and shock on her now ashen face. Maybe I'm imagining things. Maybe I'm overthinking in the way my mother used to tell me off for so often, but there was something about how the woman's ears pricked up when Aidan spoke that stays with me until it's almost time to leave.

I've a feeling Mabel may have sent us here for more reasons than we have yet discovered, but I decide to take my time to find out. The woman behind the bar definitely stopped in her tracks when she heard the Murphys of Ballybray mentioned. Did she know them? I want to go and ask her, but something about the look on her face tells me to leave it at least for now.

Aidan finishes his meal, oblivious to what's going through my mind, and I don't want to change the mood of what has been the most charming day together so I say nothing and soon I'm enraptured again by his conversation. He has me in stitches with his tales of settling into New York when he was just twenty-one and very wet behind the ears to life in a big city.

'Can I get you anything else?' our waitress from before asks us when she comes to clear our table. 'Dessert? Tea or coffee?'

'Roisin?' he asks me. 'Go on.'

I shrug, but he nods at me convincingly.

'OK, yes, we'll see the dessert menu, please.'

'That's my girl,' he says and my stomach gives a leap. 'We may as well go the whole way, no half measures!'

He winks at me when he says it and I wonder if there was a double meaning in his words just now. Our knees accidentally touch beneath the table and my head spins a little at the very possibility of what could probably only happen in my dreams.

Aidan has already told me how much he values my friendship, and I won't allow any distraction to get in the way of that, no matter how appealing it might be in my overactive mind.

As Aidan sorts the bill, I make my way to the Ladies before we begin our journey home, filled to the brim with elation and satisfaction at what has been such a fruitful day on such a simple level.

We didn't change the world as we sauntered around admiring the scenery and talking so much I'm surprised we didn't run out of things to say. And that's the thing about Aidan and me when we're together. We never run out of things to say, always finding a topic that needs to be covered and discussed, or a funny story that needs to be told, or a secret from our past that we feel the need to share with each other.

Maybe it's the wine going to my head as I walk away from him, or maybe it's because I can feel his eyes on me with every step I take in the opposite direction, or maybe it's the way there's a tug in my heart for him that I can't deny, but something has changed today between us and I think he knows that too.

I go into the tiny bathroom that's located at the far end of the bar, noticing how the decor in here is so different to that of the main restaurant we passed through when we first arrived. It's like stepping into a different time zone with its beige and brown tiles on the walls, one small cream-coloured sink and two cubicles and, although impeccably clean and tidy, I can tell that this part of the bar is probably from an era that Peter and Danny Murphy would have known much more than the cosmopolitan feel of what must be an extension to the original bar.

I hear a shuffle in one of the cubicles and the flush of a toilet, and when I come face to face seconds later with my company, we both freeze and stare at each other. It's the woman who was staring at us earlier from behind the bar. She goes to the basin to wash her hands and I greet her with an awkward smile, then nudge past her to use the ladies myself.

'Excuse me?' she says just as I'm about to enter the cubicle, and I can't say I'm surprised at all to hear her try to make conversation. 'I know this is going to sound very strange, but – but I couldn't help but overhear you and your husband earlier.'

She glances at my hand, I assume for a wedding ring, and I hide it deliberately.

'Yes, I noticed,' I say, waiting for an explanation. 'Do you know him?'

She shakes water off her hands now and dries them on an old-fashioned towel that sits on an oversized bulky radiator attached to the wall. It reminds me of a brief spell in a state foster home in Dublin, which sends a shiver down my spine.

'I can't claim to know him, no, but I have to ask,' she says, 'is he a Murphy? From Ballybray in Donegal?'

I nod, wondering now how much I should give away and how much I should hold back so I can hear more.

'He is, yes. He's Danny's son, Aidan Murphy,' I say, our eyes locked now as we play a game of cat and mouse, without me knowing what's at stake. 'Would you like to meet him? You seem to know his family?'

'No, no, I don't want to meet him, not now,' she says, her face draining of colour. 'Look, I've said enough for now. I'd better go. Forget I even mentioned it. Sorry.'

'No, wait!'

She goes to leave and I can feel my heart thumping in my chest. My skin prickles and I walk towards her, but she makes for the door.

'Who are you?' I call after her, not really knowing what to say, but she scurries off so quickly, leaving me standing there utterly confused. 'You can't just leave like this! Who are you and what's the big secret about the Murphy brothers?'

She makes her way out of the Ladies, and I stand there, up against the wall, not knowing whether to follow her and make an almighty fuss, or to play things cool and see what we can find out next for ourselves.

I knew Mabel was sending us here for a reason. I knew there was more to it than a simple trip down memory lane or some crazy bonding exercise between me and Aidan, which has very much worked anyhow by the way! But what else could it be? I don't want to alarm Aidan, but I do need to tell him what I heard, so I freshen up at the retro basin and go out to try to find the right moment to do so, but on my way back to him I go into the main bar and I leave my name and my phone number with the woman, assuring her that she can contact me anytime if she feels it's the right time to talk.

The flurry of possibilities of what I overheard spins around within me and as we walk to the car by the pier, I have gone quiet, which Aidan notices. The wonder of who this lady might be has stuck with me, but Aidan seems on such a high that I don't want to ruin his day by telling him something I really don't know an awful lot about.

'You've something on your mind, Roisin,' he says, and I shiver a bit as the cool of the late afternoon gets under my skin. 'Is it Ben?'

'No, no, everything is fine with Ben,' I say, trying to mask the weight that now sits on my shoulders. Do I tell him what I know or do I not? What *do* I know? 'The last I heard from Camille, they were toasting marshmallows by a campfire in true Boy Scout fashion. He's having a whale of a time.'

'And you?' Aidan asks me. 'Are you?'

Now that we don't have the confinements of a table between us as we stand face to face outside with a breeze in our hair and the sun in our eyes, I want to reach across and touch him so badly. I want to hold him so much. I want to protect him from whatever this woman knows about his father.

'I had a really, really lovely time with you here,' I say as he looks at me in a way that makes me fear the hunger I have for him is mutual. 'But I think there's more to discover here in Breena, Aidan. I think we should come back here sometime soon and see.'

'Really? What makes you say that?' he asks, a slight touch of fear on his face that threatens to dampen the end of a wonderful day.

I take a deep breath, shake my head and smile, trying to convince myself that I've said enough for now.. My gut instinct wants to protect him, to reveal what I know gently until I figure out more.

A truth left untold, I recall Mabel telling us in her message. Was sending us to Breena linked to that truth, whatever it could be?

'I'm just saying it's likely your dad and Peter had friends and more of a story here,' I tell him quickly. 'And it might be nice to try to discover that next time, just to deepen that connection and carry on his memory.'

'Of course,' he says when his eyes meet mine again. 'Why am I not surprised you'd think of such a thing?'

My heart skips a beat when I feel Aidan take my hand and hold it before I get a chance to say any more.

My eyes move to meet his and he closes his eyes briefly as if he is trying to find the right words to say something that's itching to get out.

I've told him, albeit in a roundabout way, that we should

223

go back and look up some of his dad's old friends, should they exist, and that will include the lady I just met, whoever she might be, when the time is right. I've left contact details with the woman behind the bar, so I've done as much as I can without upsetting Aidan in any way.

I want to say more, but my hand is still in his and I don't want him to let go.

'Roisin,' he says, rubbing his forehead with his other hand. 'Look, I have to tell you something.'

'I have to tell you something too,' I say, not knowing if I should, but he places his finger on his lips and hushes me.

'I'm sorry if this comes completely out of the blue,' he says, 'but I feel I have to say it to you and now, after our day together, it . . . maybe this is the right time.'

My eyes widen and I hold my breath for what is to come. I feel goose bumps rise on my arms and on the back of my neck at the simple touch of his hand and I automatically put my other hand on top of his as I hang on his every word.

I close my eyes too as a mixture of elation and fear runs through my insides – fear that I'm going to be told something I don't want to hear, and elation at the idea of perhaps being able to tell him how I really feel when we're together. And when I open my eyes I just nod at him as he smiles, trying to let him know what I'm thinking without saying a word.

'You asked me earlier today about what a couple should

have to stay together,' he says, biting his lip, 'and when I was replying to your question, all of the things I said . . . Roisin, all of the things I said were about you.'

I try to respond, but I don't want to interrupt his flow, plus I don't think I'm even able to find the right words yet to reply.

'I don't think I've ever felt so close to anyone before like I do when I'm with you, Roisin,' he tells me with a nervous smile that I can tell comes from deep within him. 'The past months have made me feel like a new man and have been exactly what I needed. I think Mabel might have known it was what you may have needed too.'

I swallow hard, unable to disguise the way my eyes fill up and my skin tingles with the anticipation of knowing how he feels about me, but deep within me there's a tug of guilt and the knowledge that nothing can ever come of this. I want it to so badly, but it can't happen.

He leans across and holds me close in his strong arms, my head rests on his chest, and in this moment I realize at last just how powerful a hug can be. As I stand here entwined with Aidan, endorphins radiate within me and relieve the aches and pains of my past. It's therapeutic, it's magical, and when we finally let go, he tilts up my chin, I part my lips and he leans towards me once more, the warmth of his mouth filling me up so much that I rise closer to him, my hands reaching and clawing his shirt. I close my eyes and savour the taste of him for just a few seconds, this feeling that I've waited on for what seems like for ever taking all my fears away, if only for this moment, and if only for today. I wish I could stay in this wonderful moment.

'We can't do this, Aidan,' I whisper, almost breathless under his spell. 'I want to just as much as you do, but we can't.'

'We can, Roisin,' he tells me. 'Please trust me. We can.'

23.

We leave Breena behind, two very different people from who we were when we first arrived there. Everything has changed within me, as if I've been shifted to a higher level of emotion than I've never felt before. I don't recognize it as coming from me. It's almost euphoric, as though I'm on top of a mountain and I'm totally untouchable. It's like running a marathon and realizing you did it against the odds, and even though you're so tired and sore and you just need food and rest, you know you could easily do it again.

It's the fuzzy feeling of that connection that occurs when you smile at a stranger and they smile back, or when you hold a newborn baby for the first time, and I know it's so wrong even though it feels so right.

But no matter how high I feel, it's also like standing on the edge of a cliff, looking down at an almighty fall, and I know a fall is coming my way if I give in and let all my inhibitions go. I'm not a married woman any more. I haven't been for years, and Aidan claims his short-lived marriage is over, so maybe I should just enjoy it for what it is?

I want to, but can I really let go of the fear of my past making sure I make a mess of it all? Attachment is unhealthy, it's destructive and it's unsafe, and I know I'm already feeling so attached to Aidan and all he represents. He is the opposite of Jude, he is a reminder of Mabel and a real-life link to her, and we have so much in common, yet we live in worlds that couldn't be further apart.

I want to give in, but I can't. I check the time. It's just gone six in the evening and yet I feel as if this day has gone on for ever, in the best possible way. A pang of feeling I'm doing something so wrong rests in the pit of my stomach, but I swallow hard, trying my best to push it away. Why shouldn't I have some fun for a change? Why shouldn't I just let go and give in to this, whatever it is? Why do I always have to over analyse everything that comes my way? We've had such a lovely day. Aidan has told me he's a free man who was trapped in an unhealthy and unhappy marriage for too long, so why shouldn't we now just go with the flow and see what happens?

'Have you ever been to Belfast city?' he asks me, and I can't help it. My eyes light up at the possibility of making this day last as long as we possibly can. 'I've an idea, if you're up for some spontaneity to finish our trip?'

My first reaction is to say no, of course I can't do that, as the familiar weight of non-stop responsibility to be home for a certain time comes naturally. But then I realize of course that I don't have to be back for any particular reason today. I can have fun, and I will put myself first for a change. I can deal with the consequences, whatever they may be, later.

'I'd love that,' I tell him, and as we drive, not to Ballybray but towards the city in the warmth of the car, I find myself singing along with the radio, and when Aidan puts his hand across and leans it on my leg, I hold it there, not ever wanting to let him go.

We park up in the Cathedral Quarter of Belfast just half an hour later. It's a trendy and hip cultural area, packed with pubs, Mediterranean bistros and cafés, with live music spilling out onto the streets as people eat al fresco. The cobbled streets play host to a multicultural vibe that feels like a different world to sleepy Ballybray, and I drink it all in, not knowing where we are going exactly but high on excitement as to what is coming next.

This is so not me, and it feels so damn good!

When we reach the steps of the Victorian glamour of the Merchant Hotel, Aidan leads me inside and orders me a cocktail. I sip it and watch the hustle and bustle outside, savouring city life from the comfort of such grandeur, wanting to pinch myself in this moment that is so far removed from my own real life or responsibility or past. When he returns, Aidan looks like he has something up his sleeve as he can't stop smiling. He joins me at the table and then kisses my hand.

'Roisin, I don't want you to feel pressurized in any way,

but would you like to stay here tonight?' he asks me, and my heart skips a beat. 'I'm not saying we have to share a room, but just thought you might like to kick back and let me treat you. We can have dinner, listen to some music, and do whatever you want to do. I think you deserve a break, so if you're up for it, it's all on me.'

I look around the magnificent surroundings. The hotel is five-star opulent luxury, with its art deco interior, and I'm in heaven, and there's nothing more in the world I'd rather do than let my hair down and enjoy myself with Aidan tonight.

'I'd love that,' I whisper to him, and then he leans across and kisses me tenderly. It's been so long since I've felt like I've deserved to just be me, and not Ben's mother or Jude's widow, or someone who has to keep all the balls in the air. I feel a trickle of guilt creep in again, but I know what Mabel Murphy would say if she caught me considering saying no to something I'd really like to do.

I glance at my phone to see a picture message of Ben and Gino pop up in my inbox. They are decked out in their equestrian gear now and both pull funny faces into the camera. 'Two very happy and excited boys,' writes Camille. 'Hope you are having a relaxing time with Aidan. You deserve it.'

The 'mummy guilt' pang eases and I can see Mabel nodding in approval, just as she was about to launch an inner verbal warning to me from beyond the grave.

'Thank you,' I say to Aidan in advance of whatever he has planned for us this evening. 'This is a lot more than I could ever have expected for today. I'm looking forward to it already.'

We check in to the hotel and my jaw drops when I see the room I'll be staying in for one night only. It's the ultimate in high-end luxury and nothing like I've ever seen before, with velvet throws, silk curtains, silk voiles, and antique furniture on deep pile carpet. The bed is a mahogany four-poster, the bath is free-standing and has a roll top framed with chocolate marble, and a display of fine art looks down on us from the walls. I feel like Cinderella and Pretty Woman rolled into one. I want to stay here for ever. I sink into one of the pillows and Aidan joins me, then we laugh like giddy teenagers.

'I don't think I've ever seen anything like this before,' I admit to Aidan as the rush of his spontaneity and generosity blows me away. 'It's so beautiful.'

'Like you,' says Aidan, kissing my forehead. He pulls me in closer and I can feel my own hunger for him rise. He holds my gaze, making sure every move he makes is to my pleasing, and I nod in approval for him to go ahead. It doesn't take us long to undress each other, and my mouth waters for his taste, which sends me straight to heaven, as does his touch when his fingertips explore my body and then his tongue, and soon we are as one.

It's slow, it's so intimate, it's gentle, and it's hard, and I close my eyes in wonder at how perfect it feels to be here with him, naked and in full abandonment, yet so confident and sure.

I barely recognize myself, and as we both stand under the rain shower afterwards, I keep thinking of my younger self and how I'd never have imagined I'd experience someone who looked at me the way Aidan Murphy does. It's not his money or his status, but how he does everything with my feelings in mind. There's nothing arrogant or showy in any of his actions, just pure love and affection, and I don't ever want this day to end.

And the surprises keep coming . . . we spend an hour sipping champagne in the hotel's rooftop hot tub after a heavenly massage, something I'd never have dreamed of doing.

We dine under Ireland's biggest chandelier, where every mouthful of food is orgasmic, and then finish our night tucked into a cosy corner in the jazz bar, where we manage to sneak in a dance cheek to cheek to the sounds of the band singing one of Mabel's favourites, Ella Fitzgerald's 'They Can't Take That Away From Me', and as we sway slowly to the music, I close my eyes and feel a tear trickle down my face. I can hear Aidan hum along to the music, and I thank Mabel for sending me a man who makes me feel so special and so worthy of every single step I take on this earth.

But deep down I know that when this all sinks in tomorrow I'll be absolutely terrified of how vulnerable being so open with Aidan leaves me, and how I'm still holding back the conversation I had with the lady in Sullivan's and the possibility of a truth left untold.

I know that when all that has happened today hits me tomorrow, I might be more frightened than I've ever been in my whole life at how I've let myself become so involved with a married man, of being subsequently let down again or by having my patched-up heart broken.

SUMMER

24.

'Why do I feel like you're already gone, like a dripping tap with every drip, drip counting down the seconds till you disappear?' I ask Aidan as we picnic on Killahoey Strand on our last Sunday together before he leaves to sort out his affairs in New York. 'It's like you've already gone even though you're still here.'

'That's deep, for a Sunday morning,' he says, staring out to sea. 'We're not losing anything, Ro, how many times do I have to tell you? In fact it's the opposite. I'm putting plans in place. Let's just try and enjoy our last few precious moments.'

I only wish I could enjoy them and relax for our last afternoon together but I can't shake off this feeling of impending doom. Aidan's bags are packed, his flight is booked for this evening, and a long era of at least a few months apart looms ahead, plus he's been insanely quiet for the past few days, constantly on his phone and hating to be interrupted.

'I know it's not goodbye for ever, but I'm so emotional at any sort of farewell, I have to warn you,' I tell him with a hint of laughter. 'I'll be a blubbering mess before the day is out, all snot and tears at the airport and wailing like a banshee.'

Ben is busy battling with a huge kite on the beach in front of us with Gino, who is claiming to be an expert on kite aviation, while Aidan and I lounge on a tartan rug beside our favourite sand dune, the perfect little cove of comfort where we're shielded from the sporadic breeze and exposed enough to catch a glimmer of the sun in the sky, which can't seem to make its mind up.

It's a pleasant day as far as Irish summers go, but my heart is weeping with every second, every minute, and every hour that ticks by, knowing that inevitably I'm going to have to watch Aidan walk away to a life that I know very little about – a life where he will try and pack up his commitments to a family business which has entwined him with Rachel and her overbearing and very rich father.

'Ah, you'd make a very sexy banshee. Is there such a thing as a sexy banshee?' he jokes, showing a glimmer of his happier side, while gently pushing my hair off my face when the breeze catches it. 'Believe me, if I could sort everything out from here I would, but I've got years and years of my past life to get into gear, not to mention tackling the present and future commitments of work. It will take time, Roisin, but we'll get there, I promise.'

I want to ask him how long it will take for us to 'get there' wherever that even is, but at the same time I know he doesn't need that pressure, so instead I try and assure myself that this is only a temporary measure and one for the greater good, even though we haven't exactly worked out what that greater good might be as yet.

Will we be together properly? Will we live here in Ballybray? Will Aidan work in property again, or will he start something new? Will he really be able to leave New York behind to live at a snail's pace in rural Ireland?

'I wish I could press forward and make it all happen faster,' I whisper, as a gnawing sensation of underlying fear starts to nip at me inside. I'm afraid of being here without him and without Mabel, as it's all I've ever known. I'm afraid of him being convinced to stay in New York for work commitments and that once they get him back stateside they won't want to let him go again. But most of all, I'm afraid that when he gets there Rachel might plead with him to give their marriage another chance and start all over again with her.

'You're overthinking again, I just know you are,' says Aidan, leaning back now on the sand. 'Please stop. Rachel has already moved on quite substantially from our marriage, so you've no worries about her trying to change my mind if that's what you're thinking.'

'What do you mean she's moved on? Has she found someone new?'

He shrugs his shoulders.

'Leave it, Roisin, please! I'm not sure about her personal

life in that way, but let's just say she's been enjoying herself on the social scene and the word is out, much to her father's annoyance,' he explains. 'Bruce Bowen has a huge wallet and a big influence on the media, so he's kept it quiet for now, but it's only a matter of time.'

I shudder to think of how different Aidan's life has been in a fast-moving city like New York, caught up in the rat race of meetings, conference calls, buying and selling for millions of dollars, work hard, play hard, don't have time to look over your shoulder lifestyle. Here in Ballybray, we tend to paddle along at a duck's pace of living, working in a slower, much more community-led environment where everyone knows your name, and yes, sometimes they know your business too.

'You know, it's quite ironic how it was Mabel and Peter's influence that took me away from here to New York almost fifteen years ago,' ponders Aidan as he watches the boys battle with their kite, slipping and sliding in the sand, 'and now it's Mabel who has brought me home again. It's like my life has come full circle. It's so strange. I'm back to the beginning.'

'You don't mean that in a bad way, do you?'

He gets up and brushes the sand off his jeans without answering, leaving a lump of worry in the pit of my stomach. There's no doubt about it, Aidan's mood has been sliding backwards the past few days and it's really got me wondering if he's having second thoughts about all the time we've spent together.

I blink back tears, thinking of the vast stretch of the Atlantic Ocean that will soon lie between us and the immensity of it almost makes me lose my breath. I imagine him seeing Rachel again after all this time, and the old saying of how absence makes the heart grow fonder plays havoc with my heartstrings at the notion they might want to get back together.

'Aidan, just promise me,' I whisper to his back as he stands now against the light summer breeze. 'Please just promise me that if you get there and decide you'd rather try and fix your life in New York and with Rachel, please don't let anything to do with me hold you—'

'Stop, Roisin, please,' he says without looking back at me. 'You've no idea how much I'm dreading what I have ahead of me, so stop with the pressure. Just let me do what I have to do!'

'OK,' I wince, crawling back into my shell again.

I don't mean to add to his pressure, but I've been trying to envisage how I'm going to readjust without Aidan, not just me but Ben, as we once again make changes in our own minds and in our practical daily ways to make life normal.

Just as we were letting Mabel's death sink in, Aidan came along and helped us heal together. For eight months now the three of us have been swept along in a bubble of laughter, fun and contentment like I've never known, but now that bubble is about to burst, if only temporarily, the idea of not having him around is almost too much to bear.

I've said so many goodbyes in my life I should be used to them by now, I know that. I've packed up my life so many times ever since I was a young teenager, sometimes running literally for my life and sometimes jumping from the frying pan into the fire, but this is different. This is a dread like I've never felt before because now that I've finally felt the love I've always longed for, the fear of letting it go, and of him possibly never coming back, is just so overwhelming.

I also dread to think of how Aidan will soon sample the rollercoaster of emotions I experienced when I had to pack up my life after Jude died when he goes back to do the same with the life he shared with Rachel. I remember how the finality of it all came at me like a freight train. I'd tried so hard to put my feelings on pause that when the day came to put all my belongings into bags and pack everything up it was like carving shapes with a dagger on my heart.

I'd tried to shift my brain into autopilot that day, but no matter how angry I was at Jude and no matter how much he'd bullied and intimidated me for years, packing up family photos showing some of our happier times together was still a killer blow to the soul.

I packed up memories of a caravan holiday where we'd both swelled with joy when Ben jumped into the swimming pool all by himself for the first time. I packed up the day of Jude's only brother's wedding in our very early years together, when to me the whole world had ceased to exist and it was just the two of us, so happy and in love.

And as I cried sore while I packed up some of these more pleasant memories, a juggernaut of flashbacks of more difficult times also raced towards me – I packed up a dress I wore to a surprise birthday lunch I'd planned with his family during which he'd pinned me up against the wall when out of sight as everyone laughed and chatted just feet away, warning me to never, *ever* plan anything behind his back like that again; I packed away the cups I used when my neighbour popped by for a coffee unannounced and he came home to find us chatting in the kitchen, after which I was made to suffer for days and was quizzed on every conversation we covered in case I had mentioned him; I packed away the scarf I was wearing to Ben's first parent–teacher meeting at school where I'd casually mentioned in conversation how we were considering a family holiday, and Jude beat me black and blue afterwards for telling anyone our business.

I packed up the ability ever to let my guard down and the willingness to believe someone when they told me they loved me for ever. I told myself that when it came to trust and love outside of the unconditional love I had for my son, I'd locked up that chance for good and thrown away the key.

As I sit here now with Aidan on the beach in Dunfanaghy, I compare the lightness I feel when I'm with him to the dread and fear I had inside when I was married to Jude. I feel like I'm looking back at a totally different person, and I can only hope that Aidan feels liberated and free when it's his turn to pack up and move on from a toxic existence in America.

'We should probably make a move,' he says when he eventually turns back to face me, both of us lost in thought and dreading the inevitable as the clock ticks away our time together for now. 'I need to be on the road to the airport by three.'

'I suppose so,' I say, as a weight of sorrow engulfs me from head to toe.

Sensing my despair, he sits down beside me again and I cling on to his jumper, grasping it tightly, allowing my fears to disintegrate if only for as long as this final moment lasts. I close my eyes and quickly drift off to a time when I dreamed that someone might love me enough to hold me every time I felt down. And I cry for how I wasn't sure I'd ever find that in real life. I was convinced that such tenderness and content-ment were for other people, but never for me, and now that I have it at last, I don't ever want to let it go.

'You're not making this very easy, Roisin,' Aidan tells me, and when I look up at him, I see his beautiful eyes are so far away from me, and it stings so deeply. 'Please don't make this any harder than it already is. I've so much going on in my head and I just want to get this over and done with.'

'I know, I know, I'm just sad,' I say, standing up and blowing out a deep breath to shift some energy. 'But let's treat it like removing a sticky plaster, yeah? The quicker it happens, the less painful it will be and the sooner it's over.'

'I suppose so,' he says, standing up to join me, then calling out across the sand to the boys. 'Ben, Gino, you call that flying a kite? Come here and let me show you. You need to untangle the string for a start. Ah, lads, come on!'

And in a case of 'one for the road', Aidan spends a last few precious moments with Ben on the beach, which makes me fill up with warmth and tear up at the same time.

We are going to miss him so, so much, but like I thought earlier, it really feels as though he has already gone. His head most definitely is already gone, and I just hope he decides to leave his heart behind.

After a brief but impressive lesson in kite flying which made Ben and Gino whoop with sheer delight, we make our way back from the beach to the cosiness of Ballybray. We drive through the village, past Cleary's Bar and Truly Vintage, past the corner shop and the various little stores of all shapes and colours and on to the familiarity of Teapot Row, and I try desperately to stay positive about what lies ahead.

As we approach the two little cottages where we've made so much history between us I feel an unexpected sense of calm at last. We've come through so much together in a relatively short space of time and have such an unbreakable bond, so I know deep down I've no need to panic over a few months apart.

At least that's what I'm going to have to keep telling myself, isn't it?

We'll miss each other, yes, but today is most definitely going to be an 'au revoir' more than a goodbye, even though we don't know how long our parting will be.

And so when we stand at the airport terminal in Dublin a few hours later, as hundreds of people bustle past us dragging wheeled cases and all sorts of luggage behind them. It's a bittersweet moment that I decide to face with a strength I've gained over the years from Mabel's wisdom and more recently from the security of Aidan's love and friendship. I'm trying to keep a lid on the usual fear that continually simmers and bubbles somewhere within me.

'So, I'll see you soon, buddy!' Aidan says to Ben when we've walked as far as we can through Departures at Dublin Airport. 'And mind your mum for me, won't you? Tell her to drive slowly and always wear her seat belt, even on short runs! Don't be afraid to tell her off for that!'

I roll my eyes as I get the hint at my forgetfulness to wear a seat belt sometimes when driving in and around the village in my pick-up truck.

Ben fist bumps with Aidan, then high fives, and finally gives in to wrap his little arms around Aidan's waist, which makes me swallow back emotion and have to look away.

'I did say I was pretty hopeless at goodbyes!' I remind him when he catches me wiping my eyes. 'OK, just go quickly! And don't look back, please. Just keep walking and we'll do the same so that it's not as painful as it could be.'

'You'll be fine,' he says, kissing me quickly on the forehead. 'I'll keep in touch.'

'I know you will, now go!' I tell him, and he finally walks away and I do my best to try to ignore the lump in my throat. I paint on a smile, put my arm around Ben, who looks up at me for some reassurance, and then we both break the rules and look back to watch Aidan disappear into the distance as he reaches the sliding doors.

'Ah man, I can't wait until he gets back,' Ben says, his freckled nose scrunched up as he watches the empty space where Aidan stood until now. He fixes his baseball cap and then stands up straight. 'But we'll be fine, Mum. I'll look after you. I promised Aidan, and you know I never, ever break my promises.'

I don't know whether to giggle or cry at his sweetness.

'And I'll look after you too, Ben,' I say, putting my arm around him again as we walk off towards the early evening sunshine. 'Let's get home and do something nice, eh?'

'Good thinking,' says Ben, and by the time we reach the car I'm smiling through my tears knowing that we've just taken our first step towards a whole new life together.

But if and when a new life with Aidan will ever begin, I have absolutely no idea.

25.

Mabel's penultimate message arrives unexpectedly on a typical Irish summer's day in mid-August, just under two whole months after Aidan's departure.

It's a day when the weather can't make its mind up between light showers and brief bursts of sunshine, but as I feel around the envelope which as before bears her very distinctive lilting handwriting, I know immediately that it isn't a video like the previous two have been. The shape of the envelope is different for a start, and it's delivered by registered post this time, meaning I have to sign for it, which makes me wonder with all my might what she could be up to next, and question who could be helping her to deliver these packages from beyond the grave?

'Have you any idea where this may have come from?' I ask Mickey, who often brings my post into my workplace these days instead of to my home address if he's passing by and sees me. 'I know who it's from, but I've no idea where it's being posted from.'

Mickey holds out the envelope and squints at the post-mark, then puts on his glasses and takes a closer look.

'Looks like it's been posted locally,' he tells me. 'It's bringing good news, I hope?'

'Yes, I think it should,' I reply, feeling a most welcome rush of excitement at what might lie inside.

I'd recognize Mabel's handwriting a mile off, but there's no way I'm telling Mickey what's been going on with her messages. As much as I like to see him and chat with him over coffee on a Monday, to tell anyone around here that I'm getting messages from a lady who died nine months ago would spark off the most colourful rumours. The whole village would soon have wind of it and before I'd catch my breath, I'd be branded some sort of lunatic, with Chinese whispers declaring that Mabel was still alive and kicking somewhere.

As much as I love village life here in Ballybray, I also know when to keep my own business to myself, apart from Camille of course, who has been on this journey with Aidan and me from the beginning. She has witnessed my mood dipping lately, a mixture of missing Aidan so badly as the distance between us becomes more and more frustrating, and lack of sleep as I burn the midnight oil trying to build up my little side-line business that I've put so much effort into.

I put the envelope from Mabel in a drawer behind the counter and go back to arranging a selection of my brand new beeswax candles, aptly named Simply Mabel, and a collection of glazed blue dishes, on an upcycled green-painted dresser as I wait to get the go ahead from Aidan to open up the small envelope to see what's inside.

'So, no big cinema viewing required this time,' he says when he eventually responds to my message by video call. He's been so busy at work lately that our phone calls have been short and to the point, and to be honest sometimes filled with tension as the reality of being apart for such a long spell really kicks in.

'Not this time, it seems,' I tell him, taking a few steps back to admire my display to make sure all is as I want it to be. 'Do you think that looks OK, or should I put the candles on the top shelf?'

I switch the camera on my phone to let him see what I mean and we both agree they would be much better on the top row by themselves rather than scattered on each shelf like I have them now. The Simply Mabel range of locally sourced beeswax candles with organic wicks and fine navy trim complements the accompanying set of handmade dishes, all of which were thrown in my spare room. I'd found a gas burning kiln online, which I'm storing in Mabel's garden shed for now, and my little enterprise is growing right before my eyes, even if my eyes need matchsticks to stay awake most days because of it.

'Congratulations, Roisin,' says Aidan. 'They look amazing. I just wish I was there to celebrate with you.'

I can only sigh and wish for the same, knowing it just

isn't possible to be together for every little milestone in our lives over the summer. Most of our conversations these days are laced with the same desires. When Aidan's company was nominated for a huge contract that will be allocated at a ceremony in November (his final, final commitment to them, I'm assured), I wished I could be there to celebrate as he toasted the prestigious shortlist announcement. When Ben celebrated his eleventh birthday in early August, Aidan wished he could be there to join us and give him his present in person instead of sending him one from afar – a very generous gift of a full set of riding gear, including a black hat, navy jodhpurs, a back brace, boots and fleece jacket, which made Ben cry with delight. I recorded his reaction on my phone, our main line of communication, and sent it to him, but it just wasn't the same.

'Thank you so much, Aidan! This is the best present ever!' Ben had said in his message. 'I really hope you come back home to us soon. I miss you.'

And although we are still buzzing from our amazing time together, and we're all keeping busy with our own commitments, there are days when the frustration of being so far apart can almost be too hard to handle.

I miss his hugs. I miss his smell. I miss holding him and kissing him. I seem to switch from telling myself how lucky we are to have found each other, to wanting to punch the wall at how unfair it is that we're so far apart.

'It's still early days, so try to stay positive,' Camille assures me when I'm having a particularly bad day. 'Just imagine the next time you see him, how good it will feel. And keep making plans. You always need something to look forward to or else you'll crack up.'

On my birthday I got a hamper of goodies and a huge bouquet of flowers delivered to the door, but you can't hug a bunch of flowers, can you? A bunch of flowers doesn't talk back or dine with you or make love with you in the night. I thanked him politely of course, knowing he meant well, but the disappointment ate at me for longer than it possibly should have and it took me a while to get over it.

'I feel like I'm the other woman,' I tell him frequently.

'Don't say that,' is his usual answer. 'You know how much I'm trying to sort my whole life out. Stay with me.'

But then there are times when I'm filled with hope and excitement as I realize that our time together can't be so very far away now that a few months have passed and we still have Mabel's summer message to look forward to.

'So, open the envelope!' Aidan tells me now, when I'm finished showing off my display of candles. 'I'm itching here. Come on! Let's see what Mabel has in store for us this time.'

Camille gives me the nod from her stool in the nook to take Mabel's message upstairs, so I do that and as I climb the narrow wooden stairs, I feel with every step I take a little lift in my mood as some hope returns. The aching I have for Aidan when we're apart is nothing that I've ever felt before, the fear I have that it will all go wrong lingers always, but the excitement at the thought that this message might be the nudge we need to finally get together again is even more powerful.

I pull a beanbag from the corner of the room into the centre so the stream of light falls right down on me, warming my soul as I open the envelope, but when I do, my hand goes to my mouth and I can hardly speak.

'What is it?' asks Aidan, from the phone I've propped up on the floor. My mouth is dry with shock and I shake my head, wondering once again how Mabel could have planned this all in so much detail as she was facing up to her last months in this world.

'She's sent us airline tickets?' I say, blinking back my utter disbelief. I pull my sweater over my head as it's much too warm in the heat of the attic room to take this all in. 'There's a letter with them too. I'll read it aloud.'

'Airline tickets?' asks Aidan, a rising panic in his voice. 'Tickets to where exactly? Where is she sending us? I can't go too far at the moment with work, and the next few weeks are crucial so I can't—'

'Calm down, calm down, they aren't for you,' I tell him, clutching the tickets to my chest as if I'm holding a winning lottery ticket.

'What?'

'They're for me and Ben!' I explain, fingering the tickets and checking the date, which is in just two days' time, my eyes wide as saucers as I try to take this in. I panic for a moment, wondering and hoping that our passports are in date as we haven't had the need to use them for so long. In fact, Ben's only trip abroad in all his young lifetime was a weekend in London to visit Jude's sister, and coughing up for that almost put Jude over the edge.

'What's going on, Roisin? Where does Mabel want you to go?'

I feel like creating a dramatic pause for effect, but I can't hold it in.

'If Mohammad can't come to the mountain, the mountain will come to Mohammad!' I say, unable to resist teasing it out just a moment longer.

I expect Aidan to cop on, but he looks truly puzzled.

'Aidan, Mabel has booked tickets for Ben and me to visit New York for the weekend!' I exclaim. 'We're coming to see you! Oh my goodness, I can't wait to tell Ben!'

I watch him on screen, sitting in his favourite coffee shop, which I now know is called Bean, and a place where they know him so well they keep him a seat at the same time every day, but his voice drops to a whisper.

'This weekend?' he asks, his mood not exactly matching mine. 'Hang on! I'm not getting this at all. Why is Mabel sending you to New York this weekend?'

I try to ignore the slight edge in his voice and focus on the job at hand.

'Let me read out her letter and see,' I reply, my hands

shaking as I pull it from the envelope. 'I'm sure all will be explained right here.'

Visiting Aidan in New York has always been on my radar, but no matter how much I tried to fit it in or work around it, there was always something to make me put it off for just another while. Ben's school commitments were a biggie, but there's no excuse for that now as school has packed up for summer. Camille had offered on numerous occasions to have Ben for a whole weekend if I'd wanted to go to see Aidan myself, but there was no way I could have done that without Ben. He is still totally absorbed in all things New York related and is convinced that we would be going there together, so I couldn't let him down. Then, there is the huge subject of money, not that I'd ever admit that to Aidan. I'd bought the cottage almost five years ago now, with life assurance money after Jude's passing (and looking back, I must admit to having a slight moment of glee at how careless and carefree he would think I was for doing so) and apart from a few thousand left over I'd tucked away for Ben's education, I've been managing nicely on my payment from Truly Vintage and am looking forward to making a little extra with my own craft collection. Jude would have hated me doing so, which makes me even more driven to succeed.

I carefully open out the letter from Mabel, putting any worries about money and passports or other practicalities to the side for now until I see what she has to say as excitement and anticipation spills over me.

My dear Aidan and Roisin, she writes so elegantly in fine black ink on thick cream, textured paper.

I'm writing to you this time using old-fashioned pen and paper, as I'm not feeling so good today and although I'd planned to make all my little messages by video, it took me a while to think of this one and to see it all through.

Believe it or not, one of my biggest regrets in life was not travelling more and exploring the wonderful world we live in.

In fact, let me tell you a secret – despite my claims to be so worldly and wise as I shell out advice to you both, until Peter took me to Ireland and showed me all the delights of his home land, I'd never stopped to believe that life even existed out of New York City!

Yes, indeed, I've lived almost eighty years on this planet, but I never, ever ventured out of my comfort zone too far – oh how I wish I could turn back time and go see the world! I wish I'd have lived in different places! Tried out new things!

When you're stuck in your own bubble of work and play, a calendar year seems like a big chunk of your time, but when you look back, you realize how it goes in a heartbeat. So make every year count if you can be bold enough to! No one is stuck in any place for ever. No one is too busy to try out something new.

One of my biggest admirations for you both, Aidan and Roisin, was your courage to make things happen, to take the bull by the horns and make the changes you needed to, to make your lives better.

Roisin, I'd love you to visit the street where I lived with Peter, the cabaret club that became my second home, the streets we walked and the places we loved so dearly, and some of the friends who made me the person I became as I grew older – oh, and make sure Aidan shows you how he lives there too. You just might like it!

I only wish I could be there with the three of you on what I hope will be a wonderful experience!

Take lots of photos, make lots of memories, smile, breathe it in, and experience as much as you can.

With all my love for ever,

Mabel

PS Roisin, I know you keep your passport in a little box in your kitchen cupboard. I checked your dates. You're all good to go! Enjoy!

I burst out laughing, partly with shock, but most of all I'm so impressed at Mabel's attention to detail and at how she even checked my passport. I know now that someone will have definitely been helping her with her little 'four seasons' project, but I've no idea who, and I'm already itching to get home and pack my bags to see the Big Apple, not to mention to see Aidan, who I've been pining for, for months now.

Yet he doesn't seem to share the same enthusiasm, and I try to ignore his look of panic and distress.

'Are you sure you can drop everything and just come here this weekend?' he asks, shaking his head in disbelief. 'What about work? I'm not sure I can change my schedule at such short notice. I've made it no secret at how everything over the next few weeks has to go like clockwork if I'm to make my escape from here, Roisin.'

My bubble bursts just a little as I realize Mabel's assumption so long ago would be that we would spend time with Aidan, but how would she have known those dates would suit someone so busy? They evidently don't.

My stomach sinks. Does he not want to see us? Is the timing really so bad that he couldn't show just a little bit of excitement at the prospect of us finally seeing the city that he's called home for so long?

'We . . . we won't interrupt you, I promise,' I tell him, trying my best to understand where he's coming from, but at the same time not letting him flatten the mood and the potential of spending even a few hours together at last. 'I'll plan loads of sightseeing with Ben and if we even get to have one lunch or dinner with you then the trip will be worth it.'

'I'm sorry, Roisin, I don't mean to be a misery,' he says now rubbing his eyes. 'I've just been under so much pressure and I can't drop everything now when it's been going so long.'

I try to hide the disappointment in my voice.

'I understand, Aidan. I totally understand,' I whisper,

feeling tears prick my eyes. 'We'll do our own thing and if you can see us for even just a little while over the weekend that will be a bonus.'

I know that deep down, despite the sick feeling in my stomach at his subdued reaction, I do understand. He's been busting his gut to work towards his big finale in November when his company, or rather Bruce Bowen's company, is in line to pick up one of the biggest contracts awarded in the property business at a glitzy hand-over ceremony, so I shouldn't be too shocked that he can't just stop everything for our unexpected visit.

'Thanks, babe,' he says, looking a bit more relieved now at last. 'OK, I'll book the two of you into a nice hotel and make sure you have a wonderful time. You're going to love the Big Apple and Ben will too, and I'll be there with you as much as I possibly can. I can't wait to see you.'

He's tired, I know he is, and he's more than stressed, so I do my best to forgive him for not exactly jumping up and down at Mabel's presumptuous timing. So I say a quick goodbye and take the stairs a lot faster than I normally do to share the news with Camille. Most of all, I can't wait to tell Ben. We're going to New York and we're going to see Aidan, if only for a little while.

26.

'Mum, did you know there are as many as 800 languages spoken in New York City, with Spanish coming second to English?' Ben informs me when we touch down at JFK around six p.m. New York time, only two days after receiving Mabel's very unexpected message.

What was equally unexpected was the envelope inside my passport when I went to find it that contained ten one-hundred-dollar bills and an instruction for me to 'treat Ben and have a wonderful trip'. I didn't have time to make any detailed plans, other than to make sure Aidan knew our arrival times. In typical Aidan fashion, rather than my idea of hailing a taxi to his address, he insisted on sending a chauffeur to bring us to our hotel via a brief sightseeing tour to get a feel of what life is like for him when he's not kicking back with us in sleepy old Ballybray.

'And it's one of the most photographed cities in the world too,' says Ben, pointing his camera out through the window on the plane as he takes in every inch of our journey. We passed the time during the flight with back-to-back movies, bottomless drinks, and never-ending snacks, having been upgraded, by Aidan of course, to first class, and I honestly feel like pinching myself that my precious son and I are getting to experience this trip of a lifetime together.

I can't help but reflect on how I never thought I'd find myself in such a place of euphoria. I want to turn back the clock and whisper in my ear when Jude was shouting at me in that other life that my path was going to take many, many twists and turns for the better very soon. I want to go back in time to remind myself, when I sat at the top of the stairs, my arms battered from his overactive fists and my eyes sore with exhaustion and from tears of desperation, that good people and kindness do exist. I was never driven by consumerism, nor did I even know what it was like to have money to be extravagant, and indulgence can frighten me more quickly than it impresses me, but to see how the other half lives and to experience kindness and love with Aidan for another few days in my lifetime makes me so grateful and thankful that I never, ever did give up or give in when my days were dark and my nights were long and terrifying.

The evening summer sky in New York is a cool, clear blue, and when our uniformed driver, John, meets us at Arrivals, I can hardly take in my surroundings because all I can watch is my son's face as he absorbs all that's going on with a magical wonder I wish I could bottle up and keep forever.

'So, let's get you two across the city and show you the beautiful Big Apple,' says John, who, I realize from the badge he wears, is in fact one of Aidan's very own private drivers and not a hired chauffeur as I'd thought.

We drive through Brooklyn, where John points out every milestone he can think of, including Gerritsen Beach along the way.

'It's like a little New England fishing village, really quaint and close-knit,' he says in his strong Bronx accent. 'It's a very unique part of the city.'

'It looks a bit like Killybegs to me,' says Ben, snapping out the window on his camera phone with every milestone we meet along the way. 'Well, apart from being a bit sunnier, of course.'

I marvel at his innocence, watching his little fingers click and click, knowing most of his photography efforts will either end up a blur as we drive past, or be deleted to make room for some of the bigger sights we plan to see, but I don't want to put him off his stride. Watching him so animated and so happy, and knowing all he has been through, never fails to make me well up.

John drives us around the scenic route, which skirts the river and takes just over an hour and a half, and when Ben spots the Statue of Liberty in the distance I've never been as glad of the invention of a seat belt, as I'm sure that without it he would have levitated out through the window for sure.

'Mum! Mum, look!'

'There she is,' says John, just in case we need to be reminded. 'It's the glorious green goddess! Man, but that sight never gets old.'

I've a feeling John is enjoying his mini tour guide role as much as Ben and I are, and he answers all my questions with such passion and pride.

'It's so good to meet some of Mr Murphy's friends from Ireland instead of men in suits superglued to their phones,' he says, when I compliment his attention to detail and enthusiasm as he takes his time to explain to us newcomers some of the lesser known facts on streets and villages, and he even throws in the odd piece of movie or TV trivia too, pointing out to me where Carrie Bradshaw from *Sex and the City* lived, and to Ben where scenes from some of *The Avengers* movie were shot.

We move through Manhattan and on to Fifth Avenue, where our journey will come to an end, and over an hour later when we arrive at our hotel, I feel my legs go weak with anticipation at seeing Aidan soon, as well as being in awe of this very different world in which we find ourselves.

I'm nervous in a way I never would have expected. My mouth is dry, I can feel my fingertips tingle with anxiety, and I feel a great fear and sense of panic of the unknown.

Yes, being here is all I imagined in many ways, but even though I'm going to see Aidan who I know so well by now, and with whom I've become completely smitten, it feels like

I'm going to meet a stranger. I've heard of all the various real estate projects he juggles morning, noon and night, I've seen and read newspaper clippings from Mabel that stretch back for years, but to be honest all of that information belongs to a different man to the Aidan I've come to know. It is all secondary, and new to me. It has absolutely nothing to do with the person I know so well, yet it is everything to do with him. This is the real Aidan, the real version of him that has existed here for fifteen years. This is the way he lives day in, day out, and the way of life he wants to eventually pack up and move on from.

'All OK? Still in conference.'

Aidan messages just before we get out of the car, so I send him a quick reply and remind him to stay focused on his work for as long as he has to.

'Thanks Ro!' he messages back. 'I hope you love it here!'

But am I really going to love it here?

Everything is so unfamiliar, even for a former city girl like me. I thought Dublin was busy, but I've never witnessed crazy busy like New York before. The streets are thronged with traffic, there are yellow taxis everywhere and, just like in the movies, there's a buzz in the air, and you can almost smell how busy everyone is.

Ben brings me down to earth immediately, as only he can.

'And this is why it's called the city that never sleeps, Mum,' he says. 'I think I like it here already.'

He launches into the famous line of the Sinatra song

about spreading the news, and I swear he is almost dancing as we follow John into the hotel lobby, which makes my heart want to burst with joy.

I can't argue with his enthusiasm, so I pull up my big girl pants metaphorically, step it up in the afternoon summer sun, put on my shades, and give it my best shot. This is New York, New York and I'm going to see the man of my dreams.

I'm petrified, yes, but I'm also excited beyond belief.

I can almost hear Mabel laugh and nod her head saying 'I told you so' as I drink in my surroundings when we open the door to the suite Aidan has booked for us on the penthouse floor of our hotel in Lower Manhattan. I plonk myself down on the super king-size bed as Ben races straight to the window, then I follow him and we both look out on to the majestic views, doing our best to take all of this in.

'Thank you, Mabel,' I whisper to my best friend in the world. 'Thank you for this experience and for bringing us here, for giving me hope in my life again and for bringing Aidan into our lives. I'll never forget you for this, ever.'

The sprawling penthouse has views over Hudson Square with its own rooftop meditation space, a gym, a 24-hour attended lobby, and a private garden to the rear. Even though we are in the middle of one of the most non-stop cities in the world, it feels so serene and peaceful in this room, with its classy decor and timeless design.

'I feel like Julia Roberts in *Pretty Woman*, I swear!' I say to Aidan when he calls to see we've settled in. He's been in conference calls all day and is only finding a minute now to call, even though it's almost midnight. 'I'm totally out of my depth here and don't know whether to laugh or cry!'

'And what does Ben think so far?' he asks me. He sounds so exhausted and his voice is full of heavy apology that he hasn't been able to see us yet. 'I know he's been fascinated by New York for ages so I'm hoping it's all he expected and more, but this is only the tip of the iceberg.'

I look across at Ben who is parked in front of a huge wide-screen TV playing from a selection of video games provided by the hotel, on his very last ten minutes of doing so before bed and after devouring a late-night snack of burger and fries from room service.

'He is in his very own version of Disneyland,' I tell Aidan. 'But he really needs to get to bed soon. And how are you? You sound exhausted, so please don't be worrying about not seeing us tonight. We're both pretty knackered and happy to chill out here for now and get to sleep if you're still busy.'

As much as I know every detail of how crazy his schedule has been lately, when he agrees we do just that I feel like I've been punched in the stomach, no matter how late at night it is, or how tired I am now too. My breath shortens and an outbreak of sweat dampens my skin with disappointment.

It's so late, I remind myself. It's not a 'vacation' for him here. It's his work and livelihood, and he's doing this for our future.

'I've this huge industry dinner event tomorrow evening with Bruce and I've to make an acceptance speech of sorts, but the words just aren't coming, so I'm going to be at this for another hour at least,' he explains as I do my best to understand. 'No disrespect to my aunt Mabel – I know her intentions were good – but I'd much rather I'd had more time to plan this visit, Ro. It couldn't have happened at a busier time. I'm so sorry this is happening. I really can't wait to see you and hold you again. I mean it. I'll get to you as soon as I can.'

I breathe out, trying to take it all on the chin, and when I think of how we are now only miles away instead of being oceans away, I feel a tingle inside as I think of spending time with Aidan here. Searching for the bright side, I'm also so looking forward to having a look around the city over the weekend and getting a glimpse into Mabel's early world, seeing for myself how it really is such a polar opposite to what I've always known.

I grew up not knowing for many years how long the bedroom I slept in was going to be my own before I had to move on. I lived in an apartment the size of the main bathroom here, where I had to budget for teabags and milk on a weekly basis in a system called 'sheltered living' for children coming out of care. And then I spent too many years thinking I wasn't made for any better, only to be told so on a daily basis by a husband who felt it was his duty to keep me exactly there, right where I came from.

And most of all, I never knew that anyone would want to know there was a look of joy on my face more than the joy they might feel themselves. Even though he isn't here yet, I see Aidan's mark everywhere in this magnificent suite, beyond the money and ability to buy whatever he wants. He knows I love pyjamas, and so there's a cosy new set folded in the bathroom just for me. He knows my favourite flowers are yellow roses, and had ordered a display for the table by the window for my arrival, and he knows Ben has a liking for doughnuts, so he had a variety of flavours waiting for him.

As soon as we are unpacked and Ben is asleep, I run a bubble bath and pour some bubbles to match into a champagne glass, put on a playlist that reminds me of the day we spent in Breena and our magical night in Belfast, and as I lie there soaking I notice how the soap and fragrances are all scented with my favourite bergamot. I lie there and wonder when all his kindnesses will sink in, and when I'll really believe I deserve this.

My hands shake as I lift the glass and taste the bubbles, knowing that if Mabel is watching me now, she'll be rubbing her hands with glee.

And after my bath as I lie down on heavenly crisp bed linen, watching the white voile that billows on the windows and falls like grace onto the polished mahogany floor, I close my eyes and I imagine Aidan's arms around me and his lips on my neck until I drift into a sweet slumber.

This may be the city that never sleeps, but young Ben O'Connor and I are officially exhausted and we can't wait until tomorrow.

27.

Our sunny Saturday morning in New York is filled with breakfast on the go, a little bit of shopping when I find an absolute corker of a vintage store on Fifth Avenue and pick up a quirky denim dress, and more steps down memory lane planned than we could have bargained for as we endeavour to follow the map of Mabel's life before she left America for her later years in Ballybray.

Meeting up with Aidan isn't quite as magical as I'd expected it would be when he turns up at the hotel at eleven thirty, looking as if he hasn't slept a wink.

'What's going on?' I ask as he puts his arm around my waist and pulls me in close. 'Did you sleep at all?'

'Not much,' he says, stifling a yawn. 'I'm OK. How are you? And Ben, so good to see you again, buddy! I've got something for you.'

Despite his nonchalance and exhaustion, butterflies dance in my tummy at the sight, smell and taste of him, and a surge of lust fills me up so much I could burst. He looks so handsome in a white shirt and jeans I recognize from before, but I notice he's lost a bit of weight now that I see him in the flesh. He's still to die for, with his dark, wavy hair, full mouth, and perfect smile, and his arms look like they could take on the world, but the stress of being here in such a fast-moving environment again is definitely taking its toll.

'You can't photograph New York on anything other than this,' he says, handing Ben an up-to-date proper Canon camera. 'Here, have a practice.'

Ben's jaw drops and I let out a sigh of utter euphoria as Aidan kneels down so that he's at Ben's height and adjusts the camera strap around my son's neck, and then helps him to point and shoot in a few practice runs before we set off to explore New York as Mabel once knew it.

'OK, so let's step back in time and do a Mabel Murphy tour, shall we?'

We clap our hands in excitement and I'm nearly sure I can hear Mabel's laughter in the air as we make our way outside, but just when we're about to step into John's car as he waits by the sidewalk, Aidan takes a call that will change our afternoon totally.

'He's a tough guy to pin down for a whole afternoon,' John tells me as we watch Aidan pace up and down outside the car, rubbing his forehead and clenching his fists. I barely recognize him and I don't like it at all.

He comes to the window of the car and leans inside.

'I swear I can't believe I'm saying this, but I'm going to

have to catch up with you guys later, Roisin,' he says. 'Bruce needs me on site at one of the new developments. It's going to take an hour at least. John knows the route. I'm so sorry.'

I'm glad of John's voice to patch over my disappointment as I feel tears sting my eyes. This is not what Mabel planned for us, surely. This is not even the Aidan I know at all.

'I'll take care of them, don't you worry, Mr Murphy,' John says as he slowly drives out of his parking space, leaving Aidan to flag down a yellow cab and take care of whatever emergency has come about.

'We can have our own fun,' says Ben, clicking his camera through the window.

'Yes, we can,' says John. 'That's the spirit.'

But I can't speak. I feel as if I have snakes inside me, eating me up and poisoning all my hopes and dreams of a future with a man I don't feel I even know any more.

John quickly drives us around eastern Brooklyn and shows us the house Mabel grew up in – a shuttered three-storey terrace with wooden slats and a flight of about ten steps up to the front door. I pause and try to imagine a young Mabel skipping along the sidewalk here as she made her way to school. She told me so many happy stories of her childhood here with her only sister who she lost so tragically to teenage cancer, and her hard-working mum and dad, who never got over it.

We drive by the street where Peter and Mabel spent their

early married life near North Riverdale in the Bronx, and when I look up at the window of the brown brick town-house, I picture them looking out at the world from their home, where love was always on the menu, but where the heartbreak of never having the family they craved often cracked them at the seams.

We catch a matinee on Broadway in the afternoon, making it Ben's choice, which he is over the moon with, and he predictably decides to go for *The Lion King*.

'Good choice!' exclaims John when he drops us off. 'It's one of the best.'

All the way to the theatre, he and Ben recite lines from the movie I could easily say I've seen more than a hundred times, and it makes me smile to hear how competitive they both are when trying to outdo one another on everything from quotes to song lyrics.

We are exhausted but exhilarated after the show, and when we pop by The Supper Club where Mabel became an off Broadway star as our last pit stop, it's there we meet the larger than life Penny Sanders, granddaughter of the original owner, who makes us feel like celebrities in our own right, even giving us a tour behind the scenes so we can see where Mabel would have applied her make-up, where she stepped into her most wondrous costumes, and the place where she prepared to entertain the masses.

The basement bar is very much as I'd imagined it from Mabel's description. Deep red velvet curtains frame a small stage, which hosts a baby grand piano and a small drum kit. The stage overlooks a host of little black polished round tables, framed with high-backed dark red leather chairs, and a long shiny bar runs up the side of the room, which is decorated with cocktail menus and advertisements in plastic stands for forthcoming shows. I just wish Aidan were here to experience all this with us.

'I'm so sorry,' he says in a text message, but I can't bring myself to reply.

Penny, a tall, voluptuous lady with a beaming smile, couldn't be more welcoming as she gives us a history of the club and how much they've tried to hold on to its authentic style down the years, which means it's more or less still the same as it would have been when Mabel was part of the crew here.

'She could light up a room without saying a word,' says Penny, enjoying the memories of Mabel as much as we are. 'I was only a very young child, but I'd sit right here at this very table and watch her rehearse onstage, lost in a world of her own while she practised her lines and sang her songs. Her husband Peter would slip in to the back just over there, smoke a cigarette and look on with pride. He'd come here in a yellow cab and he'd tell anyone who'd listen just how much he hated them!'

I laugh, remembering how Mabel once told me about Peter and his awkwardness around public transport, especially New York's yellow cabs. Hearing about Peter reminds me also of the lady in Sullivan's back in Breena and I wonder if she'll ever get in touch? I doubt it, but I do intend to follow it up with Aidan once he finds his way back home to Ireland, if he ever does. I'm in New York, the city he lives in, but so far he could be anywhere. We've barely spent time with him at all.

Ben is skirting the bar and I've one eye on him to make sure he doesn't touch anything he shouldn't, but Penny seems relaxed and encourages him to take pictures with his new camera.

She turns to face me again.

'You know, you look a little like Mabel did back in her heyday,' says Penny, really focusing my way now. 'She was blonde of course, whereas you are darker in colouring, but she was petite like you, Roisin. Bird-like, almost, but so delicate and pretty. She told me you reminded her of herself in many ways.'

I do a double-take.

'You already knew about me? Were you expecting us here today?' I ask her, wondering whether there's some sort of higher force spurring us on, or some extra planning on Mabel's behalf that may have anticipated this visit.

Penny glances at Ben and then back to me.

'Of course I did,' she tells us, letting us know that it's no surprise. 'Mabel and I kept in touch as often as we could.'

'Oh.'

'Oh yes,' she continues. 'I used to love receiving her letters.

She'd tell me of her handsome nephew Aidan and his life in New York and young Roisin and Ben next door to her in Ballybray. She said you'd come here together this weekend. I was very much expecting you, though I'd hoped to meet Aidan too. He couldn't make it, huh?'

Mabel, as always, is ten steps ahead and I can't find any more words to keep up.

'He has a lot of work commitments, unfortunately,' I tell Penny, sorry now that Mabel's plans haven't gone exactly as she may have liked them to.

After we've reminisced as much as our energy and hunger levels allow us, Penny walks the two of us out and we follow her down a tiny corridor which is framed with black and white prints of many of the club's stars in action. Ben trails his eyes along them, keeping them peeled in case he spots the lady herself.

'To think she walked these corridors on a daily basis all those years ago,' I say, sensing that deep connection to Mabel once more, one that I've only ever felt by being in her house back in Ballybray.

I can just imagine her teetering along in high heels, a feathered gown draped around her shoulders trailing on the floor behind her like a 70s version of Lady Gaga, and a sparkled bodice, which left just enough to the imagination, to whet the appetite of her attentive audience.

'She didn't just walk along here, she owned it!' says Penny. 'Oh, she was the life and soul of this place and lots more, so thank you so much for taking the time to pop by just like she hoped you would. I know it would have meant the world to her. She was a very special lady.'

Ben looks up at me and smiles, loving as always to hear nice things about Mabel. I put my arm around him protectively.

'And she asked me to give you this, young man,' Penny says, taking an envelope from a folder she's been carrying throughout our tour. 'She only kept a few of these in her dressing room and they were only given out to people she really thought deserved them. She asked me to give this to you, Ben. It's the very last one we have.'

Ben stares at the autographed black and white photograph of Mabel, which is dated 1979. She wears a paisley head scarf, tied to the side with tumbling curls that sit on her shoulders, and her hand, delicately poised under her chin, is decorated with a chunky silver ring on each finger.

'Wow, did she really want me to have this?' asks Ben, touching the photo in surprise and awe. 'This is awesome! Thanks, Penny.'

I read the writing that titles the glossy autographed picture, which says '*Truly Mystifying – Mabel Murphy*'. Her distinctive neat signature is written in a white space below the photo and I just know that Ben will treasure it for ever, as I will treasure the memory of being here this evening.

We say our goodbyes and, as I walk away from The Supper Club, I'm reminded of how mystifying Mabel was and still is in many, many ways. It's almost show-time for the new cast who will perform here this evening, but the ghost of Mabel Murphy still lingers, and her magic lives on in all of us.

'I honestly wasn't expecting to be called away again like that. I'm so sorry,' Aidan tells me when he meets us back at our hotel later. He has time for a very quick drink with us before leaving us again, and I can't hide my true feelings. New York has been wonderful so far, but not in the way I'd hoped it would be. We've only seen him for what seems like five minutes overall and he's all set to get going again. 'Now do you see what I mean about the pressure on me here? I'm sure John looked after you, though?'

'John knows all the words to *The Lion King*, even better than I do,' chirps Ben. 'He also knows even more about New York than I do, but I guess that's because he lives here and I don't. I know pretty much everything about Ballybray.'

'We had a nice day, all things considered,' I say to Aidan. I could say so much more, but I know I need to bite my tongue for now, especially in front of Ben. 'You would have enjoyed it. I loved seeing where Mabel came from, but I suppose you've seen all that before.'

'I have,' says Aidan, gulping back his pint of beer and trying to hide the fact that he's watching the time on his phone that sits on the table, constantly bleeping through message after message. It makes me dizzy and just a little bit bitter at how different his life is here. I don't like it at all.

'Tell me about your wildest dreams, Roisin,' he says to me when we get to our room after our drink in the hotel bar. He has to attend an event at 9.30 p.m., it's already gone 8, so time is, as always since we got here, against us. We've had his company for an hour, and it has gone in a flash.

The lights in our suite are low, the flames dance on an electronic screen in the huge hearth, and Ben is back playing on the in-house entertainment system, having declared his undying love for New York, with Mabel's photo proudly positioned on a cushion beside him.

'You're sounding a little bit like your old self at last, Mr Murphy,' I joke in reply to Aidan, who pours me a glass of champagne in anticipation of my answer.

'I'm not the same person when I'm here, Roisin,' he says, his eyebrows furrowed in front of me. 'It's a very, very different way of life. Now you see why I can't wait to get out of it.'

I nod, drunk on his presence and just wishing I could have more of the old him.

'I understand, but to answer your question about my wildest dreams,' I say, trying to stay in the moment, 'I think Ben's happiness will always come first to me, no matter what I do or where I go in life. I want to give him the life

I never had – one full of warmth, stability, security and every opportunity I can possibly bring his way.'

Aidan smiles and raises an eyebrow.

'You're so selfless,' he says to me, shaking his head a little. 'But I mean for *you*. What are your wildest dreams for *Roisin*? I know you want the best for Ben and from what I can see, you're playing a blinder, but I'd love to know where your own heart lives. What are your own desires?'

I put my tongue in my cheek, then blow out a long breath and look around the room as I think again. Being a mother does make you selfless to a degree, I believe, at least it has done for me so far, but maybe it's because I'm over-compensating for all I never had.

But what do *I* want?

'A house by the sea full of love?' I joke.

'And what else?'

I pause for thought.

'I suppose a lot of what I want comes from what I want to give to Ben,' I say, as honest as I can be for now. 'I remember when I was about fourteen years old and I was being looked after by lovely foster parents called Janet and Michael on the south side of Dublin in a place called Dalkey Island . . . I had a very pretty bedroom, and from where I sat at night doing my homework, I could often hear the couple who were taking care of me laugh downstairs as they were cooking dinner.'

I don't know why, but my eyes begin to fill up at the memory.

'I only ever wanted a happy home life,' I say, swallowing hard now to stop the emotion that threatens to choke me. 'When I opened my window in that cosy little room I could hear the sounds of the sea, and it calmed all my fears and reminded me that I was never really alone. I've wanted to go back to that feeling all my life.'

Aidan bites his lip as he listens. I'm not sure what he was expecting, but I'm pretty sure it wasn't this.

'I used to dream I had a brother or a cousin – anyone,' says Aidan, and once again I get a glimmer of the man I was so close to for so long back in Ireland. 'I pined for someone to share things with, so I know how you feel to want something so simple that everyone around you seems to have and take for granted. I just wanted a family. I wanted the simple things that money can't buy.'

I feel the need to emphasize just how much I agree with him.

'Aidan, I'm not an overly ambitious person career wise, nor will I ever strive to be as successful in business as you are, but I'm proud and I'm independent, or at least I once was before I married Jude,' I explain to him, my heart now running away with itself.

He never takes his eyes off me as I speak, drinking in my every word. Jude would have interrupted me at least twice by now, or contradicted me in some shape or form, or told me not to be so silly or dreamy.

'I'm a fairly simple person, deep down,' I explain. 'So I

suppose my real dream is never to have my heart broken again and to have a content and loving home life, as simple as that. I just want peace in my heart. It's something I've never had before.'

Aidan takes my hand and kisses it slowly. He then looks up at me beneath his black eyelashes, and I reach out to touch the dark stubble on his face with the back of my hand. His true beauty, although his good looks are very noticeable to strangers, is very much within his skin. It's in his heart and his soul, and that's what makes me like him more and more.

'What about you?' I ask him.

'The same,' he says to me. 'It sounds like we both want the same. All the rest is bullshit and noise. All of this life I have here is gloss and just so empty without someone to share it with who loves you and who you love in return. I want exactly the same as you, Roisin. And I think I've finally found it.'

The only lingering downside of what he says is the thought of leaving him again tomorrow when we go back to Ireland to our own very ordinary but quite blissful little existence. It already sears my heart, but we have one more day before we have to say goodbye. I don't want to have to say goodbye to him ever again.

'I'd better go and get ready to talk business over a late dinner,' he says, his eyes full of regret and pain now. 'I'll be in touch first thing, I promise.'

I walk him to the door and feel my tummy rumble at the thought of dinner, but there's also a slight tug of anxiety in there now and I can't quite place where it's coming from.

'Aidan?'

'Yes?'

'Will . . . will Rachel be there tonight?' I ask him, already wishing I hadn't opened my mouth as Aidan's face falls. He freezes, and the weight of stress once more lies heavily on his forehead.

'Look, Roisin, I can't lie to you,' he tells me before he leaves me for the evening. 'She will be there, yes, and I'll be in her company for business reasons, but you've nothing to worry about, and I mean that.'

I can't hide my terror at the very idea, and I feel like running away from all of this. It doesn't sit well with me at all. For just a moment in this hotel room, I got a glimmer of the Aidan I've grown so close to, but already he's gone again as he turns into the money-making, fast-talking corporate person he has been moulded to out here. I can't relate to this man at all.

He kisses me goodbye and I watch him walk away down the corridor until the elevator door closes and he disappears, waving as he does so. Then I close the door, grab my glass of champagne, and take it to the bathroom where I sit on the edge of the bath and have a good cry out of Ben's earshot.

All the comfort of love and excitement from our time

together today feels somehow under threat, and the loneliness that grips me in this big, anonymous city makes me want to pack my bags right now and run straight back home. I imagine Aidan and Rachel seated together at dinner, maybe her hand on his leg, her lipstick on her champagne glass, her perfume in the air.

I imagine there might be music in the background, and maybe they'll play their favourite song, and I suddenly feel like I'm in the wrong place at the wrong time. It doesn't feel like Aidan's relationship with Rachel is over, not like it did when it was just the two of us in Ballybray. I feel out of place, uninvited, and a bit silly as I sit here amidst a luxurious lifestyle that could never and will never be me.

I can't believe I'm thinking this way, but all of a sudden I've the most terrible hunch I'll be glad to leave New York tomorrow. I look around at all this extravagance Aidan has arranged for us and it doesn't feel like me at all. I'm a fish out of water here.

I love nature and fresh air, I love the beach and the sea and the wind in my face. I love vintage, and second-hand clothes that have a story to tell. I love creating something from nothing and driving around laughing and singing in my pick-up truck with its battered and bruised rusty edges. I love the things that money can't buy, like laughter and a hug and the feeling of the sun on your face.

I love the Aidan Murphy I got to know back in Ballybray,

not this slick, souped-up New York, cardboard cut-out version.

It's going to be a long, lonely night, and all of a sudden I can't wait to get home.

28.

'So, the awards ceremony and big contract pitch is at the Fitzwilliam Hotel on October 28 now, instead of November,' says Aidan, as we share our final supper in New York early on Sunday evening in a restaurant where the menu caters for Ben's love of Italian food, and I'm treated to a martini straight from the freezer. 'It's a Thursday evening and sounds like it's going to be pretty intense. I'll be glad to get it behind me.'

'October 28th? That would have been Mabel's eightieth birthday,' I remind Aidan, who nods as he enjoys his food. I'm doing my best to deny the heaviness in my stomach and the flurry of questions that run through my head as to how the big dinner went the night before, but so far all I've had in return are very vague answers as he passes it off as 'nothing exciting' and 'just part of the job' and 'another thing ticked off the list'.

Maybe it *was* just 'part of the job', but to leave us like that in a hotel in New York after travelling all this way while he dines out with his ex-wife and her father just doesn't sit well and leaves a very sour taste in my mouth. And yes I know our visit was unexpected, and yes I know he has a very full-on life to sort out here, but I don't think I'll ever forget how lonely I felt last night, long after I'd filled my emptiness with room service and lay awake as each hour ticked by, wondering what he was doing and more importantly, if he was doing it with Rachel.

'I'm so glad it's being pulled back to October, and I'm trying not to get too carried away with it being Mabel's birthday as I think that might be a good omen,' he tells me, wolfing down his meal. 'It's probably the biggest Irish– American contract pitch for ex-pats there is in the city, so it's a pretty big deal to me to get it for Bruce, and then I'm free from all my commitments to him. We're nearly there, Roisin. Just another wee while and I'll be out of their clutches, once and for all.'

Seeing his enthusiasm I can't help but lighten up a little and I'm already picturing the scene, Aidan in his smart tux, walking up onstage to accept the contract to the nods of approval from his peers in the construction world, as cameras flash in his direction and he accepts it with such gratitude, then escapes to celebrate his freedom at long last.

'Do you have to make an actual speech if you win?' asks Ben in between slurping his spaghetti. 'You should really start practising now if you do. When I won a medal for saying a poem at school, I practised every night for months in front of the mirror, didn't I, Mum?'

I ruffle Ben's hair and pat his little shoulder.

'You sure did, Ben,' I say, in full agreement. 'Practice makes perfect, isn't that what they say, so Aidan, you'd better get working on that speech right away.'

By the time we've finished our meal I have shaken off any of my inner conspiracy theories that have threatened my entire last night and day in this magical city, and I start to view our future with some hope again.

Aidan, I guess, has done his best with his time while we were here. I knew he was coming back here to New York in June to sort out his business, I knew that business meant dealing with not only his male counterparts but also Rachel as a business partner, and I knew that Mabel's mission to bring Ben and me here this weekend was totally out of the blue and very short notice to someone as busy as Aidan.

We didn't have any time alone to share together intimately, but Ben and I have made some wonderful memories, and when I see the smile on Ben's face as he skips alongside Aidan down the busy street, I remind myself just how far we've come already and how patient I'm going to have to be to see us through until that wonderful date in October when our true future can finally begin.

I hold that thought as I walk a few steps behind Aidan and Ben, unable to hide now the smile on my face as I watch them chatter as they walk, and also as Aidan points out buildings and monuments of interest along the way. We only have an hour or so left before we leave for the airport and journey back to our life in Ballybray, so I stop briefly at a newspaper stand we pass to buy some souvenirs.

'How much for the cute little teddy bear?' I ask the vendor, who is rubbing his hands at the prospect of the sale. He has Statue of Liberty branded merchandise of all shapes and sizes, T-shirts, postcards, posters, and coasters, but for some reason my eye is drawn to a fluffy white bear with an American flag on his belly. I want something to remember our stay here, and I think he'll do the job.

Aidan and Ben stop in their tracks ahead of me, noticing me when I wave in their direction, and they make their way back towards me as Ben eagerly spots a keyring of the Statue of Liberty.

'I'm getting one for Gino,' he declares, taking out his little wallet, which is still stuffed with dollar bills from Mabel's generous donation.

I banter with Aidan when he tries to pay for the teddy against my will, and then, just as he's about to hand over the dollars to the hungry and eager vendor, the world stops around me at the sight of a photograph on the front page of a business newspaper.

'Wait a minute, I've changed my mind!' I say to Aidan, stopping him from sealing the deal.

In slow motion, I turn my head towards him. He hasn't noticed it yet and when I force my eyes back towards the multiple images of the same photo printed in colour, with a headline that reads 'Bowen and Murphy – New York's Property Power Couple', I honestly think I'm going to be sick.

The photo of course is of Aidan and Rachel at the 'no big deal' dinner the night before, dressed in their finery as he kisses her on the cheek for the camera, with his eyes closed. I take a second to absorb her look as the world stops spinning around me.

Rachel is a world away from me, and I can see that in the photo I was the last thing on Aidan's mind. She is all solid gold jewellery, subtle sophistication, and bags of glamour in her knee-skimming black dress, a perfectly pert gym-toned bottom, miles of legs, and skyscraping designer shoes on her feet that will probably never be worn again. She oozes money and style. Her glossy red lips form a perfect 'O', and her bejewelled hand goes to her perfectly proportioned cleavage, while Aidan, with his eyes closed, plants a puckered-up kiss on her cheek.

I'm dizzy and I can't speak.

My heart is thumping and I can feel sweat patches form under my arms in the vintage denim dress I bought yesterday, which now feels frumpy, and I'm sure I can smell mothballs from it. I put my hand out for Ben, to try to steady my nerves, but the searing sensation I feel in my heart just won't go away, and I realize it's the pain of deep emotional hurt.

Aidan, who by now has spotted the newspaper too, is frozen, unable to speak, and it's as though he has stabbed me in the back, only right in front of my eyes.

Ben browses along the stand, lost thankfully in a world of his own, while I do my best to stand up straight in deep shock at what I've just witnessed. I hand the teddy bear back to the vendor and walk away, taking Ben by the hand and pulling him along beside me.

'What's wrong, Mum? Why didn't you take the bear?' he asks, but I can't answer him yet. Bile rises in my gut and I can feel every hair on my arms and on the back of my neck as shock engulfs every inch of me, inside and out.

'Roisin, please don't read this the wrong way!' Aidan pleads as he plays catch-up behind us, trying to reach out to me physically, but I subtly shrug him away. I'm afraid if he comes any closer I might vomit, as the meal from earlier washes around my stomach as if it's on a spin cycle, and my eyes blur in shock. 'It was all for publicity! You know how these things work, Roisin! Come on! Hear me out at least!'

'Ben, try and keep up, honey. We've a flight to catch,' I say, unable even to recognize my own voice. 'We don't want to miss our plane back home.'

I feel as if I'm drunk or drugged as I weave through people on the street, and when we reach Aidan's car, I beg myself to stay composed for Ben's sake. This is not how I want to end his dream-like trip to New York.

I think of Mabel's photo framed in his little suitcase that lies in the boot of the car, the Statue of Liberty trinket he clutches in his hand and the way he hasn't stopped humming along to the songs of *The Lion King* that he says won't leave his head.

I must stay composed. I must find a stiff upper lip until I get away from here, and most of all, I must learn once and for all in life to always listen to my gut instinct and to never, ever believe a man when he says he loves me ever again.

The journey to the airport, which Aidan insists on driving to himself even though I wanted to get a taxi, consists of him pretending everything is absolutely fine in front of Ben, and me biting my tongue from saying exactly what I'm thinking and ruining Ben's whole trip because of it.

'When can we come back again, Aidan?' Ben chirps up from the back seat as we do our best to weave through Sunday night traffic in New York. 'Do you think we could come and live here someday, Mum? I really liked our hotel room. The bed there's *so* much bigger than my own at home. And we didn't do the helicopter ride, but Aidan says we can do that next time, didn't you, Aidan?'

And to think that just last night, as Aidan and I shared our deepest fears and dreams in the hotel suite, I'd actually contemplated that moving here to be with him might be an option one day. It was a fleeting thought, and one I'd have to think long and hard about, but what's a year in a lifetime with someone you love?

I can't even answer my son as I'm afraid of being sarcastic

and hurtful, and as much as I'm so disappointed in Aidan, I still can't bring myself to hurt him before we say goodbye in front of Ben.

Aidan is trying so hard to make eye contact at every given opportunity when we stop at lights or when traffic gets heavy, but I can't pretend that nothing has changed. He has been spending cosy nights out with his so-called ex-wife, as if they're still together and was quoted in the article as saying she was 'his rock following a recent family bereavement in Ireland' and 'the one person he could turn to when the chips are down in life'.

I feel so sick.

'Can we do "best parts", Mum?' Ben asks me, making my heart bleed as he remembers a long held tradition of ours where we'd sum up our day after being somewhere new with our very own highlights. 'My favourite part was *The Lion King*! Actually, no, it was definitely the big store – what did you call it again? Spacy's?'

'Macy's,' I say, trying to add some sparkle to my voice, which is undeniably monotone.

'And Mabel's work place, it was cool,' says Ben as he grips the window, drinking in his last taste of New York. 'Yes, that's my top three. What are yours, Mum? I bet you loved the shopping best.'

I manage to fake a smile when I turn around to look at Ben, who doesn't even give me time to answer. I just know he is going to milk this for weeks when he gets back to school.

'And I can't wait to give Gino his present,' he continues. 'He isn't going to believe that I saw the real Statue of Liberty, but this little one will have to do him.'

'I'm sure he'll love it,' I tell my son, blinking back tears as I look out through the passenger window of Aidan's black Jaguar. 'You're a good friend, Ben.'

I feel Aidan's pleading stare on the back of my neck, but I just can't look his way. I bite my fist and watch as the New York skyline flies by and says goodbye to us, reminding me of how alien I feel here right now.

I can't wait to get home.

When we get to the airport, the reality of saying goodbye to Aidan again, despite my inner heartache, hits me like a ton of bricks, but it's a different type of sadness from our last goodbye.

This is final, this is heart-stopping, and this is as though my whole future has been ripped out from beneath my feet without warning or without giving me time to catch my breath.

I can see in Aidan's eyes that this is killing him too, but I can't bear to be physically near him right now. He reaches out for a hug from Ben and I watch them embrace. I wonder if he can really explain his way out of this, and even if he does, if I can ever forget how seeing that photograph and reading that article made me feel today.

'I'm so sorry, Roisin,' he whispers into my ear when it's time for our final farewell, but I can't listen to him now. 'I know we can't talk this through right now, but I want only you, and I *can* explain everything, I promise.'

I look up at him with glistening eyes.

'Save your promises for "your rock", Aidan. You know, the wife who got you through such hard times,' I say through a false grin and gritted teeth. 'God, I've been so gullible. Now I know why you weren't keen on us coming here, and I feel so ridiculously fooled and so stupid. Goodbye, Aidan. I'm so bloody disappointed. You've broken my heart all over again. Goodbye.'

'I'm sorry!' he says, looking right into my eyes with pleading sorrow. 'I'm so sorry, Roisin, but believe me I can and I will explain if and when you want to listen.'

I feel like I've been once again led into a fog, just like I was with Jude, where I was so trusting and vulnerable, so willing to believe that I was loved, when all the time I was being hoodwinked again. The searing sting of embarrassment burns a hole in my stomach and I hear Jude's laughter in my head at how easily I was tricked again. I see him shaking his head, smirking at me, telling me how easily lured I am by the promise of the love and security that I've been so desperate for all my life.

'Never,' I say, smiling through my tears, then I take Ben's hand. 'No man will ever hurt me like this again, and I know it's clichéd, but I did think you were different. I've been such a fool.'

We both walk away, without stopping or turning around

as we go through the security gates, and when we are finally out of Aidan's sight I want to scream and cry at how much my love for him is tearing me apart. But I can't do that now. I have to keep wearing this mask for my son's sake and that's the only thing that stops me from giving in and breaking down right here, right now in this busy airport terminal.

It's like a tsunami of grief; it's as if my heart has cracked open a little more every time I'm treated this way by someone, and I don't know how much more of it I can handle in my life.

My heart can't take any more bruising. It just can't do this any more.

29.

'Yes, you can,' Camille instructs me as we sort out a new line of clothing she's ordered in from London a few days later. 'You *can* do this. You're not giving up on this, no way. I won't let you, and neither will Aidan. What does he say? Have you at least heard his side of the story? There's bound to be a story behind the story if you get what I'm saying. Things work differently in New York, and business is business.'

I slip a rose-gold beaded dress onto a hanger, but it keeps sliding off, no matter how I try to manoeuvre it, which doesn't help with my darkening mood. The sun is splitting the trees outside and my anxiety levels aren't up to much, meaning I can't focus on the job at hand at all, never mind trying to patch up my broken love life. I can't concentrate on anything. When I'm at home I'm tetchy and irritable, and when I'm at work my mind is all over the place.

'I'm not taking any of his calls to hear about any of his business,' I explain to Camille, who looks on with such pity. 'Camille, my heart broke, and I swear I felt like he was in complete denial of what I was looking at right in front of me. It was so hurtful. I don't get it. How could he live such a lie to me? We talked every day and we messaged right up until my bedtime every night for the whole summer since he left, but I guess the time difference allowed him to play his very clever balancing act between the two of us. I'm so gutted. I really thought he was different, you know. I really did!'

I drop the gold dress on the floor again, and this time I lean my head back and count to ten to stop myself from totally breaking down. Since I got back from America I have a very short fuse, and I've even begun talking to myself when I'm at home, trying to work my way out of destroying the best thing that has ever happened to me.

'It won't work out so there's no point wasting your precious time for any longer,' says one voice in my ear, while the other tells me to hang tight. 'Just because everything else turned to mud in your life, Roisin, doesn't mean it has to do so for ever. Grab this by the horns and fight for the answers. What would Mabel say?'

'I really wish we could get over this,' Aidan tells me one Friday night when I give in and take his call. He even suggests he books a flight to come to see me for a long weekend to try to mend things. 'What do you want me to do, Roisin? I can call Rachel and ask her to tell you everything if it makes you feel better? Is that what you want? Just tell me what will make this all go away and I'll do it!'

I pace the floor of the kitchen, my veins bubbling with frustration at how I don't know how to get rid of all these insecurities and the self-doubt that is running through my head and keeping me awake at night. I picture Rachel in my head, comparing her tall, willowy figure to my ordinary, average Joe height even when in heels; her tanned and toned legs, and her solid gold trimmings. She looks as if she hasn't had a day of hardship in her whole life. She looks as if she was born with one of those gold bracelets on her arm. How could Aidan love someone like her and then claim to love someone the very opposite, like me?

'That's like saying how could you marry someone like Jude and then be with someone like me?' he retorts, scoring a point that makes absolute sense.

I hate the person I'm becoming, but I know it all stems from the long distance between us and how it feels like for ever since we said goodbye in New York. The days are dragging on and on, my mood is dropping deeper and deeper, and I'm becoming a person I don't know any more, or like for that matter. I even went into Mabel's house and scoured the place for the newspaper clippings of Aidan and his life before me, to really test my own limits, and when I read about him and his 'former beauty queen wife' it almost sent me over the edge. It's as if I've pressed the self-destruct button and I've lost the instructions on how to switch it off again.

'Do you really want us to break up over this?' Aidan asks,

when I've pushed him as far as I can, asking questions about Rachel that bear no relevance to where we are now and how far we've come. 'Just yes or no, Roisin, because I'm doing everything I can here to convince you that this is all going to be worth it one day. It won't be like this for ever. I don't intend it to be, and I'm sure you don't either.'

'We can't "break up" when we were never really together!' I say to him, unable to look at his face on my phone screen. 'You're so tied in with Rachel still, and I'm not doing this any more, no matter what I feel for you. I can't!'

I want him so badly and I love him so deeply, but it's killing me and it's making me into a monster. I want to run away from it all, and that's not good. But most of all I want to run to him. I've no idea what to do.

I've never wanted to be with someone so badly, yet the challenges it brings and the weaknesses it brings out in me are so ugly and I hate it.

He sounds as shocked as I am, but the vulnerable state I've driven myself into is a one-way street and I've just hit a roadblock. I bite my lip. I can barely breathe.

'Roisin, do you love me?' he asks, his own breath stilted and uneven.

My heart stops when I hear the 'L' word mentioned. Do I love him? My God I do. I love him so much and it's killing me to do so.

'Because I love you,' he says, his eyes glistening now. 'I love you and I can't believe you're doing this! Maybe if we

300

see each other again soon we can work this all out? Trying to sort it out by phone is a nightmare, so if you just give me a chance to get there . . .'

I sniffle and wipe my puffy red eyes. I want to see him, of course I do. I want him to hold me so close and take all this pain away, but the thought of saying goodbye again and sliding down into this hole of despair every time is breaking my heart over and over and over again.

'You know, you're not that person any more,' he tells me, a bit more determined now when he realizes I can't find the words to answer him in the way he'd want me to. 'You think that everyone is out to hurt you or destroy you, but not everyone is like that, Roisin. Not everyone is Jude or your mother. There are plenty of people like Mabel or Janet and Michael in this world, if you are just brave enough to let them in. I love you, but you've made it crystal clear lately that you aren't prepared to fight for this, even though I'm the one trying to come up with solution after solution. I hope you have the sense to change your mind, but in the meantime you need to decide what the hell it is you want in life, because at the minute it doesn't feel as if it's me.'

He hangs up and I sit there in silence, wondering what I have just done. I claw the carpet on my living-room floor. I crawl on my hands and knees and beg for the strength to get me out of this self-destructive fog.

I am numb. My heartbeat slows down as I pull myself up off the floor. I've no idea what to do next or who to turn to. Everything is silent and numb. It's too late to call Camille, and I can't think of anyone else who cares.

I don't have anyone else. I've blocked out the world to protect my own heart, and yet here I am, feeling it smash into pieces once again. Why can't I believe Aidan when he says that we can make this work? Why can't I just enjoy what we have instead of always wanting more? Why am I so afraid that just like Jude, he will hurt me or leave me a broken mess?

I stumble into the kitchen, where I reach to the top shelf in the cupboard and I take down the bottle of whisky that's only here on reserve for cold and flu season. My fingers slip on the glass I take from the shelf below, then I pour myself a hefty measure and I sink it in one.

I hate whisky, but right now I hate myself even more.

The next morning when I wake up feeling like a foggy mess and I've got a missed call and a text message from a number I don't recognize, I'm not in the mood to read it never mind reply. But I hold my phone out and squint to read the message.

'Hi Roisin, you may remember I spoke with you briefly in Sullivan's Bar in Breena a few months ago and you left your number. I'll try calling you again, but I thought I'd text to say that I'm ready to talk now about the Murphy brothers. It's time for the truth to come out at long last. I look forward to hearing from you in your own time. Thanks, Bernie Sullivan.'

Maybe it's my rising anger, maybe it's the idea of cold revenge, or maybe it's a hungover decision I'll later regret, but I type in an instant reply and then toss the phone onto the empty pillow beside me, before willing myself back to some extra minutes of sleep before Ben wakes up.

'Wrong number,' I tell the mysterious Bernie from Sullivan's in my vengeful response. 'I hope you find who you're looking for. Sorry, but it's definitely not me.'

AUTUMN

30.

For the next few weeks as balmy September days slip by into autumn and the days become shorter, I slide deeper and deeper into a darkness that engulfs every part of my existence. I ignore Aidan's calls, I turn my head when I hear Camille's voice of concern, I isolate myself from anyone or anything that doesn't involve existing in a world of feeding Ben, making sure his homework is done now that he's back to school, and waiting until he is asleep so I can self-medicate in order for me to sleep too.

It's only when Ben walks in one night wanting a drink of water that I see in his face a mirror image of myself at his age and it scares me enough to put the bottle down and take a whole new approach to how I'm going to get on with a life without Aidan.

I have a glass in my hand, I'm mid pour when the innocence of his voice rings in my ear and launches me back to reality and the fear that I could very easily turn into my mother.

'I can't wait to tell Aidan that I jumped Mr Magoo today in the paddock!' he says as he pours water from the tap.

The flush of water hitting his glass and then splashing on the sink rings in my ears and a wave of shame washes over me. 'He bet me when we were in New York that I wouldn't be able to jump by the next time I saw him, and Aidan said he'd give me a ten-pound note all for myself if I can. When is he coming to see us, Mum? And why is the *For Sale* sign back up next door? I thought he wanted to keep Mabel's house for ever so he'd be close to us?'

I push the glass away and stare at the wall. What am I becoming? Why am I destroying everything I've worked so hard for since I came here? Why am I unrecognizable, if not to my own son just yet, but to myself when I look in the mirror? I can't eat, I'm losing weight by the day, and I need a dose of alcohol to cradle me to sleep at night. I sniff, I close my eyes tightly and then I turn to face Ben with a cheery smile.

'It's time you were asleep, mister,' I say, walking him back upstairs where I tuck him into bed, praying he doesn't smell the whisky on my breath and trying to ignore that I too had noticed the *For Sale* sign in the garden. I lean into his little neck, nuzzling into his warm sweetness and inhaling his familiarity and scent of home.

'Are you OK, Mum?' he asks me, his voice croaky with tiredness. 'You seem really sad. It scares me when you're sad.'

I wish I could pull myself together. I know I have to pull myself together. I told Aidan I wanted everything for Ben that I didn't have myself in childhood and yet here I am, showing my darling son the opposite, causing him to worry about me when it should always, always be the other way around.

'Don't you worry about a thing, my precious,' I say, kissing his forehead and tucking him in tightly. 'Mummy is fine and loves you very much, so you don't have to worry about me, ever.'

He looks up at me, with longing and raw vulnerability in his eyes.

'You love Aidan too,' he says, reading my whole sorry set-up with a lot more intuition than I could ever give him credit for. 'I like how you smile when Aidan is around. It makes me feel happy when you're happy too. It makes me feel a bit fuzzy inside.'

I swallow, I smile, and I ruffle my baby boy's hair, then I go to the top of the stairs and I can't go any further, so I sit there and recall how I used to do the very same thing when I lived with Jude and when I needed to find answers from within.

I'd sit on the top stair of our marital home and I'd will myself to have the strength to make the changes I needed to. I would hug my own waist and rock back and forth, breathing deeply and deliberately as my mind raced with possibilities. Where would I go if I packed up and left him? What would I do next? What would the neighbours say? What would Jude do without us? Would Ben ever forgive me?

And now, as I sit here in a similar position in a place that has been a lifeline to me after a life of hell, I know that this is similar in that I've only myself to blame for this loneliness and despair I've found myself in, because this time I can't blame Jude or Aidan. I'm inflicting a lot of this upon myself with my late nights wallowing in self destruction.

My spare bedroom door where I once loved to escape when life was going so well has been closed for weeks now and I've had no interest in opening it again. My violin, which Mabel had presented to me with such determination and delight, hangs on the wall in there, overlooking unfinished pots and blocks of beeswax that were once going to be candles.

I hear Jude's voice, laughing at my failure again. He had such a distinctive laugh. Some might have called it hearty, but to me it was always laced with gloating and a warning that he was winning again as always.

'*You actually thought you'd be able to find a life better than the one you had with me,*' I hear him saying, his mouth twisting into a threatening shape of disgust with bullets of spittle hitting me in the face. '*You're second-hand goods, Roisin O'Connor. You're a reject. A scrapheap kid, and without me you'll go right back to where I found you, just where you deserve to be. On the scrapheap! No one will ever want you! Even your own family didn't want you.*'

I hear Mabel's voice, cross and angry at how I'm turning into that woman who believed him again – that weak, broken person who thought the world would always be against her and that it was as much as she deserved.

'Push those shoulders back and stand up straight, for goodness' sake, Roisin,' I hear her American sing-song voice with a pinch of warning that only she could get away with. *'You can't and won't settle for anything but the best and you'll get it if you work hard and be counted! You are worthy of just as much as the next person in this world. Prove it to yourself! Prove it to your mother and to Jude, who both dragged you down to this level in the first place!'*

I feel my blood pumping now and I pull myself up using the bannister for support. The whisky in my system makes me wobble ever so slightly and the smell on my breath now makes me sick. I stand there, my heartbeat throbbing in my ears as the room spins around me, all these voices in my head sobering me up and driving me on.

I hear Ben.

'You seem really sad. It scares me when you're sad. When I see you happy, it makes me happy too.'

And then Aidan.

'You think that everyone is out to hurt you or destroy you, but not everyone is like that, Roisin. Not everyone is Jude or your mother. There are plenty of people like Mabel or Janet and Michael in this world, if you are just brave enough to let them in.'

But loudest of all is my own voice, and it's one that shouts so loudly now I have to block my ears with my hands. And that voice tells me to open up the spare-room door and do something useful to tire out my overactive brain so I can sleep without alcohol to ease my pain.

So I turn the handle, I switch on the light, and I put on some classical music to ease my soul. I slip my apron on over my pyjamas and I sit down at my pottery wheel where I smack a lump of clay into the centre, splash it with my fingers with water from the bowl and I pump the pedal to make the wheel spin as I focus on the wet, moving mixture and mould it with my fingertips and the heel of my palm. I close my eyes, letting the familiarity ground and soothe me, and I don't stop until I've a new creation ready for a new day.

I need to get my life together again. I need to change my own world so that I can once again create things in this little room, and then I can start to believe in myself again. But as the night draws in and the clock ticks back the hours, I can't help wondering what Aidan is doing now, so many miles away in New York, where his world has crashed down on him just like mine has.

I lift my phone. I want to call him so badly, but I can't destroy myself any more than I've already done, and I've already made my decision.

I can't let any man win me over like that again. I've been bitten, torn, lied to and ripped apart far too many times.

I leave my workshop and go to the bathroom where I wash my hands, unable to meet my own reflection in the mirror above the basin. I never thought I'd sink as low as this again and I get a horrifying flashback to when I was a very young child and my mother disappeared during the night in search of a bottle, leaving me wandering around the house alone, looking for her, crying in the darkness, with nothing except my own echo to keep me company.

I'm that child again. I'm wandering around, with no idea where to go next.

I fall onto my bed and pray for sleep, hoping as I drift off that tomorrow might bring the answers I need so desperately before I reach rock bottom and forget how to bounce back again.

Aidan calls once a week for the whole month of September, determined to keep trying to convince me to hear him out, but our conversations are like taking a knife and slowly carving deep patterns on my heart every time I hear his voice.

'I miss you and love you,' is how he ends every call, during which he tells me about his day and asks about mine, and I squeeze my eyes tightly with my fingers to stop the river of pain from flowing when I hear him speak.

'You'll be fine,' I answer him. 'You're destined for big things over there with the Bowen family. You'll be fine.'

It was Camille's idea that I give in and pick up his calls again when she found me in the garden one morning, unable to make it into work because I was simply too exhausted to function.

'Ignoring the one person you want to talk to more than anyone isn't the way out of this,' she told me, coaxing me to eat the end of summer strawberries and organic yoghurt with honey she'd bought in a healthfood shop, along with bags of other goodies in her effort to help me find my lost appetite again. 'I know you don't want to forgive him, Roisin, but just see if some light conversation with him will give you some focus. It doesn't take a rocket scientist to see how cutting him out is affecting you.'

'Have you been speaking to him?' I asked her, my eyes wild but heavy with tiredness.

'I haven't, darling,' she said, putting her hand on mine, which looked cold and pale in comparison to her tanned Italian skin. I felt ugly and unworthy of her attention and wished she would give up and leave me alone. 'But I'm sure he is very, very worried and just wants to talk to you. Roisin, Aidan loves you deeply and he misses you as much as you're missing him. Give him a chance to explain properly and maybe you'll see that?'

She bent her head down to try to look into my eyes, which were now staring at the daisies that covered the lawn at the back of my house. Mabel's new gardener, employed from afar by Aidan of course, has offered to cut the grass for me on numerous occasions, but I politely refused, partly because its wildness marks my own state of mind. I hadn't washed my hair in days and my love of pyjamas had gone a little bit too far as they were all I seem to want to wear.

A pile of washing was cleverly disguised in a kitchen cupboard, and it was only when Camille filled the sink and washed some dishes that I realized how neglected the whole house had become.

'He's too caught up with his life in America,' I told Camille, even though the thought of him makes my partially empty stomach lurch. 'It's too complicated for me right now, but yes, I'll speak to him. We can still be friends, even if it makes me sad to think how much I'd hoped we could be so much more.'

Camille shook her curls and we stared at the garden together.

'You know,' she piped up just when I was getting used to the silence. 'When I first met Paddy, I thought I'd died and gone to heaven. Like you, I'd been let down and broken by a rotter beforehand and I believed that no one would want me.'

I leaned back in my wooden garden chair and felt the September sun on my face, listening to what new revelation Camille was going to come out with to knock me into shape when it came to my own life.

'I pushed him away at first,' she said, laughing now at the memory. 'But he persisted. The more I pushed him, the more he insisted that he wasn't going away and that he would prove me wrong. He told me I was the most beautiful woman he had ever met at a time when I felt frumpy and down, but it was only when I could look in the mirror and see what he saw that I knew I could believe him and give our love a chance.'

I opened my eyes and looked across at Camille.

'Aidan Murphy can't change your mind,' she told me. 'And I can't change your mind by coming here and making you eat when you don't want to, or convince you to talk to him when you don't want to. Only you can do that, Roisin. So, sit in your pyjamas all day every day if you want, skip work if that's what makes you feel good, and drink your whisky until it comes out of your ears, because until you can see what I can see, you'll never do a thing about it.'

She stood up, holding her coffee cup with both hands.

I realized right then by looking at her with her dangly green earrings, her multi-coloured Moroccan style dress, her freshly applied make-up and her present way of thinking, that she was in a totally different world to me. I was lost and trapped in a dense fog, and she was right. It was only me who could find my way out of it.

I realized that it was never going to be all about what Jude said, it wasn't about blaming my mother, it's not about Ben or Mabel or Aidan.

It's all down to me.

At the end of September I unroll the map of Ireland I keep in a drawer up in my spare room and I pin it on the wall. I slip a hairpin out of my hair and close my eyes, and then

I stab the map with my makeshift weapon and open my eyes in anticipation.

I do it again, and again and again, but no matter how many times I try to replicate my bravery from before, it just isn't happening. I don't feel inspired by any of the places I land on, nor do I feel the desire to find out anything about them, and it's only when I tear the map with frustration that I realize, I've no idea where I want to go next, but what I do know for sure is that my chapter here in Ballybray has ended. I need to move on.

So I pull on a dress from my bedroom floor, I brush through my sticky hair, pull it back into a bun, and leave the house quickly so I can be back in time for Ben coming home from school.

'You might remember me,' I tell the ruddy-faced estate agent who picks up on my out-of-town accent immediately. 'I bought No. 3 Teapot Row from you about five years ago.'

He puts down a brochure he is holding and looks up at me over his glasses. He is almost retirement age, I'm guessing, but dresses like he's ten years older, with trousers that go way up his back, held up by braces, and a shirt that needs to be tucked in at the sides.

'Of course I remember you, and if all my customers were as decisive as you are, Miss O'Connor, I'd have a lot more hair on my head,' he says, laughing out loud at his own joke.

'I'd like to put my house on the market,' I tell him, barely able to hold back the sadness of my decision as my eyes well up at the thought of another new beginning. 'I'd like to put it on the market straight away. I want to leave Ballybray.'

31.

'But where will we go?' Ben asks me over breakfast the next morning when I tell him my plans to pack up once more and start again. 'I don't want to leave Ballybray. I want to stay here with Gino and my friends at school.'

My head races with so many options and paths to choose in life next, but I know what Ben is saying is true and that his happiness has to be paramount in whatever I decide upon.

'Look, nothing is for definite yet, but I just think it would be nice to maybe live by the sea?' I suggest. 'Gino lives out in Dunfanaghy, which is just a few miles away. Oh, I'm sorry, Ben, but I just think that with Mabel gone almost a year now, there are too many memories here that I'd rather try and move on from. We can remember her always, but I'm finding it hard to be here without her.'

Ben walks to the sink and rinses out his cereal bowl, puts it on the draining board with a little more force than he probably should and looks at me with tear-filled eyes.

'You were happy in Ballybray when Aidan was here,

weren't you?' he says, pleading with me. 'Why doesn't he come here any more? Why did he have to go back to stupid New York anyhow? I hate New York and I hate you for ruining everything! It's not fair!'

I stand there open-mouthed as he grabs his coat from the hallway and makes his way towards the front door with his schoolbag dwarfing him on his back as always. He is eleven years old now and has much more to say than the little six-year-old I once led by the hand up the garden path outside.

'Ben!' I call after him, following him up the hallway. 'Ben, don't run off on me like that!'

But he has already slammed the door behind him and is making his own way to school. I should go after him and try to explain more, but it's safe for him to walk down to the village this term, and he's been enjoying the independence so far, so instead I plonk down on the sofa, curl into a ball, and cry for some direction.

Damn you Aidan Murphy and your precious business in America. Damn you for making me love you like I still do.

The days pass by in a hazy blur and, as the season changes fully into autumn in October with the most magnificent display of red, gold, green and amber leaves falling on the footpaths of Ballybray, as always my mind turns to Mabel and the prospect of her final message.

In just over a month it will be a full year now since we last saw her, and the gaping hole she's left in our lives becomes more evident as each day passes as her house lies empty next door.

I go through each day like a zombie, trying to ignore the symbolic *For Sale* signs that sit now in each of our gardens on Teapot Row. Their presence irritates, frightens and excites me all at the same time, but most of all they make me feel so sad as I prepare to close up another chapter and start again.

'*With every new beginning, there has to be an end,*' Mabel used to tell me so often. '*It's never too late to start all over again if you feel it's for the best.*'

And Mabel was right of course. There are no rules, and nothing lasts for ever. So I go to work and I function on autopilot, and I do my best to ignore the pull and tug at my heart every time I think of Aidan, how he used to make me feel when he held me, the laughs and fun we had together, and the hopes and dreams we'd planned ahead. The pain hits me worst on Sundays when I remember our mornings on the beach and I sometimes find the longing for him so hard I can barely breathe.

On this particular Sunday, as the autumn wind howls down the chimney and the rain pelts onto the window, Ben and I are sitting here in the living room when I receive a message that makes my heart skip a beat.

'Fancy a walk on the beach?' it reads and I do a double take when I see that it's from Aidan. 'Meet me there in an hour in our usual spot? Please?'

My jaw drops and I look around me, searching for answers

as if they'll jump out from somewhere and hit me in the face, waking me up and letting me know this isn't some cruel trick of fantasy.

It's Aidan.

'Hang on! Are you in Ireland?' I text him back quickly, baffled to my very core as pins and needles of anticipation run through my veins.

'Quick visit,' he tells me. 'Please meet me there if you can.'

Stunned yet excited, confused yet exhilarated, I ask Ben to get ready, but he insists he is OK to hang out and watch some TV while I go to see Aidan.

'Did you know he was here?' I ask him, confused now as to how I could have been so oblivious to all this.

'Yes, I saw him this morning when you were still sleeping,' he tells me as my eyes widen. 'He got here really early so we had tea in Mabel's kitchen and he asked me not to tell you he was here. He said he would surprise you later.'

I'm in a daze as I clamber around the house, almost falling over myself as I quickly try to find suitable footwear for a rainy day on the beach, a raincoat that will keep me warm, and a waterproof hat to fight off the elements. I give Ben strict instructions not to touch the cooker or anything electrical while I'm away, listing off rules that I can say without thinking for times like this when I've to pop out briefly without him.

'I'm not a baby, Mum,' he tells me. 'And I do have a phone now, so just go and talk to Aidan. Maybe you'll be happy again when you do.'

I instantly forget my hurry and rush to my son's side, crouch down beside him where he sits on the armchair and I shake my head emphatically.

'Ben, it's not as simple as that, honey,' I explain to him. 'It's not just being away from Aidan that's making me unhappy, and being with him today briefly isn't going to make me happy. I've a lot of things I need to take stock of right now. Please don't think that seeing him is going to be like a magic wand that will make everything better again. I can't promise you that, I'm sorry.'

'You're always *sorry* these days,' he says, sulking slightly, and he lifts the TV remote and stares at the screen, which gives me a clear cue to go.

I drive towards the coast as the windscreen wipers sweep from left to right, remembering how I've dreamed of this moment so many times during my darkest hours as I lay awake in bed, tossing and turning and gripping the tear-sodden sheets as I yearned for Aidan to make this all better.

I only thought my heart had been broken before, but as I replay that night in New York as I lay in the hotel room, wondering why he couldn't be with me more than he was, and then picture him clinking glasses, kissing cheeks, holding hands and laughing and touching a woman who I'd been told was part of his history, I was physically sick many times. *Actually* sick, not just feeling sick – the type of sick that comes with shock and with no warning when a simple thought could trigger my stomach to heave and retch as I imagined him talking to me one minute and then laughing with her the next.

Never did I believe that rejection and betrayal could hurt so badly, not only on an emotional level but also on a physical one, to the extent that I don't even look or feel like myself any more. I've lost almost a stone in weight, so my cheeks are pale and gaunt, my usually thick, glossy dark hair is outgrown and unkempt, and my clothes don't hug me like they used to.

I don't want Aidan to see me like this; a broken mess in comparison to the strong, vibrant woman he first met when I tackled him under the falling snow last year in November, but I need to meet him face on, no matter how much I'm dreading it.

I need to tell him just how much he has hurt me and why, no matter how much he pleads or tries to brush it all off today or any day going forward, I cannot ever trust him or anyone else again. And then I hear Mabel, trying to steer me out of my own cloud of negativity and the web of lies I'd accepted from Jude.

'*Don't push away love when it comes your way, Roisin,*' I hear her tell me once more. '*Don't let the ghost of Jude and his past ways ruin your future.*'

I only wish I had the strength to believe her. I only wish I had the strength to believe in Aidan.

* * *

I park up the pick-up when I get to Dunfanaghy and walk down the lane that leads to Killyhoey Strand under a grey sky that completely reflects my mood. I can't deny how much the thought of seeing Aidan again in the flesh is going to tear me apart, and my insides fizz with dread and anticipation.

Then I stop when my feet meet the sand. The wind is in my face, and I shiver under the breeze, and when I look into the distance I see him standing there, looking out onto the dark, angry sea on this blustery autumn day.

He spots me instantly, as if he's been watching for me since he got here, and when his dark figure walks towards me as I go to meet him, I pray for the strength not to fall into his arms like I really want to. I ache for his touch and for his kind words, for his encouragement and his humour and understanding. I plead for everything to be the way it was, but just as the wind and rain batters my face, so does the reality of truth as it eats me up inside and spits out the true facts that he was living a lie in America while I waited for him here.

'Roisin!' he calls to me as he walks more quickly towards me now, wearing the same grey jacket he wore on our sledging day almost a year ago. 'I was afraid you wouldn't show up. My God, it's so, so good to see you.'

He reaches out to touch my face and, although I want to step back or brush his hand away, I just stand there in the rain and let him, with my eyes closed as hot tears fall onto his cold hand.

'Why are you back here, Aidan?' I ask him, still wondering if this is all just a cruel dream. 'Why are you doing this to me? This is so hard and it's not helping to see you in person again. I've told you I can't do this any more. It's not fair.'

He shakes his head, his dark hair soaked through in the rain that patters off his broad shoulders, with his hand still on my face.

'This is our special place, Roisin,' he says, taking my sodden hands in his and holding them tightly as the waves crash and roar in the distance. 'I wanted to meet you here to remind you of how we used to be and how we still *can* be. It's you I love, not Rachel, I promise you. I need you to believe me.'

I want him to kiss me.

I long to take him home and lie together in the warmth of my living room like we used to as Ben entertains us with stories and games, or as we watch movies and argue about silly things that we'll later laugh and hug over and forget about, but that was just a fairy tale, one made of imagination and false hope. Those days, as perfect as they were at the time, weren't real, and the love I feel for him now will disintegrate soon, won't it? I wish someone could tell me that this deep, gut-wrenching pain won't last for ever.

'I believed everything you told me,' I tell him, searching so desperately to stay strong and true to myself, but looking at him now with his beautiful face tilted, his lips that I once thought were mine, and the person I thought I knew so well, is making me feel as if I'm fighting a losing battle.

'And everything I said was true!' he says, his voice rising above the noise of the sea and gulls that fly above us on this blustery, dark autumnal day. 'I never lied to you, Roisin! I just had to play the game over there, but that's all it was. It was just a silly PR game composed by Bruce and Rachel to pull in the biggest contract of their lives that will all come to fruition in just a few weeks. They need me on this job pitch, and they need us all to pull together and show a united front of happy families so they can clinch the deal. After the awards event on October 28th I'm free! You've got to believe me. I can't lose you over this. It's killing me!'

'I want to believe you, Aidan!' I sob like a baby now. 'Heaven knows how much I want to believe you, but I can't go on feeling as vulnerable as I have lately. I need to look after my heart, and the only way I can is for us both to move on. I'm sorry. I'm so sorry, but I just can't let this ever happen to me again.'

Standing here with him is making me dizzy with frustration because deep down of course I do believe him. Deep down, I know what he is saying is true. I know that he's been living a lie with Rachel and that she is bleeding every ounce of time she has bargained with him for business reasons before their big deadline. I know he wants to be with me as much as I want to be with him.

'I'm struggling, Aidan,' I sob. 'I want this just as much as you do, but I don't know how to fully give myself to you when part of me is still so full of fear.'

And deep down I know that I'm not really angry at *him*. Instead I'm angry at *myself*, for allowing the demons of my past to continue to choke me. I long to give in to him as my heart so desires to, but my head is working overtime with reminders of a flurry of mistakes from my past. Jude is haunting me, I know he is. He is reminding me that he hasn't totally gone away and that he probably never will. The scars he has inflicted are still raw and, despite all the love I have for Aidan and how much I know I want him and need him in my life, I fear those wounds from Jude haven't been healed as much as I thought they had.

'Just give me a little more time,' he pleads. 'I'll show you everything you need to see to trust me. I'll do everything you want me to do. We're so close to being together properly, Roisin.' I stand there helpless and frozen on the spot as Aidan breaks down right in front of me, holding his hand to his eyes as he pinches back tears, but the way his breath catches when he tries to speak tells me his emotions are no longer in his control.

'Do you know how much I longed to find someone like you?' he asks me, crying now in the rain, his gorgeous mouth unable to disguise the pain we're both feeling as he tries to find the right words. 'Do you know how many nights I wished I'd a proper relationship, one that didn't make me feel lonely in a crowded room, one that I felt complete and content in and where I knew I'd my best friend in the world by my side? I wished for you, Roisin!

Don't do this to us and destroy what we had over some old insecurity, when we're this close to being together in the way we've always dreamed of. You're breaking my heart and I know your heart is breaking too! Please! Just let me prove it to you. Give me one more chance, please!'

The pain I've been denying for so long now scalds me inside again and I feel tears spill uncontrollably from my eyes at how unfair this is. I want to be with him so badly, but I can't let my guard down again. I want him to hold me, I hunger for his arms to hold me tightly. I yearn to rest on his chest right now and let the world pause for just a few more blissful moments of heaven, but that will only set me right back to the start of all this, and I'm trying to heal myself.

'*This is what love is meant to feel like,*' I hear Jude's voice from years ago before we were married, when he too was filling me with lies about his ex-wife who he was still meeting up with right up to our wedding day. '*All my mistakes from before just disintegrate when I look at you. We are meant to be. We are perfect.*'

I really did believe that we would be Mr and Mrs Perfect from the sincerity of his promises. I believed him when he said we were yin and yang. We were Jude and Roisin, we were everything.

But very soon we were nothing. And in the end, we were a big fat lie.

'*And Jude is gone for ever,*' I hear Mabel whisper to me

329

now. '*So why are you letting him control you from beyond the grave? He doesn't deserve that power, Roisin! You don't deserve this and neither does Aidan. Let Jude go! Let him go once and for all and live the life of love you've always longed for.*'

I can't breathe. Aidan reaches out to touch me again and I wince and gasp for air, shaking my head as flashes from the past come back and grip me in a fist of fear.

'*You'll never let me go! You're just not good enough,*' Jude roars again. I physically block my ears. '*You'll ruin this because you're weak and a runaway. Runaway Roisin! Run away again!*'

'I can't! I can't do this, Aidan,' I tell him, wiping my tears with the back of my hand. 'I love you too much and I'm hurting so badly, but I can't risk my whole sanity and undoing all the good stuff in my life since I came here. I'm too scared. You have no idea.'

'But I do, Roisin! I do have an idea. We're both hurting. Don't do this, Roisin. Don't walk away!'

But I have to. I have to do just that. I have to walk away.

And so I take a deep breath and I leave him standing there, a grown man crying in the rain, and when I get to the pick-up, I lean my head on the steering wheel, gripping it with both hands, and I howl for all this hurt to go away. I scream for some relief from all this heartache and pain. I long for the mother I never had and for her to soothe the despair that is breaking me into millions of pieces inside.

I yearn for Mabel's advice, for her strength and for all the good work we did together to find its way back to me as I come undone.

And beneath all that, I know I'm longing for people I can never have to save me, and I know that all these faces that race through my head now as I sit here in a steamed-up pick-up represent the one person I want most of all.

I still want Aidan. I still love him. A love like this will never disintegrate. It might linger and it will settle someday, but it will never, ever go away.

And I know I'll want him until the day I die.

32.

I stare at the envelope when Mickey hands it to me at work the next morning, frozen in time and with deep sadness as I know this is the last seasonal message we'll ever receive from Mabel.

The brown envelope in my hand contains her last words of wisdom, our last connection to her in this lifetime, and a good reason for Aidan and me to put our feelings to one side and pull together to hear her final goodbye.

I distract myself for as long as I possibly can to put off contacting Aidan, who is due to fly back to New York tonight after signing off the sale of Mabel's home, a task that I'm sure he isn't taking lightly. In fact, just picturing him signing off on something so final makes me feel a little weak inside.

I sort out clothing rails that don't need sorting. I replace price tags that don't need replacing. I make coffee I don't even drink. I ask Camille questions about stock that I already know everything about. I want to prolong the moment, I want to savour it, knowing I've still got it all to look forward to because as soon as I've watched it (it's another DVD for sure) I fear that I'll plummet again into a deeper darkness than I'm already feeling.

When I get home I find myself staring out through the rear window into the garden, thankful now that I finally gave in to the enthusiastic gardener and had the grass cut, to see patches of gold, red and amber leaves covering the grass like a patchwork blanket. I'm going to miss this place a lot, and I have moments when I wonder if I've made the right decision to move on, but I also know that the longer I stay here, the more I'll hold on to memories from a past that can't ever form my future. My lessons here have been learned. The pain I feel being in this cottage without Mabel or Aidan next door is simply too much to bear.

I gulp back a whirlwind of emotions as I picture him at his table at his big event next week, standing up as his name is undoubtedly called for the contract award that would attract him the publicity in his field that he deserves, and also give him the freedom afterwards to walk away from his recent past, if that's what he still intends to do.

And then I stare at the envelope that holds Mabel's final message, knowing that I'm going to have to bite the bullet and call him. I lift my phone and I hold it to my ear, waiting for him to answer.

'Roisin,' he says with the same urgency as he always does these days when I hear him say my name. 'How are—'

'Mabel's message is here, Aidan,' I tell him quickly, not answering his casual conversational question and speaking before he tries to chat any more. 'It's the last one of course, and it's another video message for us both, so if you want to call over, we should probably watch it together like she'd want us to.'

'Oh God,' says Aidan, his voice reflecting the fear I also feel at hearing from her for the last time. 'It's bittersweet, but I guess we both knew it was coming. Have you already had a sneak peek? Tell the truth.'

He laughs, winding me up like old times.

I stall. 'Of course I haven't,' I tell him, a bit nipped that he thought I would, even though I know he's making fun. 'I wouldn't watch it without you, Aidan. I'm not that hard-hearted.'

He laughs at the term 'hard-hearted', and I do too as it brings back memories of that very first day we met outside Mabel's house in the snow last winter.

Hearing his voice makes me gulp back a choking sadness as I know that the end of Mabel's messages will probably mean the end of our friendship. We'll no longer have these reasons to hook up and chat, and my heart sinks into my stomach at the reality of never hearing from him again when he goes back to America this time. The house has been sold, mine is on the market, and now that we've got this far, the thought of the future is dim and I'm wondering what the hell I'm doing all over again.

'Well, just call over when you can and we'll see what she has to tell us for this last time,' I say to him. I hope and

pray that Mabel's final message will give me the guidance
I so desperately need, yet know that seeing her for the last
time is going to be a killer blow, and I'm not sure I'm totally
prepared for it.

As I arrange my living room now once more for our final
viewing, reorganizing the furniture again for old times' sake,
it's really kicking in just how much I'm going to miss the
rhythm of each season and how much Aidan and I have
held on and waited for each of Mabel's messages.

I think back to the first one in winter where she told
us to lean on each other, to keep in touch in her memory,
to do something that makes us feel alive, and to rest our
hearts. She left me the dress that I've still never worn and
a photo to remind Aidan of the look of love. In spring
she spoke of the importance of truth and how we should
always say how we feel before it's too late, which led of
course to our wonderful time together in Breena, to the
mysterious truth that has still never been told, and to
Belfast where we admitted we were falling in love. And
then in summer, she sent Ben and me on a surprise vacation to New York where we had such fun following in her
footsteps, exploring her home city, until being there ulti-
mately ruined everything about my relationship with
Aidan and caused the unbearable pain I've been suffering
since. I can't imagine where she is going to guide us on
from here.

Aidan knocks on the door within minutes, with Ben at his heels.

'I was wondering where you'd got to,' I say to Ben, feeling ever so guilty that I hadn't known his exact whereabouts. 'I hope he isn't holding you back, Aidan.'

Aidan steps inside and I try to ignore the thumping beat of my heart and how it hurts so badly to be so near to him and yet so far.

'We've had a really good chat actually,' says Aidan, looking up at me with eyes that I could almost fall in to. 'We're going to do our best to stay in touch, and I've promised Ben that should I have to rob a bank, I'll take him on a helicopter ride one day very soon.'

Ben slides his hands into his pockets and looks at the floor.

'And I told Aidan that I'd much rather get to spend Sundays on the beach playing ball or Frisbee with *him* again than a helicopter ride any day, and *that* doesn't cost a thing.'

I can't answer that and neither can Aidan, so we make our way into the sitting room while Ben disappears upstairs, refusing again to take part in anything to do with Mabel's messages.

'You look lovely,' Aidan tells me as I put the DVD into the player, fumbling clumsily with the remote control as I feel his eyes on my body and the longing for him that engulfs me no matter if he's near or far.

'You don't have to say that any more,' I remind him,

determined not to make this exercise any more emotional than it already promises to be.

I sit down on the sofa a few feet away from him, eager now to get this over and done with, as I know it's going to be painful, and I try to convince myself that I'm ready to move on even though I have adored this little place I've called home for five years.

Teapot Row will always be special for so many reasons.

The grey woollen rug on the floor was chosen by Ben one day when he decided it would make the room cosier and I bought it for him even though it didn't exactly match the decor I had in mind. The retro fringed pink lamp in the corner was taken from a winter sale at Truly Vintage, the bottle-green sofa is worn with fingerprints, and its arms are a bit tattered and torn, but it's the place where I sat and talked to Aidan for hours on end. It's the place he soothed me and held me tightly on so many nights back in spring where I felt I was finally in the arms of someone I could always trust. I will miss so much about this beautiful little cottage, and I will leave it with bittersweet joy and a heart full of memories.

'Oh Aidan,' I say, lost in a haze of sentimentality and sorrow for how things have turned out.

'What's wrong? Are you OK, Ro? You look a bit—'

'I'm fine, I guess I'm a bit overwhelmed that this is it, you know,' I say to him. 'I'm just hoping I can make it through this without totally collapsing. I know that's not your problem. Sorry.'

My breathing is shallow and the rush of fear and frustration that engulfs me actually makes my body ache for him. Seeing his face never fails to move me, and I can't help but smile when our eyes meet. Like a chain reaction, he smiles too. I look at his blue eyes, his dark lashes, his full mouth, his white smile, and the longing I have from deep inside I fear will never go away.

'I'm nervous,' I confess. 'Are you?'

'Totally,' he says. 'I'm looking forward to this, but dreading it too. OK, let's get it started.'

And so just like before, I grab Mabel's cushion for some moral support, focus on my breathing, and decide to put my absolute faith that Mabel and only Mabel can guide me on my way from here on in.

33.

'Welcome to my birthday season and to the beautiful fall!' is her opening line and I can't help but gasp when I see how frail and old she looks in comparison to her previous bright and breezy video messages, which must have been made much earlier in the year before her passing.

She is wearing the purple sweatshirt I bought her for her birthday in late October last year, which bulks her up and disguises just how tiny she had become beneath her clothes as her illness rapidly took its course.

She takes her time, she licks her lips, and she chooses her words so carefully. She is tired and frail and I'm guessing this was recorded on or around her birthday, as she left us just a few weeks later. I'd gone shopping for groceries one day and had returned to find her wearing it, but she was so cagey as to what she had been up to while I was gone, with her make-up on and her bright sparkly new sweatshirt . . .

'I've always loved the fall or as you know it here, autumn,' she continues slowly and I listen with intent, 'not just because it means I get birthday presents, although that does make it very special, but I also love the visual change of season from green to golden colours, the orange, misty hue in the air, and the smell of chimney-pot smoke when out for a crunchy walk in the forest.'

She speaks so much more hastily and I'd forgotten just how transparent her skin had become in her last few weeks, how sunken her cheeks became as they sat beneath her razor-sharp cheekbones, and how dark her eyes were, even though she always topped up her look with make-up to try to disguise how sick she really was.

'I hope you enjoyed New York, my dear Roisin, and I hope you enjoyed having company out there, darling Aidan,' she says, her voice so much weaker and quieter now. 'It's a strange one when you realize you've no more birthdays left and that you've just blown out the last candles on your cake. My time here with you is almost up.'

She pauses to catch her breath.

'I hope you mark what would have been my eightieth birthday in style when it comes around,' she says, trying her best to lilt up her tone of voice. 'Please do something nice for me, won't you both? You know I always loved a fuss and a celebration, so please do make a fuss.'

A tsunami of tears threatens to wash over me as I listen to her, hanging on to her every breath and to her every word. I think ahead to Aidan's awards ceremony and how proud she will be of him next week when he celebrates his evening on her birthday, but what will I do here in Ballybray to mark it?

I'll get a cake, I decide. I'll go to her grave with some flowers, and then I'll blow out her candles when I come back; eighty candles – no more and no less. Eighty candles for her seventy-nine laps here in this world and the extra one she travelled with us this year through her messages.

'I've thought long and hard of how I'm going to say goodbye to you both, my darlings, now that your first trip around the sun without me is coming to an end,' she says, dabbing her eyes every now and then and touching her heavily powdered nose. 'I hope you have developed a friend-ship, quite literally, made in heaven.'

She laughs at her own words, but I shift uncomfortably in my seat and when I look across at Aidan he is staring at the floor, leaning forward with his hands clasped in front of him as if it's too painful to watch her or hear her voice for this very last time.

'Aidan, I totally understand why you wanted to keep the truth from me about your marriage, but darling, I was always your biggest fan and I'd have supported you through thick and thin,' she exclaims, shaking her weary head from side to side. 'Fear is never bigger or more powerful than love, please remember that. I just want you to be happy.'

She pauses. I can barely breathe.

'And Roisin,' she continues. 'Yes, you're an independent little warrior who can stand on your own two feet and I just know you're learning to do that again, but don't let your stubborn streak rule your head or more importantly your heart, do you hear me? When your heart screams, you have no choice but to listen. No matter how much you try and drown it out, your heart will always speak the loudest. Follow it. Always follow your heart, every single day.'

I bite my lip and look at the floor now too, then back at the screen, feeling as though I'm being told off by the person who knew me better than I even know myself sometimes. It's as if Mabel had predicted exactly what my reaction would be to Aidan's attention and kindness. She knew I'd be stubborn and afraid. She knew I'd push it away.

'Let me leave you with this, my darlings,' she tells us, clasping her tiny hands together. 'You can buy and sell houses, you can buy and sell cars, you can spend holidays in the sun as much as you like to. You can buy fancy clothes, you can buy the best jewellery, you can eat the finest foods and you can drink the best of the good wine. You can strive to get to the top of everything you do, but what if you do all that only to find that when you get to the top, there's nothing there? What if you realize it all meant nothing?'

She pauses and wets her thin lips.

'Ambition and success are marvellous traits, and we should always aim to do our very best in life, no matter if it's tackling a blocked sink or cutting a multi-million dollar deal,' she tells us, 'but when you come to the very end of your time on earth like I am now, all those material things you busted your ass working for are not what's on your mind. They make nice memories, yes, and they make life easier at times, yes, but only if they're combined with the one, most beautiful thing of all – love.

'As I sit here clinging on to every last second of life that I have left, the fear and panic I have of saying goodbye to the people I love is often the only thing on my mind,' she explains. 'But – the fear of saying goodbye will never beat the joy of love I feel for you. Never. If the love is there, the fear of saying goodbye will soon fade into the darkness, and love will save the day.'

She speaks every word like she means it, leaving no room for misinterpretation.

'*This* is life. Right now, today, where you are sitting is your life. Don't wait for tomorrow, or next week, or next month to live how you want to live, because living is now,' she says. 'And one day, on a time and date that you will never know, you will face the end of your life like me, and you won't have a choice any more. Goodbye will no longer be a choice, but right now, you do have that choice. Do you choose love, or do you choose goodbye?'

Her voice is brittle and weak now, and she sits still with her eyes closed, then she opens them again and smiles, looking directly at us both.

'Goodbye, my darlings,' she says as her face folds into tears. She lifts her little hand and blows us a kiss, her hand shaking and her breath low and shallow. 'Remember that before every new beginning, there must be an ending. This may be the end of my time with you, but it's the start of a whole new chapter for you. Take care of each other for always. I love you, my little family. Goodbye.'

She waits again and we wait too for the recording to stop, but then she looks to the side of the camera as if she is talking to someone else in the room and I strain my neck as if I'm doing the same.

'I'm finished,' she whispers, wiping her eyes. 'Thank you.'

My eyes almost pop out of my head at the familiarity of the voice that speaks back to her as I sit on my sofa, frozen and stunned.

I knew she had a partner in crime to pull this all together, but I'd never have guessed who. Someone technically savvy, with an eye for an angle, and who loved the camera from the other side. I hear a shuffle and the camera angle sways, and then he comes into view as he unclips a little microphone from Mabel's purple jumper.

'We've done our very best, Ben,' she tells her cameraman. 'The rest is for the future, and that future is up to Aidan and Roisin. You'll just have to wait and see.'

34.

Later that evening, after making his official announcement that he was Mabel's helper in making the videos, Ben's big reveal of how he pulled it all off is plunged into deep sadness when Aidan tells him he has to say goodbye for good.

'But I thought when you watched the videos together that everything would be OK again?' he asks, his freckled face crinkled in defeat and despair. 'Mabel said you'd be best of friends and that you might even like each other a bit more than that. I don't understand. We did it all for nothing!'

He bursts into tears and I can't look as Aidan takes him in his arms and sheds a few farewell tears beside him. I go to the kitchen and put on the kettle, leaning on the worktop as I try to catch my breath and face up to the reality that this is really goodbye.

By the time I get back to the living room, Ben has raced away to the cocoon of his bedroom and when I go to check on him, my heart burns when I realize he's cried himself to sleep.

It's going to take me a long time to forgive myself for breaking his heart as much as this all is breaking mine.

'Needless to say, I won't beg you to change your mind or meet me in New York on Mabel's birthday when I'm a free man,' Aidan tells me outside an hour later. 'I've my own pride and my own heart to protect, so I won't exhaust this any further except to say that I wish things had turned out differently and I also wish the best for you in every way, Roisin. I mean that.'

We stand on the footpath under the moonlight by Mabel's gate and stare towards the house that holds so many memories within its bricks and mortar for each of us. Years of early childhood visiting with his parents, his teenage years when he lived there after his major loss, and the place he called home right up until now when he's set to leave Ballybray behind once and for all.

'Aidan, I don't know what else to say to you either,' I tell him, shaking my head. 'We had something wonderful for a very short time and maybe that's what we should remember most out of all this. Mabel intended for us to be like her family, but maybe we took it further than we should have? Maybe we just weren't meant to be after all.'

'You don't mean that,' he says, and I lean towards him to bid him a last goodbye. He kisses me on the forehead, long and slowly, as if his life depends on it, and I swear I don't breathe for at least six seconds until he lets go.

'I'm probably worse at goodbyes than you are, and that's saying something.'

My eyes glisten as I look up at him, all packed up and ready to go to serve out his final chapter in the USA before he starts all over again in something new.

'I'm going to miss you so much,' I gasp.

'My sweet Roisin.'

'But who knows where this new start will lead us both?' I say, trying to sound just a little bit optimistic. 'I might even get my house by the sea after all this, and you—'

'Don't,' he says, breaking my attempt at lifting our mood. He runs his hand through his hair and speaks with fierce determination, but the way his eyes glisten can't disguise his true feelings. 'I can't even think about what I'm going to do past the awards night, but what I do know is that I plan a very dignified escape once the formalities are over. I'll hand over the contract to Bruce and Rachel and I'll walk right out of that hotel and take my first steps towards my new future, wherever that might be.'

'Back to Ireland?' I suggest, doing my best to keep the tone practical and purposeful. 'Dublin, perhaps?'

'Probably,' he says with a shrug. He bites his lip and looks away. 'Though I don't have an awful lot to bring me back here either, do I? It's not like I've a family here any more. It's the end of an era for the Murphys of Ballybray.'

He kicks the wet ground beneath him and then just as he is about to leave, he gently pulls me close to him one more time. Then he cups my face in his hand, and with urgency, he kisses me full on the mouth making my legs go weak and my head spin. I feel his fingers press gently on the nape of my neck and goosebumps rise on my skin. I close my eyes, savouring, tasting him and praying to God inside that this won't be our last kiss. I pray for some divine intervention, for courage and for strength to accept the love he is offering.

When our lips finally part, we are both breathless with hunger and our eyes sting with tears.

'Goodbye, Roisin,' he says, looking up to the heavens as if for support, then he gives me a quick peck on the cheek. 'Take care of Ben and take care of you.'

He chokes back tears as he leaves me standing there in the early October drizzle and I tilt back my head to let the rain wash away my tears as he gets into his hired car and drives away towards his new beginning, then I go inside and lie down on the sofa where I cry from the pit of the stomach for all the damage from my past that has torn apart my future. I love Aidan like I've never loved before, and yet this claw in my stomach and this doubt instilled in my mind from years of abuse and mistrust with Jude still has a control over me. I reel over events from my past, trying to put old ghosts to bed once and for all, and I pray for the strength to give Aidan and our relationship the chance I deep down know it deserves, but I fear it's too late for that now.

This is when Mabel would give me a shake, would straighten me up and would nudge me in the right direction, but Mabel is gone and if I don't get my life into gear then I run the risk of Aidan being gone for ever too.

A text message interrupts my pity party for one and I can't help hoping with all my heart that it might be a sign of some sort about where I go from here and what I do next.

Its content almost takes my breath away and shakes me back into focus on an untold secret that had been left in the past.

'My name is Bernie Sullivan, from Breena,' reads the text. 'I'm looking for Roisin O'Connor. Maybe you could give me a call back when you can – that's if I've got the right number this time. It would be so nice to talk to you about the Murphy brothers from Ballybray, just as your message said you'd like to, as soon as you get a chance.'

I sit up straight on the sofa and push my hair back from my tear-stained face, then I stare at the text on my phone and read it over and over again until it sinks in. This Bernie lady is not giving up, it seems, and it would be foolish of me to ignore whatever it is she has to say.

It could change Aidan's life. It could change mine too, who knows?

So this time, through my sodden teary eyes, I manage to respond properly just like I should have done when Bernie first messaged months ago on my return from New York.

Maybe it's because Mabel's birthday is just around the corner, maybe it's because she asked us both to do something special, and maybe it's because I'm secretly hoping for a reason to speak to Aidan again, but this time I don't hesitate. I press dial on the number I received the message from and Bernie answers almost straight away.

'Bernie?' I say, as soon as the other woman says hello.

'Roisin?' she asks timidly. 'Is that you?'

I hear the tremble in her voice and I grip the phone, pacing the floor as I wait to hear what it is she wants to tell me.

'Yes, it's me,' I confirm, closing my eyes and biting my lip as my heart races with anticipation. 'I was with Aidan Murphy in your bar back in spring and I left my number. I've a feeling there's something you might know about his father and his uncle from their time in Breena – I'm guessing it could have been around forty-five years ago?'

'I remember you,' says the lady who I assume was the one I spoke to in the Ladies of Sullivan's Bar that day. 'I was hoping you'd get in touch. Can you talk for a while? I think it's time.'

I look at the clock, thankful that Ben is sleeping soundly so I can deal with this without interruption.

'I can, yes,' I tell her, marvelling at her timing and how she has tried to connect again on the day of Aidan's departure and of Mabel's final message. 'I can talk.'

* * *

'I'm really sorry, Camille, but is there any chance I could have the day off?' I say to my boss and good friend the following morning just after I get Ben out to school. 'I'll explain all when I can, but believe me this is so, so important.'

'Of course!' says Camille, as understanding as ever of my topsy-turvy life lately. She's listened to me cry, she's wiped away my tears, and she's tried her best to steer me when I lost my way, but she was right that no one else can do it for me, only myself, and the time for that is now. I have a chance today, a real chance to make a difference to so many lives and I want to take the bull by the horns.

I jump in the pick-up and, as I drive the two and a half hour journey to Breena, back to the village where Peter and Danny Murphy spent so many carefree days, and to the place where Aidan and I first kissed and told each other of our true feelings, I have that urgent feeling of wanting to be there already to see proof of what I've been told before I break the news to Aidan.

This is Peter and Danny Murphy's secret that was never told. This was a life they lived long before Mabel and long before Aidan and his mum. This was a secret that they held against each other to the end of their days, and one that Mabel never learned of but wanted us to find out so badly. This is what threatened to come out on the night of the tragic accident – perhaps it did come out, but Aidan and Mabel had left to get ice cream and weren't there to hear it. This is the secret Peter Murphy held from Mabel to protect her heart from knowing he already had the only thing he could never have with her.

The drive soothes me in so many ways, much more than I could have imagined. I hear Aidan's voice as I cruise along open coastal roads, I feel his hand on my knee as I listen to the songs we once shared as I inhale the memories of so many wonderful days and nights together.

But this mission is not about me and I don't even know yet if it's even about Aidan, but there was urgency in Bernie Sullivan's voice that made me want to get to Breena as soon as I could. I think of Aidan, lying in bed now in New York during the small hours after his flight, oblivious to my mission and what it might bring his way.

The winding roads remind me of my life, with their mixture of steep curves, sharp bends and long open roads that go on for miles and miles before coming to an abrupt stop at a junction, and the necessity to decide whether to take a right or a left or turn back and relive it all over again.

I crank up the radio, I sing along to the songs that remind me of happier times, and I decide once and for all what I want in life after this journey today is made. I want the smooth open road for a change, that doesn't come to an abrupt stop. I want the curves that bring unexpected excitement and joy, and I want the sharp bends that teach me lessons, whether they be to slow down or to take caution. I realize that everything that has come my way so far on my journey over forty years has made me the person I am today and, as painful as it may have been, there's no point in looking back and wishing to change a thing.

As Mabel said, this is life – right now. There's no point waiting on the big moment or the big reveal or the hero to save the day. You have to accept that every bump and bruise you feel is there to teach you a lesson, and by God I've learned my lessons lately and I'd learned a lot before I ever set foot in Ballybray.

I pass the picnic spot where Aidan and I thought we'd spotted the happy family, and I laugh out loud at the very idea of perfection in life. We're all flawed, we've all got secrets, we've all got little things we hide behind, that mask our creases and edges that we don't want to show in public. And so what if we do? It's what makes us human and it's what makes us real.

I park the car down by the harbour as before and, as I walk along the cobbled streets, I wish I'd worn flat shoes, but a quick glance in a shop front window tells me I'm starting to look a bit like my old self again. I still need to gain some weight, I could be doing with eating and sleeping a bit more, but all in all I'm feeling stronger and more purposeful, and a lot of that is to do with why I've been asked to come here today.

I've no idea what lies ahead as I do my best to remember my bearings in this beautiful place where Aidan and I shared our first dinner alone, where we ate ice cream by the pier, and where we finally admitted our true feelings. I try not to get sentimental as I remember it all, knowing that I'm here today not for myself but to reveal the truth that was left untold to Mabel – a truth that will hopefully now be passed on to the last Murphy boy, who has no idea any of this is even happening yet.

'Roisin!'

I'm greeted outside the bar by Bernie, who I feel by now is like an old friend after having chatted to her for so long the night before, when I told her all about my connection to Mabel and Aidan, and to how Mabel asked us to come here to retrace Aidan's father's footsteps from all those years ago.

She was too young to remember them of course, but she shared stories from her ailing aunt Carol, whose terminal illness means she can't be here to meet me today, but who has sent her blessings to me through Bernie and her trust that I will be the keeper of this information before telling Aidan in a way that only I can.

We go inside, not into the restaurant like before, but through a different door that leads to a stairwell, and I follow Bernie upstairs as she chats non-stop along the way, asking me about the weather in Ballybray and how I found the journey and if I'd any bother with finding a parking space when I got to Breena, as it's always been a problem with visitors.

She turns the key on the lock of what looks like the front door to a private apartment and calls out to say we have arrived. I feel jittery inside and wish now that Aidan had been here for the reveal of this long kept secret, but in a way I'm glad that I can act as an intermediary when it comes to telling him all about it.

I will call him and tell him, I've already decided, and after that what he does with the information is entirely up to him. I will call him and explain how I initially wanted to protect him from any bad or sad news, whatever it might have been, when I first bumped into Bernie in the bathroom of Sullivan's back in March.

It's a secret I have held for far too long within me, for so many reasons I can no longer explain, but I've always known from the moment I saw Bernie look at us from behind the bar that day that there was so much more to Mabel sending us to Breena than we could ever have imagined.

And when I step inside the plush sitting room of the apartment above Sullivan's Bar I have so many questions as to why Danny and then Peter Murphy would have kept this secret from Mabel, even to his dying day.

I stand there, holding Bernie's arm to steady myself, and I burst into uncontrollable tears.

'Roisin, this is my cousin Cain. He is Peter Murphy's son,' she says, but she doesn't have to explain. The man in front of me is about forty-five years old, he has dark hair and the most beautiful eyes, which are so familiar to those I've looked into for the past year. He is the image of Aidan. He is the cousin Aidan never knew he ever had. He is Mabel's stepson she never knew about. I can barely breathe.

'Oh Mabel!' I whisper, closing my eyes tightly and feeling the weight of so many lost years plunge down on my shoulders as Cain welcomes me into a warm embrace. 'You should have known this. You really should have known. You would only have loved him even more.'

35.

I wake up on the morning of Mabel's birthday around six, which is a lot earlier than usual, and make my way downstairs to the kitchen where I sit in the darkness, a cup of coffee in hand and the sound of silence in my ears as I plan for the day ahead. The cake, just as I'd promised myself, is covered with eighty tiny candles. When we baked it last night, Ben and I took our time to really reflect on what has been a wonderful five years here in Ballybray.

'I wonder if the people who live here next will have as much fun as we have,' he asked me, and the way his eyes lit up reminded me that moving on now that Mabel's messages are over is probably for the best. I just can't imagine us here any longer, and I've already begun to pack up as I wait for those bidding on the cottage to reach their final offer.

It comes in before nine, when Ben and I are leaving the house for school, and when the estate agent calls me it's like everything is falling into place so perfectly that I've no doubt the lady in heaven is guiding me as always.

'Congratulations,' he tells me when he breaks the news that I've reached the asking price and a few quid more, which will come in handy if I ever find the right place to move to next. I can rent in the meantime, but for now this is a step in the right direction.

I feel a rush of adrenaline wash through me and as always I feel the urge to call Aidan as he is always the first person I want to break good news to. It's his big night tonight, and I know when he wakes up he'll have an action-packed day ahead, but I can't resist texting him to tell him my news and I also send him a photo of Mabel's cake, which I plan to give out to customers at Truly Vintage today in her memory.

He responds immediately, which tells me he isn't sleeping like he should be.

'Can't sleep, too nervous and excited for my freedom,' he replies. 'But that's amazing news, Roisin. Huge congrats! I'm so thrilled it's all working out. It's all looking like it's meant to be.'

I walk down the path of the cottage on Teapot Row and feel a wave of nostalgia sweep over me when I see the two *For Sale* signs stand side by side in the two gardens where so many memories were made, not only in my time here but also in the years before.

I think of Mabel taking a young Aidan out through the yellow door to get ice cream on that fateful evening, not knowing when they returned his whole future would come crashing down. I think of his parents leaving in the heat of an argument around that same time, getting into their car with tempers high not knowing that they'd never come back to pick up their son again. I think of Peter, Mabel's husband, and his ageing parents as they got the news just hours later. I think of Aidan's teenage years, and how he grew up to be such a treasure to them all as he wore his heart on his sleeve and strived to be the best he could be, but all the time wanting to capture what he once had before that dreadful night so many years ago.

And then I think of Mabel and Peter's return here to live out their twilight years, of how Aidan moved away to the city they left behind, and of Peter's passing and then Mabel's more recently, taking all their secrets with them.

Now, it's time for Ben and me to move on, and who knows what's around the corner for the people who will live here next?

I take Ben's hand on the way to school, which he casually slips out of my grip as discreetly as he can without wanting to offend, and I realize how much he too has grown up in the years spent here in Ballybray. He's no longer the fragile, frightened little six-year-old boy who clung to me. Thanks to Mabel and this wonderful community he spent his primary years with, he is now a confident footballer, a keen photographer, a flamboyant horse rider, a lover of trivia and geography, and even a skilled artist when he takes the time to doodle or paint, which I like to believe he gets from me.

And I see Jude in him sometimes too, as much as it pains me to admit it. He has his father's agility in a football game, and a strong, fine figure that will grow to attract a lot of attention when he's older. With my guidance, and with all he learned from Mabel, I know he'll use his talents and his traits in the most positive way possible.

'We're quite a team,' I say to him as we walk to school, a new spring in our step despite the light drizzle of rain that will never dampen our spirits. We are two people who now know exactly where we are going in life and, as long as Ben feels safe and happy, I know I'm doing the right thing.

'No kisses, Mum, I mean it,' he tells me when we get to the school gates. I don't normally walk him to school these days, but feel a need to do so today and, as it's on my way to the cemetery where I want to lay the flowers I have in my carrier bag, it makes all the more sense to see him off properly this morning.

'You'll soon be taller than me,' I say, wanting to ruffle his hair but knowing I'd better not or he'd never forgive me. 'OK, I'd better get going. I love you, Ben.'

'I love you too, Mum,' he whispers, looking around to make sure no one is watching him, and then just like he can't help it or maybe it's because deep down he doesn't care if he's seen, he wraps his arms around my waist and gives me a tight, albeit very quick, hug. I think he knows I need it today more than ever.

I watch him as he weaves his way through the playground, high fiving a younger pupil on his way past, and I know that today is going to be a sad day but a good day.

I can feel it in my bones.

Mabel's grave is a place I've both avoided and longed for the courage to spend time at, so it feels poignant and important that I come here on her eightieth birthday to pay my respects to the woman who has very much shaped my life.

The headstone that reads her name in gold text alongside Peter's stands proud and tall in black marble, and as I sit sideways on the ledge that frames the plot where they lie, I can't help but regret how I didn't have the strength to come here a lot sooner.

I've always found cemeteries to be upsetting places, although I understand fully that others find it to be a comfort to sit by the grave of a loved one, and as I sit here now where Mabel was laid to rest, I find some of my grief wavering to make way for a peaceful, calming feeling I wasn't expecting.

Two matching white porcelain angels sit in each corner across from me and I just know they are from Aidan as I remember him coming here quite a lot when he was in Ballybray. He did the rounds of his parents' grave, his grandparents, and of course his Uncle Peter and Aunt Mabel, and every time he returned I could tell he had been crying. I can't imagine how overwhelming it must feel for him as an only child to know the only place you can go to visit your whole family is under the clay in a place of rest.

I check the time on my phone. It's just gone 9.15 a.m. here in Ireland so with any luck Aidan will have fallen asleep after our brief messaging earlier and will have a few hours more before he has to get up and get ready for his working day and the events that will follow at the Fitzwilliam Hotel in New York tonight.

'He's so excited,' I say out loud, not knowing why I feel the need to, but I'm beginning to feel closer to Mabel by being here. 'It means so much to him, especially when he realized the ceremony fell on your birthday. I just know you'll be watching over him, so proud of him as always. He's finally made the decision he has longed to do for years.'

I run my hands through the soil under which Mabel lies and hope that she's also proud of me for the decisions I've made in the past few days.

She wanted us both to celebrate her birthday today, and while Aidan has his very important event tonight, I can only ask for her blessing as to how I plan to celebrate the wonder of the life she lived and the wisdom she gave me in my very own way.

'Sorry, I didn't expect anyone else to be here.'

I hear the clicking of heels that come to a sudden stop, and when I look up to see I have company, I squint in the slight ray of sunshine at a young woman in a grey mac with a London silk headscarf tied beneath her chin. She stands over Mabel's grave just across from me and blesses herself under the shelter of a see-through plastic umbrella.

I spring up, dusting the soil from my hands. I recognize her, but I've no idea where from at first and then when I look closer it all comes back to me.

'I'm an old friend of Mabel's,' she says, extending a fine manicured hand that feels cold to touch. 'My name's Ingrid, but I doubt if she's ever mentioned me. When I say I'm an old friend, I only met her once, but sometimes that's all it takes with certain people.'

'Nice to meet you, Ingrid,' I say in return. 'I'm Roisin. I lived next door to Mabel for a few years. Didn't I see you at her funeral?'

She nods and smiles at how I recognize her, despite the change in her appearance since then. She was the lady I mistook for Rachel that day.

'Yes,' she says, 'I saw you there too. You're Ben's mum, yes?'

I take a step back. How does she know me and my son?

'Mabel told me all about her wonderful neighbours and how much you'd changed her life for the better,' Ingrid tells me.

She's wistful-looking, ghostly almost, and her presence, although it makes me wonder where she turned up from like this out of the blue, is a blanket of serenity and calm.

Her blonde blow-dried hair, so glamorous and smooth on the day of Mabel's funeral, is gone, her cheekbones that were high and defined back then are now puffed and grey, and her eyes, even though they are painted with eyeliner and beautiful green eye shadow, are home to dark uneven circles.

'Do you – do you come to her grave a lot or did you know it was her birthday today?' I ask Ingrid, unable to take my eyes off her. I realize the time, and that I really should get going. I'm on such a tight schedule and can't afford to waste a minute. 'Mabel would have been eighty years old today.'

'I didn't know that. Wow. I try to call in when I'm passing through the village, which isn't very often any more,' she explains, and then she lays a small bunch of wild flowers on the soil. 'I was Mabel's hairdresser just once, but her words to me that day as I styled her wispy curls just may have saved my life.'

'Really?'

'Yes, I'll never forget her,' Ingrid tells me. 'I was in such a fragile state about my health after my cancer diagnosis, but she told me to try and look at it not as the end of something, but the start of something new when I come out the other side. Just hearing those words from her gave me great strength and most of all, she gave me hope.'

My eyes widen.

'She was a great believer in that theory,' I say to Ingrid.

We stand there side by side in the rain, both looking on at the resting place of a woman who has touched more lives than she may have ever known. I have the world at my feet and my health to enjoy it.

'I'd follow her guidance to the end of the earth too,' I tell Ingrid before I leave her, standing there lost in her own gratitude and thoughts. 'Before I go, can I ask if you bought your headscarf locally? It looks very familiar.'

She touches the multi-coloured silk scarf and nods her head.

'I did actually,' she says. 'Isn't it beautiful? I bought it in the vintage store in the village a few weeks ago. I love it.'

I smile at her, and we hold each other's gaze for longer than what might feel comfortable to others, but then this is no ordinary moment.

'You'll never believe it, but that scarf once belonged to Mabel,' I tell Ingrid, and I watch as disbelief takes over her beautiful face and tears spring up in her eyes.

'Really?' she says, her hand going to her chest.

'Yes, really. It was hers when she was probably about your age. Who knows, maybe this is her way of reconnecting with you? I think she knows you wanted to say thank you.'

I walk the few steps between us and do something I don't think I've ever done to a stranger before. I hug her, and we stand there together, lost in a precious moment as the rain dries up without us even noticing.

'I'd really better get going as I've so much to do today to mark her birthday,' I say to Ingrid, 'but it's been such an honour to meet you.'

As I walk away on this damp autumn day, I am filled by

the knowledge that Mabel's words and legacy continue to live on around here in so many more ways than she could ever have imagined.

36.

I always try to find a window seat when I go to a new café, and I deliberately leave room for my handsome companion who has gone to make a phone call as I take the opportunity to take stock of my surroundings.

I like to think of an hour in a café as my ultimate me time, with a view that I can take in or switch off from as I choose, and today, even though the view through the pane of glass where I sit is something I'd usually revel in, today I'm more focused on the thoughts that are swirling through my mind and the task I've set myself for the time I have here before I move on.

Camille keeps me updated by regular texting with how our customers at Truly Vintage are enjoying the birthday cake I left with her in memory of Mabel. This morning's events seem so long ago already and I'm so grateful to Camille for allowing me some time out today to get everything organized as I plan the next chapter of my life.

I like to look at life like that now. Little chapters of a much bigger story, and when one is over, we turn the page and we keep going. I'm excited for this next chapter, more excited than I've ever been for those I've already lived through. I'm not approaching this next one with fear or any expectation, as I've learned from Mabel's advice that everything is worth a try.

And that's what brings me here today with my new friend Cain who I nervously await to come back and join me at our table.

It's dropping down dark outside and I'm keeping a close eye on the time. Everything about today from my early start this morning, to walking Ben to school, to chatting to the estate agent about my next move, to visiting Mabel's grave and now my time here in this café has all been meticulously planned to a tee.

I take a notebook from my handbag where I've written out my timetable for today and a list of people I need to contact right here, right now, to say what I want to say.

I start with Camille, the woman who has been my rock over the past twelve months with support and advice at the drop of a hat. I pick up my phone and write her a message.

'Camille, I just want to say thank you for all your support in recent times,' I tell her. 'You picked me up and pushed me forward, but at the same time you gave me space and some tough love to remind me that if I want change in my life or to make things better, it's all down to me at the end of the day. Thank you for being such a great friend and confidante, and for helping me get to where I am today. I'll never forget it. Roisin x.'

I press send, feeling like I've done a really important thing to show gratitude, and then I move on to the next one, my son. The thought of him makes me well up as I picture his freckled nose, his wise little head on such young shoulders, and all the ups and downs we've shared in this life so far.

'Ben, you are the light of my life, my reason for being and my wingman,' I tell him. 'I'm so privileged to have a son as brave as you are. Thank you for keeping me on my toes, for being so honest and true, and for helping Mabel have a voice when she wanted to say her final words to me. I had no idea you were so good at planning and posting off packages, but you never cease to amaze me! I look forward to our next adventures together. We have so much to look forward to. All my love for ever, Mum x'

I send the message to Ben's phone, knowing he will be surprised to receive it, but I'm determined to take all of Mabel's advice from the last year and put it into action today in her honour. I will rest my heart and follow its calling, I'll be honest and true, I will say what I need to say to others without waiting until it's too late, and I'll never put the fear of saying goodbye ahead of love.

The next message I want to send is an email that I should have sent a long time ago, but Mabel has coached me in the power of now and of how to act so we have no regrets, even though my hands tremble and a feeling of being so far away from her threatens to make me shake inside.

I can look at my life with my mother from both sides

now, as I've the life experience and knowledge from being a mother myself to understand that parenting is a complex, frightening and sometimes very lonely job. I've been a lone parent for five years now, and even though the words I could have said to my mother before would have had the power to hurt her deeply, I'm choosing words instead that have the power to heal, if not her, at least me.

'Dear Mum,' I type into my phone, feeling all the ghosts of my childhood come back to haunt me as I write these words. 'I don't know what to say to you except that I forgive you and I love you. We are all fighting our own battles in life, and I know you struggle so deeply with yours, but please know that your daughter is still finding her way in the world and she is determined to always do you proud. You did the best you could, and I know that life was a cruel and hard place for you, and that you just couldn't cope with the responsibilities it gave you when I came into your world. You thought I'd be better off without you. You thought the world would be a better place without you, and even though we will always disagree on that one, I understand you better now, as well as the demons you fought and still fight daily. My anger has simmered away. I'm a different person. Mum, I'm not that little girl any more. Please be kind to yourself, knowing that I'll always love you, no matter what. You are loved. Your daughter, Roisin x'

I press send and three sharp intakes of breath catch the back of my throat as I feel that overwhelming sensation of bursting into tears that is so familiar with childhood, where you can't breathe and you can't speak. You can only cry and cry. I stare through the window as the rain pelts with determination against the glass. Outside, the shoppers and workers are running now, umbrellas going up, car brakes screaming, and the world is a very different place, at least it is for me.

I feel free. I feel that I've got some things out in the open that always needed to be said, and should anything ever happen to me, those who love me and who I love will know exactly where they stand with me.

There's only one more person I need to clarify my feelings to, but this one will be done tonight in person. Cain returns to our table and I pack up my belongings, pay our bill in the coffee shop, and we go out to face the busy street where I hail a taxi – a yellow one of course, and Cain links my arm as we cross the busy pavement and slip inside it, headed for a night that will change both our worlds for ever.

'Damn New York traffic!' he says. 'I hate these yellow taxis.'

I burst out laughing.

'You'll never believe this, Cain. But so did your father.'

I go to the bathroom in the Fitzgerald Hotel in New York City and stand at the basin, where I take a really good long look in the mirror.

My hair is damp from the rain and I touch my earlobes as I stare now right into my own soul knowing that I am, for the first time in a long while, being totally honest and true.

I'm doing the right thing by me. I'm taking a chance, I'm putting my heart on the line, but if I don't do it now I will only ever learn to regret it. I have an hour to get ready and, when I think of Aidan's reaction to this surprise I've planned by coming here, my tummy fills up with butterflies and I feel almost sick, but in a good way. I'm nervous as hell, but the thought of seeing him again can and will overcome any fears that nudge their way inside me.

I'd said goodbye to Camille and set off for the 13.20 flight from Dublin that saw me arrive into New York just after 16.20, glad of the four-hour time difference to let me get organized for the evening ahead. It all worked like clock-work, and Cain met me at the airport just as he promised to, and we made this journey together.

As I sit here in this hotel room now, applying my make-up and fixing my hair, I wonder what Mabel is thinking, if she's watching over me. I can see her beaming smile, her turquoise eyes twinkling with joy, and her lips pursed as her head nods in approval. I close my eyes and I see her giving me a cheeky 'thumbs up' for good luck. I put in my earrings, which are long, glitzy and gold, I sweep a shade of red over my lips, which brightens up my whole face and complements my long, wavy dark hair which I spread across my shoulders.

I wait for an alternate voice in my head, but to my relief there is only joy and silence. Jude is gone. His grip has loosened. I have finally let him go.

I haven't worn red in what feels like for ever, but then

this dress that I've brought back to its home place of New York was always only meant to be worn on a very special occasion. It was Mabel's, but now it feels very much like it's meant to be mine.

I slip it on and it feels as good as it looks. I gulp back the waves of emotion as I look again in the mirror and realize how far I've come. The beads of the dress accentuate my hips and I honestly have never felt so good about myself. So this is what being true and honest feels like. This is where following your heart can bring you.

I put on my shoes, feeling tall and confident, and then I make my way to Cain who offers me his arm to link, and we walk towards the foyer where the buzz of the awards ceremony has already begun.

We weave our way through a sea of black and white tuxedos and glamorous women in every colour of the rainbow. Champagne glasses clink, a string quartet plays, canapés are served from silver trays held high in the air, and chatter with hearty laughter is in the air.

And then I see him.

He fidgets with his cufflinks, he runs his fingers through his hair, and his eyes dart around him as he greets people with air kisses and strong handshakes as well-wishers pat him on the back.

He looks like a dream in his black tuxedo, and the shadow of stubble on his chin makes me want to reach across the room and touch his face.

Rachel links his arm, her eyes scanning her surroundings and her sky blue evening gown glistening under the chandeliers. She looks my way, but of course she doesn't know I exist. Her eyes widen and she nudges Aidan to pose for another photograph.

'How you feeling?' Cain asks me as I squeeze his arm to try to kill the pain of seeing Rachel and Aidan together in real life.

'I need a drink,' I confess to Cain who grabs two glasses of champagne from a passing tray and we clink them together, lost in the crowd of spruced-up businessmen and -women who shout over each other in loud American accents.

'Are you sure this is a good idea?' Cain asks me as his eyes skirt around the bustling room of strangers. 'I swear I'll die for you if this plan all falls flat on its face.'

'It won't,' I assure him as the room falls to a hush. 'Believe me, it won't.'

'But he doesn't even know we're here!' Cain says, speaking so close to my ear that anyone would think he was whispering sweet nothings to me. 'What if he sees us?'

'Shh!' I tell him as a small stout man in a tuxedo that should really be at least two sizes larger takes the microphone on the small stage. 'This is the big moment of truth right now. OK, here we go.'

The MC tells a few jokes, some a bit close to the bone for such a prestigious event, and eventually he cuts to the chase of awarding a massive contract to an Irish–American company that will apparently go on to make such a huge dent in the industry, its ripples will be felt across the city for decades.

'When choosing the recipient of this contract, we were looking for a company that had family at heart, because after all, to build over a thousand new family homes across so many districts, it takes a family man to know what he's doing, and there's no better family man in the business than the one and only Bruce Bowen!'

The tuxedo-clad, mostly male audience and the beautifully dressed ladies who are dotted through the crowd applaud with vibrant enthusiasm as a glitter ball spins above the microphone and triumphant music plays at full blast throughout the room.

I've never seen anything as contrived in my whole life, and, when Rachel and her father spit out a well-rehearsed drivel on the importance of family, my heart almost stops with nerves for Aidan, who is due to speak after them.

'I'd like to thank my husband, Aidan Murphy, without whom we would never have clinched this deal for our company, Bowen Developments,' she says. 'He is the epitome of what New York business is all about. He's hungry, he's harsh, he's cold as ice when he needs to be, and he'd do absolutely whatever it takes to push a contract over the line, even if some people get hurt, and let's face it, in this business they often do.'

Everyone seems to find this hilarious and they burst into applause. I can't take my eyes off Aidan. He has gone a whiter shade of pale, and his lips are pursed tightly. I know that face. He shakes his head slowly.

Now it's his turn to take the mic. My stomach churns.

'Ladies and gentlemen, it has been an honour to have worked on this pitch with Rachel, my, ahem, my wife, and alongside my father-in-law Bruce for the past few months,' he says, shoving his hands in his pocket in a way that tells me he's more nervous than he's letting on. 'I just know that the future of construction and development in this part of New York City is in very safe hands. But my family is . . .'

He sees me now. Oh God, he sees me, and this wasn't supposed to happen. The mic screams out feedback and everyone in the audience puts their fingers in their ears until the stout man in the small suit tries to take over and make it all better.

Aidan sees me, and he breaks into a huge smile, his hands go to his face and he wells up as I wave shyly towards him, shrugging apologetically for taking him by surprise.

'I'll leave you to it,' Cain says with a smile.

'No, don't go!'

'I'll be in the bar next door. Enjoy your moment with your man.'

My head spins back towards Aidan again and my stomach flips.

'What I wanted to say is that my family is in Ireland, and that's where I want to be from this very moment on,' says Aidan, without the amplification of a microphone now, and the audience gasps. 'I'm absolutely nothing like the person my ex-wife just described. In fact, I don't recognize myself in anything here tonight.'

A wave of disbelief and shock ripples around the room. I think my own heart has stopped beating. Rachel and her father stop air kissing well-wishers to listen now to what he is saying, and Rachel shoots him a dagger look to stop, but I can see that he has only just started.

'I can't do this any more, folks,' he says, smiling now as if he has won the lottery. 'I'm not hungry and harsh, I'm not cold-hearted, and I'm certainly not out to hurt anyone in the name of another man's business. What I am, though, is out of here, and I'm glad to say goodbye to a life of false air kisses, back stabbing, and a world where money makes you popular. Goodnight, everyone. Rachel, we'd agreed this would be the very end, so that's it. Bowen Developments, thank you and goodbye!'

A slow trickle of quiet applause comes from the far end of the room, but it seems that others are too frightened to join in.

'Aidan, if you walk now you can never come back, I've told you this!' screams Rachel, but her father nods at her to be quiet. 'You'll regret this! You could have just played along and lived a really comfortable life here!'

'I'm tired of playing your games, Rachel. I'm gone!' he tells her. 'This is not the life I want to live. Goodbye.'

He walks towards me with determined strides past well-wishers and those who are shocked into silence by his announcement, and for the rest of my life, I don't ever think I'll have anyone look at me the way Aidan Murphy looks at me right now. His handsome face is filled with longing and a mixture of pleasure and wonder in his eyes as we both push our way through the sea of bodies to find each other.

The string quartet strikes up a tune, much to the relief of onlookers, who now turn to each other as a low hum of conversation fills the room once more.

'Roisin!' Aidan says to me when he reaches my side. 'Oh my God, Roisin! I can't believe you're here! You look stunning. You're wearing the dress!'

He pulls me close and we just stare into each other's eyes as the room swirls around us. He shakes his head in awe, unable to find any further words, so I take the opportunity to explain.

'Someone once told me that the fear of saying goodbye would never be stronger than the love I feel for you,' I whisper to him as tears fill both our eyes. 'And they were right to say that when your heart screams, you've no choice but to listen. I love you, Aidan. I love you so much and we'll find a way just as Mabel would have wanted us to.'

Aidan glances around the room and offers me his arm, which I link as the people around us look our way in confusion.

'Let's get out of here,' Aidan says with a grin. 'You've no idea how much I've longed to say those words to you. Thank you for coming to support me. I don't think this night could get any better.'

We walk through the crowds towards the door that leads to the hotel foyer and, as soon as we get out of the heat and the hustle of the party and their guests, I stop and turn to face him, knowing that his night is indeed set to get better.

'Look, Aidan, I didn't come here alone,' I say to him, trying desperately to find the right words to announce what I have to tell him.

He looks as puzzled as I thought he might be.

'Ben?' he suggests, his eyes lighting up at the thought. 'Did you bring Ben with you?'

'Not Ben,' I tell him, leading him towards the hotel bar, where I see Cain in the distance, lost in thought as he contemplates a pint of beer in front of him. 'There's someone very special I'd like you to meet, Aidan – a brand new member of your family. It turns out you're not alone after all when it comes to family. I'd like you to meet your own flesh and blood, Aidan. Your cousin, Cain.'

* * *

I only wish I could capture the look of utter shock that washes over Aidan's face when he first sets his eyes on his uncle Peter's son Cain. It's as if he is looking in the mirror, and it's a true moment in time when two hearts have been connected, like missing pieces of a jigsaw puzzle.

'But – but I don't understand?' says Aidan, as they automatically embrace in a jovial hug. They stand back, they stare, and then they hug again.

'Take a seat and let me get you a drink,' I say, leaving them to it for a moment and giving them a chance to absorb this massive change in both their lives. By the time I come back, Aidan is wide-eyed and in awe of how their paths have finally managed to cross.

'Cain is what Mabel sent us to Breena to find, Aidan,' I say, trying to add to the explanation. 'He is the truth untold. The one thing in Peter's life she never knew about.'

'I had absolutely no idea,' Aidan says, shaking his head. 'Did you know about me? That I existed?'

Cain's lilting northern Irish accent is a joy and another affirmation of their strong family connection.

'I grew up knowing very little about my father or his background,' explains Cain. He is truly like a carbon copy of Peter Murphy, right down to the sultry, movie star looks and charming smile. 'My mother brought me up alone, and it's only recently when she was diagnosed with a terminal illness that she decided to tell me the truth, and then you two arrived in our pub, and the rest is history. Good timing, eh?'

'Good old Mabel,' I whisper, even though I know she had no idea of what we were to discover there in Breena. She must have had a hunch, an instinct that the secret between the Murphy brothers was something worth looking into, even if she couldn't have faced up to it herself.

I can feel Aidan's hand shake in mine now and the world spins, but in the most magnificent way as I look on at these two Murphy boys who have been united so much later than they should have been. I remember Aidan's pain as he thought he'd left Ireland and any connection to his family behind for ever, and now he has so many reasons to return and to start a new life if he still wants to. I remember how he longed for a sibling, for a blood relative, just like I have Ben. I remember how he ached for a sense of belonging after Mabel's death, and now he has found it all over again.

'I have a cousin,' he says, gulping back tears and shaking his head. He can't take his eyes off Cain and he can't let go of my hand, which he keeps squeezing for gentle reassurance. 'This is . . . Roisin, did you go back to Breena to find him? I just can't believe this.'

Cain and I nod to him and then both men stand up, locking in a warm embrace again and looking so alike they could be brothers.

'We're your true family, Aidan,' says Cain, looking so tall, strong and protective beside him, 'and we're here to ask you to come home.'

I catch Aidan wiping tears from his eyes and I can't help

myself as my carefully applied make-up is streaming down my face, tears falling onto Mabel's beautiful red dress, which I'd saved for this very special occasion with the man I really love – a man who looks at me like no one has done before.

'Happy birthday, Mabel,' I say, taking a sip of my champagne and toasting my dear friend up in heaven. 'I think we've made quite a celebration and fuss of your eightieth birthday after all, don't you?'

CHRISTMAS

37.

I stand here in the little kitchen of the house in Dunfanaghy, watching Ben, Cain and Aidan on the beach in the distance fly a kite against the wintry elements as they run along the sand. Michael Bublé sings on the radio, and I'm hugging a mug of steaming coffee as the smell of Christmas dinner fills our new home by the sea.

The table is set, not for two and not for even for three, but for seven family members who will gather around soon and toast everyone who brought us to this wonderful moment here today.

'How did you two find this place?' Cain asked me earlier over breakfast. 'It's heavenly.'

'Mum and Aidan stuck a pin in a map,' piped up Ben, to which everyone laughed, including Cain's two young daughters who have been a great source of company and entertainment for Ben since they arrived. 'Mum did that before and we ended up in Ballybray, but I think she cheated a bit this time, didn't you, Mum?'

I held my hands up in surrender.

'Well, maybe I cheated just a little bit!' I confessed, as Aidan kissed me on the cheek on his way past to bring some fresh tea to our guests. 'We decided it would be best for Ben to stay in the local area, but couldn't believe our luck when this little gem right on the mouth of the ocean was ready and available to move in to straight away.'

The cute little two-storey thatched cottage sits on a hilltop. There's a stained-glass circular window above the front door that caught my heart as soon as I set eyes on it. The four bedrooms are spacious and generous for all our needs, and the little shed out the back will serve me well for my crafting.

I open the patio doors that lead out onto a little deck that overlooks the blustery Atlantic Ocean and I breathe in the fresh sea air and take stock of how a long personal battle has taken me to this wonderful place in my journey of life.

Mabel taught me so much during our friendship, but most of all she reminded me how it's important to take chances sometimes, and that it's OK to take risks because none of us knows when our days in this world will be over. There's nothing worse than living a life of regret, never knowing if we made the right call when it comes to love, life and happiness.

Now, when I close my eyes and hear the sounds of the sea and the boys' laughter in the distance, I feel cosy and warm in my heart knowing I'm being true to myself and to those I love.

Cain's wife Ruby and their two daughters Megan and

Isabel tiptoe down the sand dune below our kitchen window and make their way to join the rest of our family to make new memories of this wonderful new beginning that lies ahead of us all.

I recall our conversation this morning when, just after we exchanged Christmas gifts, Aidan told me how he felt being here with me and Ben, back on the coast of Donegal so close to where he spent such a beautiful childhood with his family.

'I feel complete and true to myself at last, Roisin,' he said, holding me close to his chest in our bed that has a view out to the Atlantic Ocean. 'The pain is gone and I can see that yours is gone too. All this time, the answer to the void that was within me was right here at home beside Mabel. I'm so glad I found you.'

I glanced down at the engagement ring that sparkles every day on my finger, a promise to a future together, and snuggled closer to his warmth in our king-size bed.

'And I'm so glad I found you too, Aidan,' I whispered, looking forward to a beautiful Christmas celebration like I've never experienced before. 'I feel safe in this moment. I feel safe and secure, like I haven't been in a long, long time.'

I once promised myself when I was just fourteen years old as I sat alone in my bedroom in my foster home to always look for this feeling in life as the sea crashed outside. I once promised myself that I'd get to feel like that at least one more time, even if it took me for ever to find it.

And just like my darling friend Mabel Murphy advised me to so many times, I'm going to welcome love into my life and embrace it. I'm going to hold on tightly to my precious family from this day forward, and I'm never, ever going to let this feeling go.

Acknowledgements

To everyone at HarperCollins – thank you for your belief, encouragement, inspiration and support, especially my amazing editorial team Charlotte Ledger, Kim Young and Emily Ruston who I simply adore working with on each and every project; to the fantastic publicity machine that is Rachel Quin, Becca Bryant, Ciara Swift and Patricia McVeigh; to Holly MacDonald who designs such breathtaking covers, to Fionnuala Barrett in audio, to Emily Yolland and all in the rights team, and to everyone at HarperCollins Germany and HarperCollins Canada.

To my wonderful agent Sarah Hornsley (The Bent Agency) and her super colleague Nicola Barr who is looking after me so well while Sarah is on maternity leave. Thank you for minding the business side of my writing and for being such great cheerleaders! Thanks also to Jenny Bent, Molly Ker Hawn and Victoria Cappello and all in the Brooklyn office.

Thank you to all the super loyal readers who keep in touch with me from near and far through social media with

your stories of how my books have helped you through
some happy and not so happy moments in life. Please do
continue to keep in touch as I love hearing from you always!
And a special hello to my new readers in Canada who will
be reading *Secrets in the Snow* this year x

I'm so lucky to have met and forged friendships with
many other authors throughout the years who I love meeting
up with and chatting to online. A shout out to my long
time writing buddy Claire Allan, to fellow Irish authors
Carmel Harrington, Carolyn Jess-Cooke and Fionnuala
Kearney and to Cressida McLaughlin who I had great chats
with at the Christmas party!

I'm so grateful for all the media support and to those
who help me spread the word each year with every new
story, be it online, in print, on the radio or on television,
so a big thanks to:

~ Patricia McVeigh (Walking Updates), Cliodhna Fullen,
Michelle Donnelly (Sweet Momma Simons), Annette Kelly
(Little Penny Thoughts), Seána McCrory (The Syngle Girl),
Charlene Greensword (The Hyp Midwife), Laura Hamilton
(Books and My Brain), Siobhan Murphy (Shivonstyle),
Sharon and Emma (Shaz's Book Blog), Linda Hill (Lindsay's
Book Bag), Kaisha Holloway (The Writing Garnet), Yvonne
Tiernan (The Couch), Trish (BetweenMyLines), Claire Bridle
(BookReviews4U), Jo Jackson (Tea and Cake for the Soul),
Kira (BooksandtheBrummie), Audrey Davis (TheBookClub),
Jennie (GirlMeetsBook) Linda Green (BooksOfAllKinds),

Acknowledgements

Áine Toner (*Woman's Way*), Martin Breen & Stephanie Bell (*Sunday Life*), Gail Walker (*Belfast Telegraph*), Jenny Lee (*Irish News*), Annamay McNally, Ian Greer, Robin Elliott (NVTV), Pamela Ballantine (*UTV Life*), Cameron Mitchell & Dearbhail McDonald (BBC Radio Ulster), Lynette Fay (BBC Radio Ulster), Red Szell and Lynne (RNIB Radio) Mags McGagh (Salford City Radio), Anne O'Brien (*Del and Murray Show*), Fiona Ellis (*The Irish Sun*), Vicki Notaro (*Stellar Magazine*), Keeley Ryan (*Her.ie*), and the books teams at *Prima, Closer, Heat, Bella, Woman's Own, Woman* and *The People on Sunday* ~

Thanks to all the librarians and bookshops across Ireland, the UK, Germany, Hungary, Holland and Canada who promote and sell my books. A special mention locally to the team at Dungannon Library (Elizabeth Synott-Telford, Debbie Trotter and Goretti McCaughey), TP and Madeline at Sheehy's Cookstown, everyone at Easons in Ireland, and to Ciara and Mike at SIAR, Kinvara.

Thanks also to those who invited me to speak at their events recently: Mary Anne Pamplin Dooley, Mary Ferris (Dungannon WI), Joan Reid at Good Companions, Cathal Coyle at St Patrick's College, Dungannon, Glenda Leonard, Michele Doran and all the ladies of Royal School Dungannon PTA Book Club, Seán Leonard and all the team at the Claddagh Books Festival Galway, and to those who kindly sponsored me clothes for special occasions – Diane at LaDeDi in Draperstown, Helen at Be Yourself, Kinvara Co Galway.

I've tried to remember everyone but deepest apologies to anyone I've accidentally left out!

Finally, a huge thanks as always to my family for all their never-ending support; to my dad Hugh, my brother David, sisters Vanessa, Rachel, Lynne, Rebecca, Niamh, to Irene, to all my aunties and cousins (a special mention to Roisin who I've named my main character after), and last but most of all, to my partner Jim and our children Jordyn, Jade, Dualta, Adam and Sonny James. Thanks for all your patience and quiet while I've been working on *Secrets in the Snow* xxx